THE IN BETWEEN

THE IN BETWEEN

BY CATHERINE CONVERSE

The In Between

Golden Dot Publishing
Kalispell, Montana

First Edition
golden dot publishing
Print Edition © 2012
ISBN-10: 0988225115
ISBN 13: 978-0-9882251-1-4

DEDICATION

To my parents, whose generosity is abundant on several levels.

CHAPTER ONE

The teacher's voice faded, his words jumbled and entwined. Adie Brighton's pencil slipped from her hand and danced about on the tile floor. Adie found herself on a houseboat on a Colorado lake. The shore was unfamiliar. Tall Aspens loomed over narrow rocky beaches. She stood on the bow and took in her surroundings.

The boat's captain stood before her as a bullet shot through his right temple. She wailed in horror, but her voice was silent. The shooter didn't see or hear her because, of course, she wasn't really there. And the event had yet to happen. But his face was vivid. Wide, wild gray eyes. Simple black wool hat. Lanky build. Missing his front right canine tooth.

The captain's head hit the wall beside him and a paint stroke of blood followed him to the ground. A large splash indicated that the shooter had retreated overboard, leaving no trace. Adie locked onto the victim's barren eyes, as she did in every dream that rivaled this one.

"Are you okay?" Mr. Morrison, math teacher and soccer coach, peered at her over his thin reading glasses.

Adie woke with a sore neck, slouched in her seat. A wet sensation dripped from the right side of her mouth. She scooted forward to straighten up, wiped the embarrassing drool from her chin, and pulled her long chestnut hair back from her cheeks. "Yeah, sure, I'm okay." She squeezed her lids tight, the captain's empty stare still beneath them. She could feel the waves bouncing off the side of the unsteady boat. Adie shook her head and wondered just how long she'd dozed off.

Mr. Morrison continued, his face pale with apparent shock. "It's just, well, you were screaming."

"I was?" Her cheeks flushed hot and red as she felt all eyes on her. Like no one else had ever drifted off during a lecture on cylinder coordinates.

Yet it had never happened at school before.

"Yes. Kind of an awful, wretched scream, actually. You sure you're alright?"

"Um, yes. Yes. I just—I'm sorry. I didn't mean to nod off. I guess I'm a little tired. It's not you, I promise." Adie squirmed in her seat and glanced at the clock in hopes of a dwindling hour. The classroom burst into strange whispers.

Mr. Morrison managed a nervous chuckle. "Adie, dear, I am quite aware that calculus is not exactly an adrenaline rush for most." Adie caught the hint of a few more sneers. "I'd like you to go on to the nurse's station, anyway. Sometimes nightmares indicate something viral coming on."

Payton, Adie's best friend and soccer co-captain, shot her hand into the air.

"Yes, Payton?" Mr. Morrison asked.

"Shouldn't I go with her? After something like that, I'm sure she needs some emotional support." Payton grinned, winking at Adie. Adie glared at Payton for trying to take advantage of the situation, as usual.

Mr. Morrison strolled toward the chalkboard and picked up a small piece of chalk, barely long enough to sit in his pencil grip. "Nice try, Payton. You're excused, Adie." Mr. Morrison turned his back to the class, raising his hand to the chalkboard. He attempted to write on the green matte surface when the tiny chalk twisted in his hand and fell to the floor. Muffled giggles filled the classroom as Mr. Morrison bent down to pick up the nub of chalk.

Adie gathered up her books. Before she left she looked over her shoulder to the back corner. Of course he was still staring — the odd student-teacher, Mr. Palley, who had been observing Mr. Morrison's calculus class for the last month. He never talked to the students, barely seemed to acknowledge Mr. Morrison, and looked to be at least a college junior. His body language demonstrated nothing beyond boredom — not the best qualities in an aspiring high school teacher.

Adie would catch him staring at her as if he had read her thoughts and found them horribly elementary. Yet still, she hated how tight her chest got any time she would sneak a look his way. It made her breathe funny. He rarely made any gesture toward her. But today, a simple nod.

She stood and excused herself. "Thank you, Mr. Morrison."

Mr. Morrison yelled something about a scrimmage after her, but she had already reached the hallway stairs.

For the next two weeks, Adie avoided the morning papers scattered across the kitchen table and stayed late at spring soccer scrimmages to be sure to miss the news her parents would always have blaring. This kind of stalling would last until she was sure that the story had lost its luster, and the captain had faded from the initial public sympathy, and held strong only in the memory of loved ones. Sometime in that two weeks, the captain would be found, and headlines would tell all about it.

Adie already knew the case would go unsolved. The family would not have closure and the city would have one more evil maniac running rampant, with no evidence that the incident was a solitary event, or if he would strike again.

Like all of her other dreams, Adie was haunted by the victim's eyes. She caught a glimpse of them on every stranger she passed. The empty stare replaced the happy expression on the model on a billboard. She even found them in the eyes of her own family when she held contact too long.

Adie had toyed with the idea of going to the cops. But no one really believed in psychics or prophetic dreams anymore. She'd be labeled a loony, probably start finding tarot cards in her locker, and voted "Most Likely to Pull a Scam for Money" in her yearbook. It was hard enough to keep it hidden, but to have the world know would be as difficult as those calculus equations she wasn't equipped to solve.

Each time she woke with the victim's eyes everywhere she glanced, her gut felt like she'd taken a high kick to the stomach, cleats and all. She walked through her day with the knowledge she might have saved someone. What made her most nauseous was that she felt like she was a coward to go on this way, but she didn't have the courage to do anything else.

But it had never happened at school before. Only in the safety of her own bedroom. And for this reason, Adie knew something had changed. She just wasn't sure exactly what.

*

Adie sprinted the length of the field. Her breath came hard and fast as she dribbled the ball between her feet. She pulled her right leg back to give the ball one last boot into the goal. Adie's grades suffered due to her lack of concentration and aloof focus the dreams seem to cause. So academic scholarships had always been out of the question, but she'd signed her name on the dotted line: full-ride soccer scholarship to the University of Colorado.

Payton lay on her side next to the field, her head on her hand, where she alternated picking at the grass and her split ends. She yelled out, "You're crazy, girl. You've already got a scholarship. Let's go."

Adie dribbled the ball right up to Payton and stopped it with her foot two feet from Payton's head. Payton curled into a ball and moved her hands to her face to block the blow. Adie laughed. "What? You don't trust me?"

Payton stretched her body out again and rolled her eyes. "You're good. But not *that* good."

Adie gave Payton's gut a gentle shove with her cleat. "Thanks a lot!"

Payton smiled. "Okay. Yes, you are. Can we go now?"

Adie wiped at her forehead with the sleeve covering her right shoulder. "One more."

"My word, girl, you could *not* touch a ball all summer long and still start as a freshman at U of C. Can we go to the mall and shop for boys now please, before my school-night curfew sets in?" Payton sat up and ruffled her wavy blond hair.

"Well, there's still the state all-star game." Adie bounced the ball back and forth on her knees.

Payton lifted an eyebrow. "Seriously, you care about that? We're graduating, Adie, and you already know where you'll be next fall. Leave the showing off for those girls still hoping to nab a walk-on invitation."

Something shifted and Payton's hazel eyes seemed to turn black and hollow, sinking back into a swirling pale circle that used to be Payton's face. Adie's breath shortened and she looked away.

"What's wrong with you?" Payton asked.

Adie put the soccer ball beneath her arm, grabbed her bag, and kicked off her cleats with her heels. "Nothing. I just—I don't know. Just have a lot on my mind."

Payton stood, gathering up her things. "You're weird."

Adie inhaled deep. "I know." She put her cleats into her bag and slipped her feet into her sneakers. "I'm sorry, but I'm gonna have to go home. Too much to do."

"You sure you're okay?"

Adie nodded, tried to look at Payton but couldn't hold eye contact. "Yeah, yeah, I'm fine. Saturday maybe, for the mall."

"Okay." Payton nodded. "See you tomorrow." Adie watched Payton's tiny dancer frame stroll to her Honda Civic. Her hair bounced as she skipped to the beat of some happy sounding song she sang.

*

The next day, Adie's jaw dropped when Mr. Palley stepped to the front of the classroom. His usually grim expression had been exchanged for a gleaming smile. His light brown hair, usually flat and messy on his head, was gelled up in front like he was headed to a boy-band audition, and opposing his hairstyle was his pants and a Brook's Brothers sweater mimicking Mr. Morrison's attire.

His eyes crinkled at the edges as Mr. Morrison announced that Mr. Palley would be delivering the lesson today. Mr. Palley nodded to the classroom and asked if anyone had questions about the spherical coordinates

Mr. Morrison had discussed the day before.

Adie scooted to the edge of her seat, working hard to hide the strange mix of discomfort and pleasure that pulsed through her body and made her chest tight and tingly.

Payton raised a hand. Mr. Palley pointed to her with a nod. She stuck out her chest and bat her lashes. "Is it possible for you to assist Mr. Morrison with our soccer scrimmages as well?"

Mr. Palley chuckled a bit, then shook his head. "I'm sorry, but I'm afraid that isn't part of my requirements."

After an entire month of staring endlessly at Adie as an observer in class, Mr. Palley didn't make eye contact with her during his entire lecture. Not even once.

Something had definitely changed.

*

One month after her dream of the boat captain, Adie sipped her coffee, and spread the newspaper out across the café's tiny table. She didn't know why she even came to this coffee shop. They always made the coffee too hot, she could barely fit anything besides her drink on the tablet of a table, and the newspapers were always dated.

She glanced out the window as the spring thaw ran from the roof to the muddy ground below. If only everything could be as sure as those trickles of water. They knew their place. They fell from the sky all disconnected simply to freeze on that roof, waiting patiently for warm weather to set them free again. Why couldn't her life feel that way? Like all the loose and missing parts would come together to reveal a master plan, to help her find some sort of meaning in those nightmares, instead of causing her to be a walking zombie struggling to hide something out of fear.

She held a pen to the newspaper as her chin rested on her other palm. The classifieds weren't exactly her idea of a rainy day read, but she would graduate in a week. If she didn't find a job for the summer, she'd end up helping her mother with her landscape business, and while the work itself was not too bad, listening to her mother for eight hours a pop was more than she could handle.

Her mom was sweet and nurtured plants with as much heart as she did her children. But Adie didn't need to learn the names and proper care of every flower and shrub that had potential to bloom in Colorado, and her mother would know nothing else to discuss. She certainly couldn't help Adie improve on her last corner kick.

Adie circled a bunch of service jobs, but they didn't feel right. She tapped her pen against the hard wood beneath the paper. There was always the pool. At least she felt confident there, sturdy and proud in her red shiny swimsuit. She had been good at it, had even been a hero once. But she'd done the pool thing three years in a row now, mostly pinned to the kiddie pool checking for swim diapers, and she was ready for something different.

Of course there was the obvious. She could coach youth soccer summer camp. She had done a few in the past. Soccer was everything to her, and she was excited to live and breathe it for the next four years. But before she had that kind of responsibility — collegiate-level responsibility — she wanted to enjoy this summer.

Her coffee finally settled to a drinkable temperature as she reviewed the small print inside each black circle. She began marking thick Xs across the service jobs. *Just get any job,* she tried to convince herself. It didn't matter, as long as it relieved her from the prison sentence of long hot days digging in dirt.

She slammed back the now fully cooled latte. It still tasted fresh, sent that same strangely delightful buzz through her system. Disgruntled, she closed the newspaper and gasped as she saw the front page. The large photo in front was of the houseboat from her dream, with an inset photo of the captain, alive and well. Adie locked eyes with the happy face in the paper and bit her lip so hard she winced. Acid crept up her throat. She swallowed hard and tried to calm her quick, deep breaths.

The murder had taken place the day after her dream. The article stated that the captain had taken the boat out at sunrise to prepare it for a family that would be on board all day. The boat was found two hours later in the middle of the lake, the captain dead inside. The police had no leads. Research and background checks on the captain proved he had no reason to have any violent enemies. The boat was confiscated for investigation and the FBI had authorized local search efforts on all edges of the lakeshore.

But he would not be caught. Adie had seen it in the murderer's eyes. That look of victory, of upping the stakes of the game. Guilt engulfed her. If only she could let the authorities know, save them from those days on foot chasing dogs through woods and jagged shores. But she couldn't reveal herself. Not even to clear her conscience. The consequences of the world knowing seemed too harsh for her to endure. And she knew that was as selfish a reason as any.

She felt a presence sneak up behind her and cast a shadow over the paper. She glanced over her shoulder as she spread her hands over the article. Mr. Palley stood over her, his head tilted slightly to the right as he read the headline.

"A terrible thing, isn't it?" he said as he sipped his coffee.

"Yes. It is, Mr. Palley. A bunch of weirdos out there." Her voice shook.

"You can call me Jeff, outside of class." He reached out his hand.

Adie placed her hand in his, and they shook. "Adie."

"Yeah, I know."

"You do?"

"Yeah. Mr. Morrison kind of pointed you out. That day you fell asleep in class."

Adie nodded as heat rushed to her cheeks. "Oh, yeah. Well, that was embarrassing."

Jeff shook his head. "Not a big deal. Calculus is about as interesting as dirt."

"But aren't you going to be teaching it?" Adie stood. That tightness in her chest was growing unbearable and she was too afraid of saying something hideous.

"No. That was just a cover." Jeff put his finger to his lips. "Shhh. Don't tell anyone."

Adie glanced around, then narrowed her eyes. "Cover for what?"

"Wouldn't you like to know?"

"Well, did Mr. Morrison know?"

"Nope."

"Okay, I'll bite. Yes, I'd like to know." Adie bit the inside of her cheek and she wished her chest wouldn't flutter.

"Walk with me?" Jeff tossed his cup in the garbage.

She hesitated. "Okay, for a minute or two." She tossed her cardboard lidded cup into the appropriate recycling bin. She reached for the door, but a hand reached over hers to pull it open. She jumped, and squeezed her lips together. After taking way too long to regain her composure, she looked into Jeff's handsome face and could do nothing but fake a nervous smile.

"After you."

"Thanks." Adie stepped out onto the washed-out cement sidewalk.

He kept pace at her side. "So, you're looking for a job?"

Adie's feet skidded on the gritty sidewalk as she came to a stop. Her face tingled and her eyes hardened. He was watching her there, too? Calculus class and now this? *That's weird. He's weird.* She made sure they were headed toward a street packed with plenty of bobbing heads and traffic. She stepped up to the curb, her face within a foot of his chest. "Excuse me?"

"Sorry. Just couldn't help but notice you practically massacring those classifieds with that sharpie. Looking for anything in particular?"

"Hey, isn't this little conversation supposed to be about you and your spy gig?" Adie raised her brows. He was too young for a detective, but she hadn't ruled out that he could actually be a criminal and this was part of his deal of immunity or something.

Jeff threw his head back and laughed. "Spy gig, huh? No, nothing like that. I'm a recruiter for a big company. Sometimes we watch certain candidates before approaching them about their interest level."

"At a high school?"

"Not usually. But this time, yeah." He stuck his hands deep into his soft-shell coat.

All kinds of scenarios went through Adie's mind. The best conclusion she could draw was that he was checking into Mr. Morrison. Probably for some kind of job that required an insane mathematical mind. Mr. Morrison would be well-equipped for that, and her guess was that whatever it was would pay a lot better than teaching. She breathed a sigh of relief that she wouldn't be around to miss Mr. Morrison. Not as a teacher, but as a soccer coach.

"I suppose it's all confidential and stuff. That's all you can tell me about it, right?" Adie pushed the button for the streetlight to change. Hopefully fast.

"Not for you, actually."

Adie crossed her arms. "Really. How so?"

"It's you I'm recruiting."

"For a job?" Adie glanced over her shoulder. Something dark fell over her, like she shouldn't be where she was. The criminals in her dreams had a similar way of making her feel that she had stepped onto the wrong dreamy stage, but still had to play the part. Her grades sucked and the only career path in soccer (after the pros, of course) was teaching a bunch of rowdy kids. So what kind of job could he possibly have for her? The curiosity was brewing up a storm in her gut.

Jeff just nodded.

"And what makes you think I'm qualified?"

Jeff waited until they had crossed the street. "Let me guess. I bet you want to do something that matters."

"What are you, my psychic?" Adie felt that rush of excitement she got whenever she hinted at her secret.

"Maybe." Jeff grinned, then turned to face Adie. "Actually, truth is, I read people really well. Your facial expressions. Your movement. Your body language. How you respond to Mr. Morrison's lectures in class. Even in the way you dress. The things that occupy most people's minds are not what occupy yours."

Adie glanced down at her holey jeans and last year's ballet flats. A part of her wanted to let him have it about the way she dressed, but she was too curious. He knew something about her. She could feel it. "Okay, Jeff. Just spill it. Who in the heck are you, really?" Adie folded her arms again.

Jeff kicked small pieces of gravel with his square-tipped loafers as he walked. His face transformed, his voice stern. "Look, Adie. The agency I recruit for does really important work. I've done some research on you—"

"Whoa. Wait a minute. You've done *research* on me? What's going on here?" She turned to check her directions, tempted to just bolt. To go find Payton and head to the mall and down a large ice cream while Payton flirted with anything that moved.

Jeff gently grabbed her arm, but she jerked it back into her side. "Adie, I can assure you that it is not unusual for us to research possible candidates. All, um, businesses do it. Can't afford not to. You should feel honored, not violated. If you could just let me show you."

"Sorry, this is just so not normal. I mean, you used to stare at me the whole time in class!" Adie slapped her hand over her mouth. She didn't mean to say that. To top it off, did she actually expect anything in her life to be normal?

"Adie, look. I am a recruiter. I work for a very confidential international agency. When a potentially talented person comes onto the radar, we spend at least two months analyzing them."

"And you discover these talented people how?"

"We've got some eyes and ears in the right places."

"No way. Uh-uh. Just tell me." Adie felt her own

voice thick in her throat.

"I can't. That's the part where you take a leap, Adie."

"Look. You seem pretty cool. But all I need is something to get me through summer so I can—"

"So you can go off to your soccer scholarship and put the worries of the world behind you."

Adie paused. "What are you talking about?"

"Let me show you, Adie."

"I'm sorry. My creep-o-meter is like, sky-high right now. I've got to go home. So, nice to see you, Mr. Palley. Good luck with, um, whatever it is." Adie turned toward home.

Jeff yelled to her back, "Tell me about your dream, Adie, in class that day. Tell me about the captain."

Adie planted her feet. The streets spun around her. Cars were a blur and the only sound she could hear was the whir of the wind. She turned in slow motion, giving into the pulling force suddenly ripping through her core.

"My dream? What do you know about my dreams?" Adie's voice grew louder. Her knees folded slightly, her hands began to shake, her voice quivered. "And how are my...my...my nightmares relevant to this? How?" Adie began pacing, her stomach nauseous and her face flushed.

"Do you see murderers, Adie?" Jeff said calmly.

Adie stopped. Stared out into the ruckus of trucks speeding past sedans. She held her face blank.

"Do you? In your dreams, do you see murderers? Do they win, Adie? In your dreams, do the murderers win?"

"YES!" Adie began to shake uncontrollably. No one knew about those dreams. Not her parents. Not even Payton. This was impossible. What could he want from her?

"What if I told you that you could stop them? If you

could stop people from being killed because you dream about it before it happens." Jeff tried to grab her elbow. Adie jerked away and began to pace. *What if she could stop it?*

Wasn't that the exact thing she had accused herself of since she rolled off her bed in the eighth grade with her first nightmare, so scared she had crawled into her closet with a flashlight and surrounded herself with every stuffed animal she still had. She had cried for hours and played sick the next day to skip school.

Two days after that night, on the news her mother watched while she sautéed ground beef for tacos, was the report of the murder in her dream. A young woman who made the horrible mistake of taking a shortcut through an alley at one o'clock in the morning. Adie had received the news like she'd been trapped in a tunnel, the television talking to her alone. She had excused herself to her room, cried herself to sleep, and vowed never to tell a soul.

She had reached the point where she could avoid the backlash of the dream itself. She had talked herself into believing that if she didn't watch the news or read the paper, then she might not know if the dream was a prediction or simply a nightmare. But the distraction always kicked in when she tried to convince herself that she was not responsible. That even if she told someone, she couldn't stop it. And now this man—well, who knew who or what he actually was—stood before her to tell her that she could indeed stop it.

Adie's voice was soft and timid. "Tomorrow then. After our morning soccer scrimmage. Elevenish. Where do I meet you?"

A group of moms surrounded by small children crossed the street at the intersection. Jeff moved closer to

Adie. "Same coffee shop." Jeff leaned toward her ear and whispered. "It will be worth it, Adie."

CHAPTER TWO

The scrimmage was a train wreck. Adie missed four 'gimme' goals, had two turnovers on potential assists — which had *never* happened — and even tripped trying to reverse the ball. Coach Morrison and Adie's father scratched their heads. Occasionally Coach Morrison would mumble something under his breath to her dad.

Normally, these repetitive errors would have driven Adie crazy. She would have called for a time-out to pull herself together. But this time, the mind game in her head wasn't about trying to impress a college coach. It was about her meeting with a whole different type of recruiter.

When the final whistle blew, Adie sprinted to her bags, pulled off her cleats and shin guards, and headed to the locker room. Her dad strolled over for their usual post-practice, or post-scrimmage, or post-game chat, but today Adie would have to politely decline.

"Hey, Dad." She gave him a quick hug. "Sorry, but today I gotta go."

Her dad flipped his keys in his hand. "Really? Where to?"

"Job interview. Tell you all about it later!" She ran off, the blouse she had actually ironed this morning billowing from her arms.

*

Adie slowed to collect herself before Jeff had a chance to see her trotting toward him from the bench outside the coffee shop. She was five minutes late, and her stomach churned at the idea that her tardiness would make her seem flakey.

Jeff said nothing about the time, but rather handed her a twelve-ounce cup of steaming liquid.

Adie smiled. "Of course you know what I drink."

Jeff took a big sip of his own cup and tossed the cup in the garbage beside them.

Adie shot him a look of shock. "Really? You can't just walk five more steps to the recycle bin?"

Jeff stared at her blankly for a moment. Then he stood, pulled his cup out of the garbage and walked inside the coffee shop to the recycle bin. He tossed it in with an extra bit of enthusiasm.

"So, you ready?" He leaned back on his heels and stuffed his hands in his jean pockets.

"Sure. Where we headed?"

Jeff pointed to a patch of woods about four blocks south of the coffee shop. He headed in that direction. She trotted a couple of steps to catch up on a sidewalk that tapered about thirty yards up.

The sidewalk ended. She didn't notice where the ground beneath her feet morphed from smooth pavement to a narrow gravel lane that veered into the forest. They walked mostly to their versions of small talk between patches of silence, glancing at one another now and then. She tried to learn more about him, but he refused to give up anything about his own life. And clearly he didn't need to quiz her. So instead, they kept a brisk pace with their eyes on the path.

Adie stopped to inhale the fresh air, surprised that the fear she'd felt yesterday had turned into some kind of compelling curiosity. And maybe even hope. She closed her eyes and listened. A few birds to her left settled in. Perhaps they just arrived from the south. A soft wind whistled through branches. But other than that, just quietness. She opened her eyes. Jeff was watching her. "I didn't know such peacefulness was so close to the city." She sighed. "It's nice."

Jeff nodded. "Let's keep moving."

"When are you going to tell me what this job is all about?"

Jeff nudged her to move further down the lane. Tall trees towered on either side, creating the illusion that all that gravel and dirt might go to the ends of the earth. Maybe this was starting to feel a little weird. Even the tiny crackling of gravel beneath her feet gave her goose bumps.

Jeff placed a hand on her arm. "Adie, it's okay. I just need to show you."

Adie stared at him. His green irises had a gray ring around them and his lashes were long. She pushed his arm away and breathed deeply, as if the air were dense with the bravery she needed to keep her feet moving down that lane.

Just when the silence was more than she could stand, Jeff spoke. "We're almost there. I just need you to keep one thing in mind. One thing only. Remember that this is all about you having something very special that most people do not. You can stop evil, and not everybody can say that."

"Good enough."

"No matter how freaky it seems at first."

"Ooookaay."

"Or how unqualified you may think you are for the job."

"You know, I saved a little girl from drowning once. At the pool." She couldn't help herself. She felt a need to overcompensate. Jeff must have found her so selfish and lacking in character, that she didn't use her gift to stop people from dying.

Jeff looked straight ahead as he inhaled deeply. "Yeah, I know."

Adie grinned. "Right. Of course you do."

Jeff looked at her and smiled. His demeanor seemed to radiate an authenticity that calmed Adie's pulse. At that moment, she knew this was real. It hit her like a meteorite that this strange young man really believed that what she considered a curse was actually something very useful. Somewhere. Somehow.

Jeff stopped and peered into the thick woods. "This is it."

Adie peered into the woods. Nothing but scattered trees and branches. No path. No sign. No road. "This is what?"

Jeff put a hand out. "This is where we enter. Take my hand."

Adie stood her ground. She thought about her family. What they were doing at that very moment. Her mother was probably out in their garden, planting too many vegetables. Her brothers were probably fighting over video games, ignoring her mother's request to do homework. Her father had probably stopped by the university to grade papers until lunchtime.

"What about my family? Will it all have to be a secret?"

"Yes. But how long have you kept your secret from them already?"

Adie froze. Of course he'd believe that she could keep her lips sealed. She already had. She shrugged. "Fair enough."

"Alright, then. Let's go." He took a step down off the road into the ditch, bending his knees to absorb the drop.

Adie turned back toward the road they had traveled. She squeezed her lids tight, forcing herself to remember every murderer she had seen, every evil grin and sly expression. Was Jeff one of them? She couldn't remember. Should she know him, the way he knew her? Confusion pummeled her, made her dizzy. She put her palms to her forehead, as if their warmth would infuse clarity right through her skin.

She searched him for a vengeful twitch or a fidgety hand. But he was nothing but still. Waiting. "Just kind of curious. Um, if I turned around right now and went home, what would you do?"

Jeff dropped his chin, sighed and shook his head. But Adie could see his grin. "Yes, Adie, I would let you go. But I would know what you're missing. So I'd regret it for you."

Adie nodded. "Well, what are we waiting for?"

She jumped with two feet into the ditch next to him and followed him into the trees. About a hundred yards in, they stood amongst a mix of dead branches and vibrant spring buds. Just trees and nature and uncertainty.

Jeff turned to Adie. "Wrap your arms around me."

"No way. This is already weird."

"Adie, you have to hold onto me."

"Fine." Adie wrapped herself around him, catching a scent of something like musky cedar.

"Tighter."

"Okay, okay." She moved even closer, buried her head into his chest. She hated that her heart sped up. Her abdomen tightened and an odd warmth took over her body.

"Hold on. Here we go!"

Four walls of bamboo wrapped in vines shot up

from the ground and surrounded them. The forest floor dropped beneath their feet. Adie screamed as she held onto Jeff more tightly. Freefalling for what seemed like hours, Adie could hear her own voice trailing them, loud and frightened. She didn't look up or down. Her cheeks and her lips and her thighs all vibrated with the movement. When her eyes opened, all she saw was black. She squeezed them tight again. Was this just another dream? An abrupt thud answered that question.

"We're here." Jeff gently released her. "You okay?"

Adie slowly opened her eyes. She stepped back from Jeff to regain herself, brushed away at her tapered black pants, and pulled at her sleeves. She glanced up, curious where the forest had gone but found a black paneled ceiling instead. Her feet had landed firmly on a beautiful Persian rug, filled with repetitive patterns in blues, greens, and reds. The room was large, the walls papered in a warm gold. Intricately detailed trim lined the floor and ceiling to lend the room a Victorian charm. Deep purple couches perched in a corner, soft and welcoming. Tall vases filled with roses and lilies branched to the ceiling framing a dark wooden door.

"Jeff? Where in the hell are we? Or are we in hell? Although last I heard hell sure didn't look this good." Adie asked as she soaked up the bright colors and exquisite décor.

"Rather than being in the mile-high city, you are now twenty miles below it. You are in the Orientation room of Impire Peace Agency. Our people must do their work down here, below the surface, to stay 'under the radar'. Our agency is invisible to the world."

Adie shook her head. Twenty miles below the city? How was that even possible? Tight spaces had never bothered her before. But knowing that certain things were so out of reach caused her throat to tighten. She felt a little like the walls were caving in. Her mind wandered to things like soft breezes and trees that grew to the sky without limits. And her family.

"I'm sorry, Jeff. I still don't understand. And honestly, I'm kind of freaking out." Adie felt a strange sort of calm, actually. It just seemed like she should be leery and suspicious, so the words to match just kind of came out.

Jeff motioned toward one of the large velvet couches. "Have a seat. I'll get you some water."

His comment gave Adie an odd assurance. At least they had water. Still, she was astounded how anyone could survive in a place such as this. How did it all get here? Did food, supplies, and plush velvet couches just fall through the forest floor, too? The water tasted no different than it had back home. She drank it down completely, surprised by her thirst.

Jeff sat opposite her, pulling some brochures and books from a cabinet beneath a coffee table. The agency's name was splattered all over them, along with the title, "Information and Training Manuals."

"You need to listen carefully, Adie. You still have the opportunity to opt out. You'll have a tour, and then you'll need to make a decision. If you decline our offer, your memory will be blocked of this experience. You'll be spat right back up into the world, back into that coffee shop on 23rd Street and I'll only ever be that student-teacher who stared you down in calculus."

"Whoa." Adie sank deep into the couch. "That's kind of scary."

"Scarier than the nightmares?"

Adie sat forward again. "Okay, I'm listening." She folded her arms across her belly.

"Impire Peace Agency, or IPA as we call it, began about thirty years ago. A woman with dreams such as yours could no longer keep them to herself. Her husband, an entrepreneur, approached local government about his wife's abilities. Of course, they thought it was hogwash. So her husband starting reporting her dreams, and too many turned out to be homicide cases on their desks a few days later. They were put on contract as informants. Mrs. Blakefold would identify locations, dates, and times, and local law enforcement could schedule a random event to throw off the perpetrator. Sudden large crowds, police car drive-bys, that sort of thing. This prevention is what dropped the crime rate.

"A few other women stepped forward when they heard what Mrs. Blakefold was doing. They wanted to use their gift for the betterment of society as well. But then things got messy. Information leaked and a major drug ring locked in on the Blakefold group. They went after the Blakefolds, thinking they were some kind of moles, not believing in the whole psychic thing. Most people don't. Anyway, two of the women were killed."

Adie sat up, placing her hand over her mouth. "Wait a minute. There's, like, a lot of us? That have these nightmares?"

"Yes. But, as you can see, they can be put to good use."

Adie lifted a brow. She wanted to believe it. More than anything.

Jeff continued. "That's when the government shelled out the grant money to build the agency a protected environment. Law enforcement officials didn't want to give up the intelligence Mrs. Blakefold could offer, but the public wouldn't buy into the idea of using tax dollars for law enforcement to bring in psychic help, so they couldn't establish the agency in the city. The Feds and local government were willing to do anything to keep the agency safe and to assist in finding more like Mrs. Blakefold.

In hindsight, I'm sure it was all political. When the crime rate goes down, local law enforcement and Feds get a nice little pat on the back, and probably a little bonus in their pockets. Even DEA gets a lot of busts from it. Anyway, we don't mind that so much, because we know that what we are contributing to the world is a good thing."

"Where do I fit in? I've only got three months, you know."

Jeff nodded. "I know. Your commitment is the summer. All you do is report your dreams. Seriously, it's that easy. If you're successful, then you'll be invited back the following summer. Of course, you would always be welcome full time."

"I'm not giving up soccer, Jeff. I'll just put that out there right now."

"You don't have to." He leaned in closer, his chin on his hands. "There is an entire world just past that door, Adie. It's not only full of important work to the human race, but it's full of wonder, and excitement, and all kinds of things you could ever have up there. What I'm going to show you today will give you just enough of a sneak peak at the kind of summer you could have. You'll have to make a decision to commit or not. If you decide not to, we'll just rewind your brain to the coffee shop yesterday. If you decide to commit, then you'll go back home and have one week to graduate and prepare."

"So I have the week to mull it over?"

"Look there." Jeff pointed to the wall. A pair of earphones hung neatly on a hook alongside a couple of electrical wires with padded ends. "If you decide to stay up in the city this summer, to pour over miserable job options, distract yourself by living on the soccer field, and taking on an earful of Payton's boyfriend details, all you have to do is put on those headphones."

But the dreams will not subside. You have a gift. So when the tour is finished, I will ask you, can you go back to that world, to watch human lives being taken in your dreams, knowing you could stop them? If that's a life you can live, then simply place those earphones on your ears and attach those electrode panels to your temples. You'll hear music, and the next thing you know, you'll sit in that coffee shop on 23rd Street, and I will not be there."

Adie turned to the wall behind her.

"But what about my parents? There's no way —"

Jeff interrupted. "It will be all arranged. All you have to do is go along with a story of an opportunity to coach soccer at a youth camp in Spain for the summer. Your name will be on a national touring camp coaching roster within an hour. All the details will be prepared and taken care of by our staff. All you have to do is, well, tell them a little white lie. And be convincing. You're going to want to tell them the truth, but it just can't work that way. It's not safe.

"Also, any time you want to head up to the city for a family visit, you must pass a vigorous loyalty and confidentiality test before you go." Jeff tilted his head and smiled.

Adie thought for a moment. Couldn't help but pick at a cuticle. "Do you see your family?"

Jeff looked past her, then to the floor. "No. I don't have any."

"I'm sorry." Adie hoped he would open up. Explore. Explain. But nothing.

Instead, Jeff stood. "Well, are you ready to see what you could be missing?"

Adie looked behind her at the earphones on the wall. If it was all too much, all she would have to do is put them on and it would be over. Whether it was a dream, or it was real, it would be over. She would be back sipping her mouth-burning coffee, wondering how to avoid a summer picking dead-heads from geraniums. There was just one tiny detail Jeff had missed. There had been no discussion of money.

"What about pay? We haven't discussed the pay." Adie scooted forward to the edge of the couch, as if she were moving away from those earphones.

"I can't. Not yet." Jeff replied. "You can be sure that you will have plenty by the end of the summer. An account will be set up for you and you'll have access to it anytime you go up to the city." He moved closer to Adie. "Quite honestly, money means nothing down here." He pointed to her head. "Now that. That has value."

A nervous tickle slithered down Adie's spine. Could this all be for real? Was she really going through with it because she could help, or because of some strange attraction to him? It was all a bit much. Couldn't they have sent some beat up old codger to give her all of this impossible news? Would she have gone if they had?

Now she got it. Jeff's gift was persuasion.

He reached across her and grabbed one of the big green binders titled, "Employee Handbook." Inside was an agreement letter. She'd agree that should she decide not to accept employment after the tour, they had the right to erase her memory of all things IPA.

"Just sign this and we're on our way."

Adie held the pen to the paper and paused in thought.

"Oh, what the heck. Nothing better to do." She signed. Adie Brighton.

CHAPTER THREE

"Are you ready?" Jeff asked. He urged her toward a large burgundy door with a hand on the small of her back.

"Yes." Despite the butterflies inside her, Adie took in a deep breath and moved with the gentle force of his hand. She was smart enough to realize that Jeff might not be so touchy-feely because he fancied her. It was more likely he was just doing his job. But that didn't put a cap on the way her body responded to him. She pondered how many other hearts he'd broken just to get them there.

Jeff punched in a bunch of numbers on a keypad on the wall next to the door and a monitor dropped from the ceiling. An man looking mid-sixties appeared on the screen.

"Well, Ms. Brighton. Welcome. I am Ivan Blakefold, CEO. We are thrilled to have you. The decision you have made is a brave one. We hope that you will find Impire Peace Agency something you want to be a part of. I am anxious to meet you, but I am currently in our Spain headquarters."

Adie looked to Jeff, and mouthed 'Spain?' She quickly turned back to the screen, cleared her throat, and said, "Gracias, Señor Blakefold. Mucho gusto. Encantado."

Jeff shot an elbow into her side, leaned in and whispered 'brown-noser' into her ear. She glanced sideways at Jeff without moving her head and smiled, rocking back and forth between the balls of her feet and toes.

Ivan continued. "You are in good hands with Jeffrey, Ms. Brighton. He is head of leadership in our Recruitment Department. Should you join us, you will embark on a very rewarding experience. We thank you for considering us. Your world thanks you. If you elect to join us, we shall have dinner and I shall have the honor of meeting you. For now, enjoy the tour." Ivan nodded and the picture faded.

"Wow. He's nice." Adie smiled inside, suddenly eager to move beyond that door.

Jeff turned to Adie. "That's just the beginning, Adie." He clicked the button on the remote and the door opened.

Adie gasped as Jeff led her into a room the length and height of three city blocks. "Oh my," Adie whispered.

Jeff laughed. "Don't get too excited. This is our biggest room. Welcome to our Amphitheater. Meetings, entertainment, church, movies, you name it, we gather here for it."

Adie gazed around the enormous room. To her right, a large stage opened up to the ceiling high above. A very short adult with his hair pulled back in a ponytail swept the stage. He stopped and wiped at his brow with the crisp white sleeve of his button-down shirt. He lifted his other hand to wave to them.

"That's Oozie. Nicknamed for his hobby of building all things that blow other things up. He was part of the engineering and construction team that blew out most of the earth down here to build our agency's space." Jeff smiled and moved through the room. "He's always looking for ways to get a bigger bang, bust out more space — for when we expand."

Adie just stared at Oozie, never having seen a mature-looking person whose eyes only met her belt buckle.

On the left, theater seating sprawled to the back wall with a balcony overhead. Three large movie screens hung a hundred yards down from the ceiling in a triangle. Scoreboards were connected directly beneath them. Basketball hoops were tucked into soccer goals in a back corner. This room was equipped for anything and everything.

"C'mon. Work first. Play later." Jeff chuckled. He pushed buttons on the remote to open the next door at the back of the lower-level theater seating. It led to a room similar to the Orientation room, only the furniture was more suited for an office. A secretary sat at the desk, her reading glasses at the tip of her nose as she leaned forward toward the computer screen. Jeff pulled Adie through the door as she resisted tearing her eyes from the epic view of the Amphitheater. The woman looked up, set her eye glasses aside and stood.

"Steph, this is Adie."

"Hello, Adie. Welcome!" Adie shook Steph's hand, dazed by the woman's beauty. She had long dark hair, stood well over six feet tall in stilettos, and wore a cranberry-colored pant suit that made her olive skin look radiant.

Jeff turned to Adie. "Steph is Mr. and Mrs. Blakefold's daughter."

"Oh!" Adie nodded. "So nice to meet you." Adie could feel herself folding up behind Jeff, feeling underdressed and completely ordinary in her plain old blouse and black boyfriend-cut pants.

"We are delighted to have you." Steph buzzed something under her desk that opened the next door.

In the corner, just to the left of the open door, a young girl of nine or ten sat curled up in a green velvet bean bag, eyes glued to some electronic game, her fingers moving about it wildly. A smaller girl lay next to her, snuggled up with a brown stuffed moose. "These two little sweethearts are Maimey and Macey, my lovely daughters." Steph gave the oldest girl a small kick. The girl looked up, disgusted. "Say hello, honey."

"Hi," the girl mustered without removing her headphones. Her eyes returned to the brightly lit screen in her hands. The smaller girl lifted a hand from her stuffed moose and waved.

"It's a pleasure to meet you both as well," Adie said, unsure why she suddenly sounded so formal. As they moved on, Adie caught Maimey's eyes following her, staring at her from her now-wrinkled blouse to her worn-in flats.

Jeff led her into a large circular corridor where the hallways veered into ten different directions. A sign on the wall listed numbers and the department names assigned to them.

Adie stood quietly as the long hallways seemed to rotate around her, all melded together by deep reds and purples. In the midst of an apparent labyrinth, she wondered how on earth this all came about. How many people did it take to accomplish this? Where were they now? She rubbed her eyes and steadied herself against a plum-colored wall.

"Don't worry," Jeff said softly. "I'm going to talk you through all of this, and then I'm going to show you the best part."

The first hallway was Recruitment, Jeff's department. The Recruitment offices looked like any other business offices: papers everywhere, file cabinets, computers, music playing softly. Adie snickered under her breath, sure she heard a song by Journey or some other oldie her parents loved to listen to. Did this mean she'd lose track of modern music? Did these people even know what was going on up in the city? Did it matter anymore who won an Academy Award? Or topped the music charts? Or won a gold medal?

A tall, thin woman with shoulder length red hair and lightly freckled skin started toward them. She wore pencil-cut black pants and a melon cashmere sweater set that complimented her pale skin. She walked directly to Adie and handed over a large cup of coffee. "You look like a smart one. This guy have to bribe you with some fantasy of exotic beaches, too?" Then she extended her hand, "Welcome. I'm Lonie."

"Lonie recruits the males," Jeff said as he poured himself a cup of coffee. It began to click for Adie that this was part of the plan. It was doubtful Jeff would have much success convincing a man to join him for a stroll down an isolated forest lane. Jeff quickly added, "Her husband is a lead Analyst here." Adie felt relief at the mention of Lonie's husband. She wasn't sure what that meant—if she was happy to know that people did get still get married down here, or if she was relieved that Lonie wasn't in the probable long line of competition for Jeff.

Lonie rested a hand on Adie's wrist. "Don't worry, dear." Then she leaned toward her. "We love it here. You certainly won't find anything else like it up there." She pointed to the ceiling as if she was referring to something as tangible as the next floor up.

The next hallway was Technology, where computer monitors covered entire walls and touch screens, switchboards and surveillance equipment left little room for the people who operated them. Big whiteboards hid in the corners where blue dry-erase ink mapped out networks and databases, satellites and signals, and all sorts of C+ and Visual Basic gibberish that to simply look at gave Adie a migraine.

Five guys hovered over a large master-switch station below an opposite wall full of monitors. The head of leadership for the Department was a guy named Demry. He wore thick glasses complemented by a forced smile. He was short, with a belly that folded over his belt. His eyes seemed to cross and squirm, as if training to look at several things at once. But he greeted Adie promptly and graciously, and briefly explained the unique interface of the system.

Next were the Analysts. A room full of doctorate-level forensic psychologists who worked under the leadership of Lonie's husband, Jago. Jago offered up a nod and a huge smile as he shook Adie's hand so tightly and so long she finally winced and pulled back. He was much shorter than Lonie, which surprised her. His skin was dark, his build muscular, and he looked of some foreign decent—Greek, maybe or Italian—with big brown eyes.

"So nice to meet you, Ms. Brighton. Always lovely to welcome a bright, young Visionary." He tipped his head at Jeff and moved back to a wall full of charts.

Next they stopped by the Training Department—two rooms on either side of a glass window. One was a typical classroom, and in the other, weight machines lined the walls and kickboxing pads circled a studio floor.

"You'll primarily be trained in one of the martial arts. But you can dabble in other forms of defensive training as well." Jeff started to move on.

"Wait. Martial arts? My form of 'training' is soccer,

remember? I thought I was just supposed to tell some-one my dreams. That's all, right?" Adie looked around and noticed that just below the ceiling were photos lin-ing the walls of women of various ages, in black wide-legged pants and white uniform tops.

"It's Aikido—the Art of Peace: But trust me, you'll kick ten times more goals once you complete this train-ing. Plus, you'll learn to defend yourself on multiple levels. You actually won't be allowed to go back up for a visit until you've completed at least a full session. Blake-fold doesn't make any exceptions on this rule. It's too dangerous. Even though you're low profile, we have to prepare you. Especially if you end up going on to col-lege this fall." Jeff stifled a grin.

"You mean *when* I go on to college this fall?"

"Right." Jeff answered without looking her way.

Then he turned to Adie. "Most of the time, things are simple. You dream, you write your report, the Analysts take a look at it, and Tech sends it off to Ops—Operations. They run interference up in the city and the life is saved. *Most* of the time, it works like that." He looked away. "But some of these crime rings, they're smart and they don't stop at anything. The law gets in their way. Therefore, informants to the law—even the ones who only witness in their dreams—are considered a real problem for them. It isn't likely that your identity will be discovered, but you still have to be able to de-fend yourself. Ivan made it mandatory after IPA lost those Visionaries all those years ago."

Adie squinted at the photos, straining to see them better. The women in the pictures were all shapes and sizes. Some looked very fit, while others were over-weight and even elderly looking. All proudly sported their black belts. "Oh, yeah," she whispered to herself.

"If they can do it, so can I."

The next department was the one Adie would be working in: the Visionaries. The door to the department opened onto another long narrow hallway in warm yellow tones. As they entered, soft carpet gave way under each step. Every ten feet, there was a door to either side. A few were open to the darkness beyond them.

"Sleep rooms," Jeff explained. "In other words, your office." Jeff opened a door. "Let's check one out."

Jeff moved into the dark room. He clicked a switched, and the floor lamp gave the room a soft glow. Beside the lamp was a large melon-colored velvet recliner. Next to the recliner was a machine tangled up with buttons and screens and wires. Behind the machine a larger screen was mounted on the wall. A long bed with layers of velvet comforters and pillows sat snug against the far wall. The wall adjacent to the bed had a small refrigerator, sink, and microwave. Adie looked up to see low ceilings with no overhead lighting. Speakers and cameras popped out from every ceiling corner.

Jeff must have read the confusion on Adie's face. "You won't be sleeping in your quarters. You sleep here. A partner monitors you. Another Visionary. You take turns sleeping, then you're both off a good bit of the day. You work early evening to late morning, while you sleep. Or while your partner does. Great job, don't you think?"

Adie ran her hand along the fuzzy lime-green velvet comforter. She sat on the bed, then let herself fall into the pillows. She closed her eyes. *Wow.* She could definitely get used to this. Her eyes popped open as her mom's tone of 'too good to be true' rang through her thoughts.

Jeff stepped away from the sleep room. "C'mon. Time to meet the real boss."

Jeff led Adie to the end of the hallway where a large room similar to that in Technology awaited. Mrs. Blakefold, the head of Leadership for the Visionary Department, was stunning at sixty-five. The gray streaks in her hair complimented her natural dark brown. She was lean and fit, and the lines in her face radiated character. Adie hated to compare her to her own mother, who had taken to the idea of a psychology professor's wife who dabbled in plants quite nicely, breaking in her Birkenstocks and keeping comfortable in long, flowing dresses. Her mother was beautiful too, but this woman, this master psychic of some kind, was riveting.

Bethie Blakefold ran to Adie. "Oh, Adie, Adie, Adie. We have been waiting for you. I am *so* excited you are here. You, my dear, are extremely talented."

"I am?" Adie accepted the hug from Bethie.

Bethie stepped back, holding onto Adie's hands. Adie noticed a motherly quality in the woman. The softness in her blue eyes, the perfect shape of her bob cut. Bethie motioned for Adie to sit down across from her and offered Adie a large glass of water.

"Mr. Charming here showing you around well enough?" Bethie winked at Jeff.

Heat rushed to Adie's cheeks, but she managed to glance over at Jeff and smile. "Yes, we're getting along fine."

"Good. There's so much to learn and see, Adie." Bethie turned to Jeff. "Don't overdo it on the first day."

Jeff snickered. "I think we're done with the work part for now. I want to show her our retreat before she has to head back home."

"Ah!" Bethie nodded. "Yes, very nice idea, indeed. Well, it's back to work for me."

Adie looked around the large office, a large conference table surrounded by oversized comfy seats. Bethie's small office just beyond the larger one had just one wall to wall touch screen with multiple images and an electronic tablet on a small desk. "Where are the rest of the Visionaries, the ones that aren't on duty?"

"You'll meet them here and there," Jeff said. "Some start later and work late into the morning. Others hit the sack early, get off early. Not sure yet what your schedule would be."

Adie peeked into the room where Mrs. Blakefold was holding her finger to a spot on the screen. She shook her head.

"What is it?" Adie asked.

Bethie whipped around, jumping a bit. "Oh, Adie. Thought you'd moved on. What the heck, come on over."

Adie stepped up to the screen, where one small square had an image of Ivan leaning over a plate overloaded with enchiladas and refried beans, barely breathing between bites. "See that? He's supposed to be on a diet."

Jeff's laughter rang through Adie as she leaned closer to see that it was Mr. Blakefold.

"See, dear Adie, when Ivan is over at Spain headquarters, he forgets that I can monitor his habits. These screens here all run on GPS coordinates. And Ivan has an ear implant that gives me his exact location at all times." Bethie shook her head again.

Adie covered her mouth and giggled under her breath. She could see that his stomach stretched over his belt—even sitting up straight—as he sipped a glass of red wine.

Jeff gave his head a quick jerk toward the door, and Adie took the cue and started to leave.

"Well, Bethie, we'll leave you to scold your husband." He winked at Bethie. Then to Adie, "C'mon. I need to show you something."

Jeff led Adie down another dark hallway, same as the others, only this one had a chill to the air and a sound like a small brook passing through. Adie wondered if it was a recording, playing on speakers, to set everyone at ease. A bit of comfort so they weren't reminded they were so far from civilization. Normal civilization, anyway.

They came up to what appeared to be a one-lane train station. Instead of train cars, ski-lift type gondolas lined the track, one after the other, and the path led off into darkness. Jeff opened up the first gondola, and grabbed Adie's hand to lead her in. She sat, her shoulder against the side of the gondola. Jeff sat next to her. "Hold on tight."

Adie gripped at a handlebar just above her head. "Great, here we go again. How fast will we be going this time?"

He laughed. "Faster than before." He reached up for a wire and gave it a couple of yanks.

The gondola took off slowly at first, like when a ski lift loads, then it exploded into speed. Adie braced herself against the wall and Jeff leaned into her. Darkness surrounded them. Despite the smooth movement at such high speed, she began to feel dizzy.

"How long is this ride? I'm not feeling so well." Adie gripped her belly.

He pulled her to him. "Just about two more minutes. It's worth it. I promise you."

Adie saw some light ahead. She stood and leaned toward the front glass. Light? How could it be? She placed a hand on the glass as the light became brighter and brighter. Then she saw trees. Aspens and birches and pines. Tall snow-capped mountains. And water. Enormous amounts of water. The gondola surfaced into a wilderness wonderland. A lake spanned further than Adie could see. Spiky peaks shot to the sky and wooded beauty surrounded them.

They stepped out of the gondola. "I present to you the Agency Retreat. Over 200,000 acres of pure, and of course private, natural terrain. "

Adie gasped. "It's absolutely...breathtaking. Like Vail on steroids or something. Are you sure we're still even in Colorado? I've never seen any place so beautiful." She felt Jeff's eyes on her. But she was overwhelmed with the majesty around her. What was this place? This was her idea of paradise. And maybe Jeff knew that. Maybe this was his deal breaker. If he couldn't sell her with this, then nothing would.

Adie could see a small cabin on a knoll two hundred yards up. She pointed. "What's that?"

Jeff smiled. "The gear house. If you're going to enjoy this place, you've got to have gear. Skis, snowshoes, backpacks, camping gear, kayaks, canoes. You name it. The retreat is all about recreation."

Adie shook her head, beginning to think she must have just magically landed the best job in the universe. "Does anyone actually come up here?"

"Oh, yeah! Well, except for the Analysts. They're workaholics. But everyone else totally uses this place. Best part about working nights? You get to come here during the day." He stretched out his arms to the mountains. "Look at this place. How could you not love it? It's what sold me."

Adie could feel him watching her for her reaction. Would it be enough? She knew she'd already signed the confidentiality papers, but if they were willing to have a place like this, where a person could escape, then it was probably important for IPA to understand what type of person they were dealing with.

Adie picked up on another small barn off to the left, behind a thick batch of pines. "And over there?"

"Horses." Jeff started walking that way. "You up for it?"

Adie smiled and started skipping after him. "Um. Okay, I guess."

A tall, lanky guy hiding behind his belt buckle and ten gallon hat greeted them at the barn. "Welcome. I'm Wrangler Joe."

"Hey." Adie glanced around. "You're alone up here?"

Joe laughed. "Never. A good handful of you people come up every day to get out of that cave." Joe smiled and grabbed two saddles. He turned toward Jeff. "You riding?"

Jeff smiled. "Sure. Why not?"

Joe tipped his hat to Jeff. "Good." Joe leaned toward Adie. "This boy don't recreate 'nough." Joe saddled a stocky white horse with large brown spots for Adie and a black beauty for Jeff. "Painter's her name." Joe said as he gave Painter two love pats just below the withers. "And Mr. Reid here's got Beauty."

Mr. Reid. Of course, Mr. Palley wasn't Jeff's *real* last name.

Joe checked his watch. "Just once around the short track." He pointed to the leather strap on his wrist. "Getting late and all."

"Yep." Jeff led Beauty off and Painter just followed, without Adie having to do anything.

"Wrangler Joe seems nice," Adie said.

Jeff nodded. "Kind of the loner type. But he's been here for about thirty years, since the agency went underground."

Adie looked around, so afraid to blink and miss something that her eyes dried up. "This is amazing."

Jeff held Beauty back for a moment so he could walk beside Adie. She felt a bit nervous. What bomb would he be dropping now?

"You know, Adie, you aren't really like the other Visionaries."

"Well, I haven't met any others besides Bethie, so I'm not sure if that's a compliment or not."

Jeff laughed. "Of course it is. Most of them are just kind of, um, I don't know, strange. I suppose if your life is full of nightmares, you might go a little crazy eventually."

"Excuse me?"

Jeff laughed again. "Oh, you know what I mean. The behavior of most of the Visionaries is pretty bizarre. Even when I recruit them, they're usually pretty, um..." He seemed to be searching for the right words. "Well, most of them keep to themselves. They aren't all that chatty, or even comfortable to be around. Most just hang out with their partners. You're just way more personable than most of them."

"Oh, yeah. I meant to ask you about the partner thing."

"You'll be paired up, too. Helps to make sure you remember the details of your dream and vice versa. It's a really good system."

The long neck of the tall paint bobbed up and down. Her pelvis swung back and forth. The rhythm was like meditation. She could get used to this, too.

Adie leaned her head back, closed her eyes, and in-

haled what she could only describe as complete freedom.

Jeff pulled his horse to a stop. Adie's horse stopped
too. Jeff just stared at her. She stared back. He seemed to
be hanging onto the moment too long, even leaning a little closer. Her heart jumped to her throat. Was he about
to kiss her? Because she was far too overwhelmed already to have to process that, too. Her skin felt hot, eyes
dry.

"What are we doing?" she asked, the words scratchy
and barely audible.

Jeff smiled and nodded at something behind her.
"Look."

Adie turned slowly to peer over her shoulder and
placed her hand to her chest as she gasped. "Wow. I
mean, wow!"

A full-length soccer field with grass greener than a
Crayola crayon sat in a meadow with Aspens setting the
boundaries and huge steel bars encasing nets at either
end.

"Wait." Adie sat deeper into her saddle. "Is this for
me?"

Jeff chuckled. "There's actually a group in the
agency that plays, formed their own league, sort of. But
none as good as you, that's for sure. At least you'd be
able to keep up on your skills. For *when* you go on to college." He winked.

Adie looked out over the field, looking as if it had
been painted into the scenery. For a moment, something
rolled through her. She knew she belonged there. She
wasn't ready to let Jeff in on it, but she was pretty sure
she was going to do this.

"You want to let them ride? I mean really let 'em
go?" Jeff nodded toward a long field of tall weedy grass

ahead of them.

"Absolutely!" She had only ridden horses in the summer, at Girl Scout camp when she was younger. She hated the trail rides when all the horses were in a line just lazily strolling, each horse's nose in the tail of the one in front of them. Adie would always befriend a wrangler and talk them into taking her out for rides. Real rides. Where they would gallop, and circle around rodeo barrels, and go deep into the woods, navigating their way back by compass. She loved it most because this was where the city girl left and a savvy outdoorswoman entered.

Jeff clucked and gave Beauty a final boot. Off she went into a full gallop, and the crazy follower of a paint horse fell into stride right behind them.

"Woo-hoo!" Adie couldn't help herself. It felt too good to have that fresh mountain air blowing through her hair, against her skin.

*

Back at the barn, Jeff hopped off Beauty and handed her over to Joe, then held out a hand to assist Adie in her dismount, which she refused. Jeff let his hand drop to his side and failed to suppress a wide grin. "So, made up your mind yet?"

She wasn't ready to answer his question. "How about you? How'd you get here?"

Jeff stared forward, thought for a minute before he spoke. "I happened to be one of those dotcom guys that didn't know anything about computers but knew how to run a business. Started up a little tech biz my freshman year of college, developing real estate technology. One year later, I started to sell off my company as an IPO.

Ivan was one of the big investors. He liked me." He tipped his head towards Adie. "Offered me a *summer* job here. I never went back. Dropped out of college. Knew I'd never find anything better anyway."

"Okay. So clearly, you're some kind of smooth brainiac, but how did Ivan know you'd be a good recruiter?"

"Guess he thought I was good with people." Jeff poked at his teeth with a piece of tall grass.

Adie rolled her eyes. *Yeah, too good.*

"That and I can read people."

Adie frowned. "Read people how? Like read their minds?"

Jeff shook his head. "No, it's not like that. It's more like I absorb things. Things like character, qualities, and emotional information from people, if I focus on them. Like you, in class. That's why I had to stare at you so much. It's as if I can just feel who you are at your core just by the vibes that radiate from you. Pretty accurate, too."

"Oh, really? So, for example, what did you *feel* from me?" Adie tried not to sound sarcastic.

"Honesty. Loyalty. Integrity. Entrapment. Fear. But mostly, that you needed to be liberated, from your life and from your dreams. I absorbed a lot of tension from you, inner turmoil or something. I think you love soccer, Adie, but deep down, you know soccer isn't forever." He paused. "Am I right?"

"I guess."

"Well, it's how we know if a Visionary is ready for this. And despite your age, I knew you were ready."

Unsure of exactly which emotions Jeff could absorb, Adie's chest tightened. She hoped he couldn't sense the romantic kind. She decided to test the waters. "And what about now? What do you *feel* from me?"

He looked down and lingered on her abdomen. This reassured Adie that he had to concentrate. He likely couldn't pick out an emotion that spun through her on a whim, or a shiver down her spine that deteriorated within seconds. He lifted his head and held out a hand, letting it dangle midair. "I sense that you, Adie Brighton, are very, very, very, very....hungry."

"You're a freak." Adie punched his shoulder.

"Am I wrong?" He smiled and headed back towards the gondola.

"Okay, fine. So I'm hungry. That's not what I was asking."

"I know." He said, and loaded her into the large oval slowly moving around the end of the track. "Let's get you something to eat and get you home. I have a feeling you've got some packing to do." He winked.

"Oh, is that what you think?"

"It's what I know. Now I *have* answered your question."

"Wow." Adie rose a brow and let a small half-smile fall across her face. She gripped onto the gondola wall in preparation for the jerky takeoff. "You *are* good."

CHAPTER FOUR

Adie's parents' first hint that something was up should have been Adie's offer to make dinner, but her mother had labored away the day at the neighbors, weed-whacking and setting in mulch, and moseyed in the door too tired to ask questions. Her dad was already late after preparing a speech for an academic conference.

Adie thought a Spanish dish would be a nice complement to the presentation she would be giving them on her summer adventure to enhance the lives of young athletes in Spain. When she Googled 'best entrée food dishes in Spain,' the results were suckling pig and octopus.

She had called up Payton to see if she had any experience cooking such things, to which Payton replied, "Are you kidding me? Aren't those both registered on the People for the Ethical Treatment of Animals website?" Adie couldn't recall exactly when Payton had declared herself vegetarian.

Adie settled for something more traditional—or at least edible sounding—and impressed even herself with a huge pan of *paella* and a side dish of *gambas al ajillo* (garlic prawns). She dug out a floral tablecloth with vines winding every which way—looked Spanish enough—set out wine glasses for her parents, and poured two Cokes for her brothers in the name of bribery—they never got soda at dinner and she needed them on her side.

Her mother sat with an expression of awe at the

meal before her and placed her napkin in her lap. Her father walked in the door, tossed his briefcase into the small nook that was his office, and after a glance at the table, said 'nice work, honey' before anyone could tell him that Adie, not his honey, had been the chef. He plopped next to her mother, and Adie poured them both a glass of red wine.

Her brothers zoomed in from their game of basketball, sweaty and breathing hard. Fourteen-year old James gulped down his Coke and held it out to Adie for seconds. Twelve-year old Peter stood with his hands on his chair, smirking at Adie. Then he sat and reached for the spoon handle on the paella without speaking to anyone.

"Napkin in your lap, Peter," their mother said.

Peter glanced over at Adie, who had replenished James's cup of soda. "What gives, dude? You never cook."

James placed his napkin in his lap and scooped a heaping spoonful of the prawns onto his plate. "Who cares, man? This rocks. Thanks, Ades."

Adie sat and passed a basket of bread. She knew it would only be seconds before her dad started to pull out the psychology for this odd behavior of hers. She wanted to beat him to it. "I have some news. About a job this summer."

"Really?" her dad said. "Please, share."

Adie ignored her mother's sulking back into her chair. Her mother really wanted her to spend her last summer before leaving home pulling weeds and checking pH balances in soil.

"Hopefully it's not cooking," James said. "How about a little shrimp to go with the garlic? What did you use, a whole bulb?"

Adie paused. "It asked for a clove. Isn't that the whole thing?"

Everyone burst into laughter. Then Adie joined them. The cooking thing had been annoying and time consuming. She was equally glad that wasn't her summer job.

"Oops," Adie said. "Sorry."

Her mother poured some of her water into the dish. "That should help a little. I just appreciate the thought, Adie. The rice is delicious."

"So... about this job," her dad prompted.

Adie cleared her throat. "So, I prepared this Spanish dish tonight because I've been offered a summer job coaching kids' soccer in Spain." Adie took in a deep breath and beamed her best smile.

"Sweet!" James said.

"Where's Spain again?" Peter asked.

Adie watched her dad's reaction. She already knew what her mother's would be.

"That's fantastic," her dad said. "With what outfit?"

"National Youth Touring Camps." Adie blew out her breath. She hadn't expected this sort of enthusiasm from her dad.

"I think I've heard of them. Mr. Morrison set it up?" her dad asked.

Adie wasn't prepared for that question. It hadn't occurred to her that there would be details involved. "No, actually. I was doing a search on youth camps in the area, and this group popped up. I was sure you had to be some really epic soccer player to get hired, so I didn't say anything to you guys since I wasn't sure I'd be qualified. But turns out I am."

"Of course you are!" Her dad's face filled up with a smile. "That is an excellent opportunity, Adie. Good for you."

Adie's mom swallowed her glass of wine in one gulp and reached for the bottle to pour herself another. Adie's whole body tensed. She didn't technically need her mom's okay, but it sure would be nice.

Adie's mom took another large swig of the wine, then sat back in her chair, placed one hand on her lap and took her father's hand in the other. She smiled without showing her beautifully straight teeth, and said, "Sounds like a once-in-a-lifetime adventure, sweetie. Back early August for U of C, right?"

Adie nodded. "Absolutely, Mom." She rose and wrapped her arms around her mother's neck.

Her mother gave her a peck on the cheek. "Our rose bushes shall miss you. Guess James will have to pick up the slack."

James glanced up from his plate. "What? No fair."

Adie cleared her father's plate as well as her own. "Totally fair."

*

Payton sprawled across Adie's bed, *Glamour* magazine clutched between her fingers, glued to an article on how to make last year's cardigan *so* this year. Adie kept pushing replay on a youTube video on her laptop of Mia Hamm on a full-field dribble assist.

"So amazing," Adie said in a low voice.

"I know, right?" Payton replied. "These shoes are to die for. They totally make the outfit."

"Not the shoes. Mia's last move to seal the deal."

"Oh yeah." Payton flipped a page. "Whatever."

Adie pressed replay. Payton and Adie had been best friends since fourth grade. Adie still couldn't put a finger on how the two became so close. They certainly didn't have much in common. But Adie felt sorry for her. Payton's father was obsessed with football — watched ESPN as if he might miss something that would save the world. It was obvious he'd wanted a boy. Payton's mother bolted when she was three, and the pink-loving, tutu wearing Payton was stuck with a father that had somehow received a few extra doses of testosterone.

Adie and Payton had been partners in the first day of gym class in fourth grade and had barely left each other's side since. Payton would have never played soccer, or any sport for that matter — it might distract her from her goal of being a dancer — but Adie convinced Payton that it might help her with her dad. Adie convinced Coach Morrison to make Payton co-captain, and suddenly Payton's dad thought she was kind of cool and even started taking an equal interest in Payton's ballet.

Adie believed that Payton knew they were growing apart — Payton would love to always be hitting some party, throwing out some moves, showing off for the boys — but Adie didn't make much time for friends, and so Payton showed her gratitude by continuing to be Adie's best.

Adie froze a frame with Mia's foot cranked behind her, ready for a big shot. "So, Payton. I got a crazy killer job this summer."

Payton let the magazine fall to the bed, lifted her eyebrow. "No mama's slave this summer?"

"No." Adie turned and placed her hands on her knees. "I got a job coaching kids in Spain."

Payton's jaw dropped. "No way."

"Yeah. Can you believe it?"

"That is freaking awesome. Wait. For how long. And

when do you leave? And most importantly, will there be boy coaches there, too?"

Adie chuckled. "Day after graduation. What about you?" Adie asked, a tad afraid Payton might give her a guilt trip about spending their last summer apart.

Payton licked her finger to turn a page. "Ballet intensive workshops all summer. Daddy's paying." She smiled and raised a brow at Adie.

Adie sighed with relief. "Nice, Payton. That's great."

"Be sure to bring me back a dark, handsome hottie."

"Yeah. I'm sure I'll have them crawling all over me." Adie laughed. Payton dropped the magazine, rolled over, and giggled.

Adie stretched and yawned. "So, you ready to hit the couch?"

Payton reached her legs out long, pointing her toes to the end of the bed. "Can't I just sleep here with you?"

Yeah, right. So you can hear me sleep talk about guns, and knives, and blood, and people dying. "Sorry. You know I don't sleep well with you in the room. You don't want me all cranky tomorrow, do you?"

Payton gathered up her toothbrush and pillow. "No. We *definitely* don't want that. Good night!" Payton slipped through the door, then leaned her head back through. "I'll miss you, you know."

"I'll miss you, too."

CHAPTER FIVE

The Impire Peace Agency Dining room was filled with magnificent long mahogany tables lined with antique wooden chairs padded in velvet. The table settings were quite nice, but nothing formal. Adie was relieved that her inaugural night at IPA wouldn't be awkward with the responsibility of etiquette.

Jeff ushered Adie to a table with Bethie and Ivan at either ends. Bethie offered a sweet smile as Adie sat. Something about her made Adie love her already. Bethie put her hands together into little claps. "Oh, Adie. I'm just so happy you're here!"

Ivan stood and took her hand in a firm shake. "We are so pleased to have you, Adie. Welcome."

Adie blushed, looking down at the utensils arranged around a plate in front of her. She managed a smile and forced a glimpse of eye contact. "Thank you."

Two girls who looked a few years older than Adie pulled out two chairs across from her. They were identical, with the exception of their hair color. Long, thick tresses of hair to be envied: one blond, one dyed black. Tall, toned bodies. Neatly trimmed and manicured nails. One of them seemed to have wrinkles forming around her eyes and looked as if she hadn't sleep in weeks. The other was perky and enthusiastic. Adie nodded to the happy one. The girl waved back and sat next to her less excited twin.

Bethie made the introductions. "Adie, this is Dannika and Daylea Hadley."

Daylea's teeth sparkled and her freshly curled hair bounced as she reached over the table to shake hands, turning over an unlit candlestick. "Oops!" She even smiled as she picked the candlestick up and then stood to shake hands with Adie. "So nice to meet you, Adie."

Adie slowly lifted her eyes to Dannika. It was rare for her to feel such tension and fear even before locking eyes with someone, but there was something about this girl. Something dark. Dannika offered a slight smile and nodded to her. Adie nodded back and caught a glint of a silver loop through her brow and lip. Studs ran up the length up both of Dannika's ears. Adie glanced at Jeff to read some hint of explanation in his expression about two sisters so black and white. She could see his smile was different, and his eyes fell to his lap. He was hiding something.

Everyone was silent while the meal was brought out. Servers dressed in all black poured wine. Adie thought to cover her glass, as she usually didn't indulge in wine, even though her parents had offered from time to time. But she allowed the handsome young server to lean over her. Adie watched as everyone raised their glasses in a toast, swirled the red liquid in a circle in the glass, brought it to their nose first and then took a sip. Adie felt inferior and common. Despite these people's unusual living conditions, they seemed so worldly and dignified.

Adie noticed Dannika rising her glass to her lips repeatedly. Bethie reached over and set a hand on Dannika's tattooed forearm. "Take it easy, dear." Bethie frowned as she made sure Dannika gave notice to her instruction. Bethie straightened up and began to explain that Dannika was a Visionary and Daylea worked in Training.

They all laughed and drank and chatted through soups, salads, and unbelievable beef tip entrees with an unusual tiramisu to top off the most delectable meal Adie had ever had.

Ivan kept a steady pace over his plate, and Jeff caught Adie chuckling under her breath every time Bethie order him to slow down.

Throughout dinner, Adie stole looks at Dannika. An experienced Visionary. Dannika's eyes were dark and hallow. Her skin pale. A rare smile formed from her lips so seemingly melded in the opposite direction. Did she used to be like Daylea? Was it the Visionary work that made her so sullen?

Daylea stood when everyone had finished. "Time to hit the dance hall. Joe's playing tonight, so I wore my kickers!" She held up a foot to display shiny red steel-toed cowboy boots.

"Dance Hall?" Adie shook her head, tilting her head towards Jeff. "I guess I shouldn't be surprised."

Bethie and Jeff chuckled. "Daylea's our dancer."

"That's right," Daylea chimed in. "Let's go. We don't want to miss the first set!"

"I might sit this one out," Jeff said. "I'm really tired."

Adie looked at him like he just killed her dog and left it in the street. Her cheeks tingled from the wine and she spoke too fast. "What? You can't bow out now."

Jeff took a deep breath and looked at Bethie. Bethie nodded to him with an affection that ran deeper than Adie had noticed with the rest of them. "Go ahead, kid. You work hard. You deserve a little fun."

Adie watched as Jeff turned to Ivan, clearly seeking approval from him as well. Ivan wiped his mouth, then nodded to Jeff.

"Yeah, Jeff," Daylea nearly yelled out. "You never

come to the Dance Hall. C'mon!"

Jeff sighed. "Okay. Okay."

They all hopped up and Adie noticed Bethie piling some of the plates onto a tray. Adie began to pile up her own dishes, preparing to scoop them into her arms. Dannika took note and spoke her first words to Adie, low and firm. "What are you doing?"

Adie stood a bit stunned, realizing what she'd done out of habit. She set the plates down. Dannika was shaking her head, and whispered, "Idiot," under her breath. Daylea shot an elbow into Dannika's side.

Bethie spoke. "Just leave them, dear. Dishes, cooking, and cleaning are not your concern any more. You only have one job that you must do here."

"But I don't mind, really. If they need some help." Adie looked to Jeff for some back up.

Dannika rolled her eyes.

"Go on," said Bethie. "You kids go have fun." Jeff brought up the rear, and Adie happened to look back over her shoulder as they were leaving and caught Jeff looking at Bethie. Bethie pointed to Dannika and mouthed to Jeff, 'Watch her.'

*

Jeff led the other three down dimly lit hallways until they reached a couple of saloon doors on hinges. Above the doorway was a large sign carved from wood and framed in old iron bars that read DANCE HALL.

"Nice," Adie said to Jeff. "Real rustic."

"At least it's not purple."

Daylea burst through the doors as if her entrance meant the party could begin. The dance hall was larger than Adie's house and packed wall-to-wall. The saloon-like décor had neon backlight and the furniture was hand carved and sturdy. As soon as Daylea entered, the men in the room sat up straighter. Maybe the party really didn't start until she arrived. Dannika followed her sister to the bar. Jeff motioned to an empty table.

Joe was already on stage with three other musicians. Joe's eyes found Adie, and he nodded and smiled. Adie gave him a little wave. She really liked Joe. In this new world where everyone seemed so·perfect and untouchable, Joe was just real.

Dannika and Daylea worked their way around the room. The bluegrass brought the room alive. Daylea was giggling and flirting, while Dannika just followed her around and rarely took her eyes off the stage. Adie couldn't help but notice that Daylea was holding a drink her hand the entire time, but Dannika's hands were empty. Dannika seemed uncomfortable with her empty hands. Kept rubbing her arms or tucking her hands in and out of her pockets. Every now and then, Dannika would lock eyes with Adie and just kind of stare. Adie was always the one to look away first.

"Who are all these people?" Adie was in awe that so many people could live—and clearly thrive—twenty miles beneath the ground.

"You've barely seen any of this operation, Adie." Jeff answered. "This agency runs like a whole city. Think of a corporation. Then think of the needs of the people that work there; both when they're working and when they're not. It's all here, and so are the people to keep it all going."

Adie shook her head in disbelief. That all the people in Denver were going about their day, walking the streets, window shopping, climbing corporate ladders in high rises, reading morning papers on subways, walking their children to school, laying their heads on pillows at night — with no idea of what lay far beneath their soles.

"Something to drink?" Jeff asked.

"Maybe just a Coke," Adie said, unsure if it was wise to have something stronger.

"You got it." Jeff hopped up and wove his way through the crowd, stopping occasionally to shake hands or return a hug to one of the ladies. He came back and set a large Coke in front of Adie, a light beer for himself.

"What do I owe you?"

Jeff leaned into Adie. "You still don't get it, do you? Money means nothing down here. Everything is taken care of. Limits are placed where necessary by Bethie and Ivan, not by financial concerns."

Jeff was right. Adie couldn't grasp that concept. Her parents were always complaining about their bills losing out to their bank account. It was one of the reasons she focused so hard on getting a soccer scholarship. She didn't want to add another injured soldier to their financial battle.

Adie watched as young and old folks alike moved their bodies on the floor. Daylea kept asking for a line dance song right into the microphone until Joe finally told her he was smack out of them.

"Wanna dance?" Jeff asked, seeming timid and shy for the first time since she'd met him.

"Um. Okay, I guess." Adie stepped off the bar stool and followed Jeff closely, wishing he had asked her on a fast song. Or maybe not at all.

Jeff took one of Adie's hands in his and placed the other on her waist. Adie hated this kind of awkwardness; her stomach turned and her breath was shallow. How was she supposed to enjoy a dance when all she could think about was what Jeff might *feel* from her? She tried to stuff her thoughts with anything boring, like taking out the garbage or putting on makeup.

"This is all really so wild. It's kind of blowing me away" Her mouth inches from his ear, she hoped to ruin his concentration.

Jeff pulled her in a little closer. Adie looked up at him and smiled, while she braced her elbows on his collar bone to keep him from pulling her any closer. What if he could absorb more with physical contact? She liked Jeff. She liked him a lot. At this point, she couldn't find a single thing wrong with him. But there was too much going on with this whole new arrangement—this whole new way of life—and to get emotional involved so quickly would only alter her ability to evaluate the whole situation. She might still want Jeff. But first she wanted time.

Halfway through the longest song in the world, Adie noticed Daylea swaying in the arms of another guy dressed in cowboy attire. Her head lay on his shoulder, his eyes closed. But where was Daylea's sidekick? Adie scanned the room. No sign of her. The room was filled with sweaty, swaying bodies. Maybe Dannika got tired of this whole scene and went to bed.

A wail rang loud over the music. The crowd shuffled to the back of the room. Daylea's eyes widened as she released herself from her cowboy's grip and pushed the crowd aside to get to the bar. The wail became louder than a piercing scream. In the back corner, Dannika's body twitched and flopped around as her face twisted up and her mouth roared obscenities. At the bar in front of her were several empty shot glasses. Daylea got to her and waved at a few strong men. Jeff jumped up to run to them. Daylea reached out and put a hand against his chest. "I've got this."

Jeff's nostrils flared. "But—"

Daylea clenched her teeth. "Jeff, I've *got* this."

Jeff backed off and watched as Daylea and the other men carried Dannika's convulsing body out of the room.

Joe put down his banjo and walked over to Jeff. He spoke to him a moment while Jeff nodded and kept his eyes glued to the floor.

Jeff came back to the table. He'd ordered another thirty-ouncer. "Sorry about that." He said. Adie just stared at him. "I didn't want you to see that."

Adie looked away, choking down a big sip of her warm Coke. Why wouldn't he? Why would she care? That Dannika girl was creepy, anyway. "No big deal. Not really my business."

"Well, in some ways, Dannika is everybody's business. She's just… kind of complicated," Jeff said between huge swallows of beer.

"Apparently so." Adie started tapping her foot beneath the table, noticing that she must be more sensitive to the situation than she realized.

"Dannika, she, um, she's probably the best Visionary we have. She's very successful and she is very well-respected in her work. And most of the time, she's actually pretty cool." Jeff leaned in, spoke more quietly. "But she's been diagnosed by the Analysts with a moderate bipolar disorder. It has been causing slight inaccuracies in her dreams. Most of the time, she's still right on, but occasionally she gets it wrong. Very wrong. They put her on some medication, which seems to work, but she can't mix alcohol with her meds or she's just goes flat-out nuts. She loves to have a drink, and she begged and begged, so they did some experiments with her in solitary on her meds and alcohol. That was interesting.

Anyway, they discovered that a couple of glasses of wine were okay, but that any more than that and the mix is dangerous."

"So what was that about?"

"She must have passed out. Started having one of her dreams. Problem is, when she's drinking on her meds, her dreams are hard to decipher. They get all out of chronological order, and fuzzy. But because she's the best, they always have to check it out anyway. IPA can't run an interference on the murderer unless they know for sure, and in these cases they usually don't know until Ops is already in action."

Adie tapped her fingers against her glass. "So what were you going to do?"

"Take her to Bethie first, before the Analysts. But Daylea knows Bethie will come down on everyone. Probably stop allowing Dance Hall night. Daylea is supposed to watch her, but when everyone is dancing, Dannika sometimes steals other people's drinks. Usually, I keep a pretty good eye on her. But tonight, I, um..." Jeff looked away, then down at his beer. He smiled, "I was a little distracted." He took a sip of his beer.

Adie rubbed her sweaty palms against her jeans, tried to ignore his comment. "So, is that why she was staring at me weird? Just because she's, um, whatever you call it, bipolar?"

"Well, first of all, you're pretty," Jeff said. "Dannika always gives the pretty girls a hard time." Jeff looked down, his expression went somber. "But I do believe that the reason she was looking at you that way is because she knows you're going to be good. Maybe as good as her. Maybe better. She's very competitive." He paused, throwing back the last swallow. He set the beer glass on the edge of the table. "Also, it might be because she's your partner."

Adie's jaw dropped. "She's my *what?*" She knew her eyes must be wide as the table.

Jeff shook his head. "Normally, she's really great, Adie. You gotta believe me. You just have to get to know her."

Adie began tapping her foot harder. "Where are they taking her?"

"To specialized Ops group. They'll evaluate her dream and make a decision to move on it or not. It will be a long process since she's so wasted."

Adie took a deep breath. "Take me there."

Jeff shook his head." No way. You don't want to see this, Adie. Your first Ops interference experience needs to be your own dream. Certainly, a rational one. Not a crazy person intoxicated and completely incoherent and possibly even incapable of providing the information for success. It's not pretty, Adie. When she's good, she's so good. But this, this will not be the norm."

Adie could feel heat rising into her temples, her foot tapping so fast now her whole body shook. "Jeff, I'm in this thing now. She's my partner. Take me to her now."

Jeff blew a breath of air out of his cheeks.

Adie leaned to him. "Take me to her *now*. Or I'll go straight to Bethie."

Jeff frowned and squinted his eyes. "Fine. But then you're on your own."

Adie hopped up. "Fine."

By this time, bystanders had keyed in on their conversation. Jeff waved to them as he stood. "Carry on, guys."

Adie looked back over her shoulder. Joe glanced up from his banjo, sincere concern washed over his face. She clenched her jaw and told herself that whatever was in store, she could handle it. She followed Jeff into the dark hallway.

CHAPTER SIX

Adie could not imagine that the earth could go any deeper, yet they continued to descend to what seemed another hundred yards down a dark stairway. The door at the bottom read Confidential: Operations. Adie raised her eyebrows.

"Only the key players go into the Ops room." Jeff said as he flicked on a light switch that lit a few wall lamps along the stairway. "Lucky you, huh?"

When Jeff opened the door to the Ops room, Adie expected another large room — plush, well-lit, and office-like, as the others had been. She followed him into a chamber only twice the size of her bedroom back home. Dannika was propped up in a navy blue velvet chair. Daylea was holding a wet cloth to her forehead, and intravenous tubes were flowing from her wrists.

Three men were folded over a touch screen that ran from floor to ceiling — about twelve feet high and six feet wide. Three widescreen monitors hung from the wall to the left of the massive system, with keyboards and rows of wireless remotes beneath them. All three men wore headsets.

One screen showed nothing but a dimly lit street, apparently in the middle of a neighborhood. A trash can sat on the edge of a sidewalk, two cars parallel parked just behind it. The middle screen zoomed in on two guys dressed in tight black shirts, black cargo pants, and tall boots. They held guns beneath their armpits. The third screen looked like the outside of an old brick building.

Daylea turned and gave Jeff a scowl. "It's too soon for her, Jeff. You know that."

"It's gotten worse, Daylea. Adie deserves to know about Dannika."

Daylea glanced at Adie, then nodded. "C'mon in."

"Good luck." Jeff said as Adie stepped forward.

"You're not staying?"

"No. I meant what I said. I could have shown you around for a couple more days, but you wanted in on this, so this is where I step back."

"It's okay, Adie," Daylea said. "We'll lead you on from here."

*

Adie felt a drop in her gut, like a steep rollercoaster, as he excused himself. The thought of Jeff just disappearing made her uncomfortable. He had been the one thing so far that made it all seem somewhat normal.

Adie watched the door shut, and her heart wrenched. But he was not the reason she was here. And she was only minutes from knowing exactly what she had been hired to do.

"She okay?" Adie asked Daylea as she took a seat next to her. Adie glanced up at the screens. The three men hovered over the controls while in deep conversation. The guys in black on the middle screen reviewed something that looked like maps.

"Yeah," answered Daylea. "She overdoes it every now and then. But we can't ignore her dreams. They usually reveal something critical. Generally, she has the dreams that break a big case or assist the authorities with a big player. Everyone tolerates her because her cases usually have the biggest payouts." Daylea walked to the sink and ran cool water over the cloth, squeezing it out and placing it against Dannika's cheeks. "I, of course, tolerate her because she is my sister." Daylea sighed.

Adie hung onto Daylea's comment for a moment, churning it around. Jeff had made such a big deal about money not being a matter of concern down here. "Payouts?"

"Yeah. That's how IPA gets paid. Mostly government contracts," Daylea squinted up at the screens.

"So what's going on? Up there," Adie asked Daylea.

Dannika began to squirm and leaned forward. Daylea had set a large bowl beneath her feet. Now she grabbed it, placed it on Dannika's lap, and pulled Dannika's hair back into a ponytail. Dannika's vomit hit the bowl and splattered onto towels that had been laid around her.

Adie's stomach lurched, and she scooted back and looked away. She placed her shirt over her nose. Was she really expected to work with this girl? They were there to save lives, but Dannika didn't seem to value life. She couldn't even manage her own.

Maybe Jeff had been right. Maybe Adie wasn't ready for this. She headed for the door.

"Please, Adie." Daylea eyes were sad. "Just...just give her a chance."

Adie tried to take a deep breath, but the entire room reeked of vomit.

"Just hold on a minute," Daylea said. "Please, please." Daylea left the small Ops room, and Adie could hear her footsteps rapidly ascending the stairway. Dannika's head lay back on the chair. An ugly moan came from her throat.

One of the guys leaned toward the wall to flick a

bright red switch. Vents on the ceiling opened up and a fan started blowing. Immediately, Adie noticed a fragrant smell swirling through the room. Lavender. The stench was already fading. More at ease now, she took the seat next to Dannika.

Adie reached for the wet cloth, dabbed it gently over Dannika's forehead. Dannika slowly opened her eyes, squinted at Adie.

"Daylea?" Dannika barely let out a gargling sound as she mouthed the word.

Adie looked down, then back to the door, in case Daylea had returned. "Um, she'll be right back. She's coming."

Dannika moved back in her seat to sit up a little. "Oh, it's you."

"Yeah." Adie noticed her hand was still holding the wet cloth to Dannika's forehead. She suddenly felt awkward and prepared for Dannika to fly off the handle or tell her not to touch her. Maybe even demand that Adie leave the room. She began to pull her hand away, but Dannika grabbed her arm, pulling Adie's hand back to her head, closing her eyes to absorb the damp, cool comfort. Adie took in a deep breath, scooted toward Dannika, and dabbed the cloth along her head.

Daylea returned and walked over to Dannika. "You all right?" She ran a hand through Dannika's hair.

Dannika just nodded.

"I'm going to consult with the Analysts, see if you're free to go."

One Analyst must have overheard. "I think we're good. Why don't you get her to bed before this whole thing gets too much attention. Looks like it's gonna be a go."

"Thanks, Jago. For everything. Is it the serial case?"

Demry was opposite Jago, typing some command into a computer as a green grid began to swirl. Blinking points on random circles on the grid gave off loud beeps. He stepped in front of Jago and answered Daylea. "We think it is. Ops is already on it."

Daylea unhooked the IV from Dannika's wrist and tucked the equipment back against the wall. Adie watched as Daylea reset the device, as if to keep it handy for Dannika's next fit. She then plopped Dannika's arm around her shoulder and helped her stand.

"Should I come with you?" Adie asked Daylea.

"No. I'm just going to put her to bed. Put us both to bed, actually." Then Daylea nodded toward the screens. "You might as well watch this. See you in the morning." She started the long haul of getting Dannika up the stairs.

Dannika turned to Adie. Her eyes were sunken and red. Her hairline wet along the edges from sweat. Her black t-shirt collar had been stretched out and revealed the hint of a tattoo across her collarbone. "You just might work out." She reached down and slid an oval blue garnet ring from her right middle finger. She grabbed Adie's right hand and slipped it onto her middle finger. "I'll give you a shot," Dannika said. "Partner."

She lay her weak head on Daylea's shoulder and wrapped her arm around her waist. "They're gonna need a piece of me in this room tonight, anyway."

Adie twisted the ring around her finger, unsure exactly what Dannika meant. "Thanks. It's beautiful."

*

Adie made her way over to the screens. Jago began to update Adie on the situation as Demry kept pushing them out of his way to upload information to the Operations dispatch aboveground.

The murder Dannika had seen had been extremely violent and graphic, hence her intense screaming. When Dannika blacked out, they couldn't get a report from her, so they had to hook her up to the scanner instead. The scanner couldn't provide images, but rather sensed different body temperatures and emotions. It also downloaded her brainwaves, and the Analysts evaluated them for accuracy. Based on Dannika's level of heightened fear, as well as the brainwave evaluation, the team made a decision to go forward. Dannika's visions usually allowed for at least a three-day preparation period to plan interference. But in her fits, it might mean only hours.

Adie pointed to the screen. "So, the guys in black. They're IPA?"

Jago nodded. "Yes. We've got all of our department leaders on this one since we are pretty sure it's the Ram case. This perpetrator, we call him the 'Ram.' Demry came up with it. Mostly because that's what the guy is always driving," Jago snickered. "Most criminals like him don't fancy themselves in a pickup truck. So he's been a little tougher to profile. We're afraid he's catching on. Dannika has dreamed of him several times and we've been successful at stopping him. Based on the conversations Dannika can recall and the audio we catch when we run interference, we're fairly sure it's drugs."

"So how did you know where to send Ops tonight?"

Jago raised a brow. "Smart question." He pointed back to an electrical unit with blinking sensor lights above where Dannika had been sitting. "It's a bit of a guess, but we compared her emotional senses to previously recorded dreams, and this one matched up to a location where we've run interference before. So, we think the Ram is giving it another try. It's probably someone he feels has information he doesn't want to go any further."

They matched up Dannika's scan to the house of Jeanie Fogert, assistant to Jim Noder, CEO of First Capital Bank. Since the Ram had gone after her before, Jago had determined that Noder had something that the Ram wanted, and Jeanie had either one of two things that would help the Ram get it: information, or the potential to use blackmail to get information. Noder was likely part of the drug scheme, and Jeanie was either keeping Noder under the radar, or keeping him company.

The case was bringing in big government money for IPA, since Dannika's reports had enough to get the Drug Enforcement Agency in on it. If they could keep running interference until DEA got a bust, it would be the biggest case in IPA history.

On screen two, a forty-something guy with a hard, yet handsome face stepped up. Jago and Demry perked up. He had a short army-style haircut, with deep set eyes and a mouth that didn't seem familiar with smiling. How could he, with what he dealt with? Dreaming was one thing, reality was another. She found herself hanging onto his every word. He spoke strategy, positions of their men, and reviewed timelines. His low voice was like a drum beating against her chest, his face tense and his words firm and steady.

Adie was knocked from her daze when that boom of a voice was directed at her. The man on the screen kept his eyes on Demry. "Who's she?"

Demry stepped back toward Adie and motioned to

her. "This is Adie. A new Visionary. Dannika's partner. She's here for training purposes."

Adie put up a hand in a wave, but the cold face on the screen stayed focused, unaffected. He looked back to his map. Jago leaned over to Adie and whispered, "That's Bain Rogan, department lead for Operations."

A green light flashed across the screen two and Adie noticed five operatives were now exiting the old brick building on the screen to the right, referred to as Screen Three. The camera followed them to a large green van. On the side was a whimsical and colorful logo that read 'Eastside Floral.' IPA disguised themselves as a floral company. Brilliant.

The Analysts were glued to the monitor on the left. A white Subaru Outback drove up to the house as the garage door slowly rose.

Demry typed some commands and the screen zoomed in to the inside of a cluttered garage. A young woman in a skirt suit stepped from the driver's side of the car. The garage door was closing when Adie heard Bain through Jago's headset. "We're just outside."

*

"Let them get close to her, for the DEA's sake. We have to let them see if they can get what they want," Demry said into his headset.

A back door to the garage opened, and a hefty balding man dressed in black leather, dark sunglasses and a gun belt entered, followed by a leaner man with blondish hair, a full beard, and wearing a white tank and jeans. The skinny blond put a knife to the woman's throat.

Jago yelled over at Demry. "Okay, here we go. Volume up."

Demry pushed a button on the switchboard as far it would go and the speakers started blaring the mumbled conversation between the Ram and Noder's assistant. Adie began to feel nauseous as Demry hit a red button labeled 'Record.'

The woman's eyes were wide and full of terror. Adie had seen it many times in her dreams. It was the part she despised — the victim's eyes right before they went blank.

"We're in. I've got the static pushed to the background so the voices are coming in clear. Listen up, everyone," Demry instructed.

The Ram's voice sounded groggy and agitated, like a smoker. Adie watched as he interrogated the young woman. "So what's he got on you, huh? Why are you hiding stuff for him?" The blond man rubbed the knife against her throat, an evil smile on his face.

The woman spoke between sobs. "I don't know what you are talking about."

The Ram moved in closer. He stalled a moment, seemed to take in his surroundings. Then he leaned closer to Jeanie. "We *are* going to kill you if you can't tell us where the new codes are. And when you do tell us, you're going to resign from your job, and you're never to speak to Mr. Sugar Daddy again. You understand?"

The woman began to whimper, hugging herself and shaking uncontrollably. Adie wondered if she knew something. And if she did, what bound her so tightly to that truth? Enough to risk her own life? The bearded man in the tank pricked her throat with the knife. "Okay!" she screamed. "In the bank! He's hiding it in the bank!"

The Ram leaned back on his heels, placed a hand on

his gun. "That's a good girl. Probably in another secret vault or something, huh, pretty thing?" The Ram rubbed Jeanie's face with his finger.

"In the basement. One of the deposit boxes." She was barely whispering now, her voice frantic.

The Ram motioned to his partner to let up. "That a girl. But I'm sorry. Now you've just proved to us that you simply know too much. This is only going to hurt a bit."

Then the Ram did something odd. Adie could tell it was unexpected because Jago and Demry both tightened up their faces and frowned as they leaned in toward the screen. The Ram waved a hand over her face, then appeared to place something on her left temple. Her eyes closed and he headed out the door. His partner didn't follow.

Jago rested his chin on his fingers. "He must know he's being watched. He would have tried to kill her. Like before."

They could hear the Ram's voice, despite having moved off-screen. "Come on, you idiot." His accomplice was still twisting the knife playfully around her neckline. "We're finished with her for now."

The woman opened up her eyes, and the man grabbed her cheeks and puts his lips to hers. She began to squirm, but he held the knife to her neck.

"Rens, that's enough!"

"Just getting a little sugar, boss." Rens kept sucking at the woman's face. "Kiss me back. C'mon, give me a little sugar."

"Get out now or you're done, Rens. We have no plan to remove a body this time. So move it."

"Okay, boss. Okay." Rens tucked the knife into a sheath on his belt buckle. "You'll give it up next time, won't you, lil' sweetheart?"

The woman started to scream.

Demry spoke calmly into his headphone. "It's time, Bain. I'm sure DEA got what they need. This guy is a nutcase."

The next thing Adie heard from Screen One was a gunshot as loud as a cannon. Rens tore out the back door. The woman scooted back into a corner of the garage, put her head in her lap, and covered her ears. On Screen Three, IPA Ops discreetly followed the Ram until he and Rens were well away from the woman. On Screen One, the woman got up and scrambled inside of her house. Bain's voice rang low through Demry's headset. "Get the cops there for that woman *now*. Say a neighbor called it in."

"Right on it." Silence filled the Ops room. Adie bit frantically at her cuticles as her heart pumped blood a mile a second. Within a minute, cops were bursting into the Jeanie's door.

She ran to them and fell into their arms.

They comforted her and sat her on a couch. Jago zoomed in on her face. One cop asked her to recount the entire event. Another cop sat next to her, pulled out a sketchpad and paper. "We need all the details you can remember. Each person involved." He put the pencil to the sketchpad, ready to get it all down.

"I don't know," she said.

"Were they wearing masks? Did they leave the lights out?" asked the cop, although Adie realized that for this line of questioning was just a formality. The cop didn't know DEA would already have all of this information via IPA.

She shook her head. "No. They weren't. And my car lights were on."

"Ma'am, then you've got to remember at least something. The color of their hair. Their eyes. Maybe they were missing teeth. Or had a mustache. Anything, ma'am."

She appeared to be thinking hard. Then she shook her head lightly, tears dripping to her lap. She twisted her face into a look of confusion. "I don't understand." She turned to the cop. "I have no idea what they looked like." Her eyes widened as she wiped the tears streaming down her cheeks. "In fact, I don't remember anything at all."

Jago's face tensed. "Get that woman relocated immediately."

CHAPTER SEVEN

Adie sat fascinated by the marbled walls of the Amphi-theater, so high they seemed to cave in. IPA offered a variety of spiritual services on Sundays, running them one after the other most of the day. Adie hadn't planned on attending — she looked forward to some chill out time to take it all in — but Daylea had stopped by and nearly dragged Adie along.

Adie ran her fingers over her smooth silk skirt. An entire wardrobe had been placed in her closet, and to Adie's surprise, it was completely to her liking. Especially the shoes: shelves upon shelves of ballet flats and sneakers in every color. Plenty of jeans. Plenty of t-shirts.

Her quarters were small, no more than thirty feet wide, but made up for it with tall ceilings. Closets, dressers, and a large desk took up most of the space, along with a sink and hanging mirror above it. Twin beds with thick shabby chic bedding in a bold grassy green lined the walls. Another wall was covered with a floor-to-ceiling bookshelf complete with a ladder to get to the out-of-reach books.

Adie had slept in her quarters last night, as she was still in training. After one week, her nights with Dannika would begin if they felt she was ready. She shared her quarters with Dannika, which bothered her a bit. It was hard to imagine rooming with someone like that. Perhaps that was what the wilderness retreat was all about — not necessarily to get away from the caves but rather from one another.

Adie estimated at least two hundred people at the service today. She looked up at the left balcony and saw Ivan and Bethie in the front row, Macey snuggled up beside Bethie. Steph picked at her nails, and Maimey had planted her elbows on her knees and set her chin on her hands, her face tight and her eyes blank. Adie caught Maimey's eye and Maimey quickly looked away. Adie watched as Maimey kept glancing back to her. Adie smiled once, but Maimey put her chin to her chest and crossed her arms. No sign of Jeff. No sign of Dannika.

The pastor, a middle-aged woman with short black hair and thick make-up, stood preaching in front of a choir clad in burgundy robes. Her voice rang out in waves over the silence of the theater. Adie's family had occasionally gone to church. Well, just holidays mostly. Adie's parents had enjoyed the quiet mornings of the only day of the week they were home as a family. But Adie was comfortable enough, in that unique stillness that seemed to accompany church.

After the Lord's Prayer, Adie turned to Daylea. "So what now?"

Daylea pulled up her skirt. Underneath she wore black spandex shorts. "We train."

"On a Sunday?"

"Heck, yeah. You'll find plenty of fitness clothes in your closet. I'll meet you in the Training Room in an hour."

"You're going to take it easy on me, right?"

"Yeah, right." Daylea winked and turned to strut off toward the exit, her calves lean and defined all the way down to her cross-trainers.

Adie could tell from the first set of cardio intervals that the training was intense—might even put soccer two-a-days to shame. Didn't they just want her dreams?

Daylea smiled. "Trust me. You'll thank me someday. Everyone always does."

"Whatever."

The glass door to the training studio opened as Dannika strutted in, Maimey trailing behind her.

"Hey girls." Daylea yelled out.

Dannika locked eyes with Adie, then looked to her sister and nodded. Maimey held her hand up to wave to Adie, but her face remained solemn.

"You girls here to do some light weights?" Daylea asked, making her way to the squat bar and removing a fifty pound weight from one side.

"No," Dannika mustered, "Just a couple Aikido rounds. That's all."

"Oh." Daylea placed the weight back onto the bar and wiped her hands on her spandex. "Okay, Adie, let's move onto some tricep curls."

Dannika and Maimey did a few stretches and high-knees and jumped roped for about ten minutes. Then they stood apart from another and began to mimic one another's techniques, taking turns. Adie moved closer and sat on a bench to watch. Maimey punched her fist into a couple of jab motions towards Dannika's face and core, which Dannika managed to dodge. Dannika turned into a sidekick, which landed at Maimey's ribs, and both girls backed up and smiled at one-another. Adie began to worry for Maimey. Wasn't Dannika being a little harsh on the little girl? Dannika caught Adie's eye and seemed to purse her lips tightly as she stood facing Maimey.

Daylea plopped down next to Adie. "They're good, aren't they?"

"Not that I have much to judge by, but yeah."

Just as she spoke, Dannika rolled up Maimey into

some kind of headlock, Maimey's feet squirming beneath her. Dannika held her there as Maimey seemed to struggle.

Adie whispered to Daylea, found herself twisting the blue garnet around her finger rapidly. "Isn't she hurting her? She's so small."

Daylea smiled without making eye contact with Adie. "She'll be okay."

Adie was appalled at Dannika's behavior, even contemplated stepping in despite her fear that Dannika might put Adie into the same position, when Maimey gripped at Dannika's shoulders and flipped her over her own, leaving Dannika lying flat on her back. Adie froze, wondering if Dannika would jump up into some fury, but instead, Dannika started laughing, and reached up to give Maimey a high-five.

Daylea started clapping. "Atta girl, Maimey!"

Maimey gave Dannika a pull up, raising Dannika to her feet. Dannika nudged Maimey with her elbow gently. "Okay, Daylea, maybe we'll do some light reps. I think I've been beat up enough for one day."

Maimey's cheeks went crimson and she tucked her chin to her chest as she smiled. Then she glanced up at Adie. Adie smiled and gave her a thumbs-up, watching Maimey's smile grow bigger. Dannika glanced back over her shoulder, not saying a word.

*

The outdoor workouts were Adie's favorites, because they got to go to the wilderness retreat. With the spring thaw, the ground was damp, and the air was still crisp and fresh. A hint of an icy breeze usually snuck up on them during their evening runs to tighten the air in

Adie's lungs. They always raced the last hundred yards. It was the only time Adie ever saw any tension between the sisters. Daylea always won, but only by seconds.

Adie usually just kept her jogging pace. Dannika would glare, to entice her, invite her into their games, but Adie didn't bite. Dannika might want to compete, but to Adie, they would be partners, not opponents, and it was going to be up to her to prove that.

Dannika didn't speak much to Adie, would just slip into their quarters for clothes or books or to brush her teeth. Adie wondered who watched Dannika's dreams while Adie was training. And if Dannika was unhappy about the change, but she didn't dare ask.

No one spoke of Jeff. Like it was no big deal for him to basically vanish from their everyday lives. One day, about two thirds through their run around the lake, as her temples pounded from the exertion, all Adie could see was his face. Where was he? Why didn't she ever see him? Why did neither twin ever talk about him? She'd have to bring it up in her best attempt at a sly, round-about way.

Between heavy breaths, with Daylea and Dannika on either side of her, Adie spoke out into the open air. "So, does anyone know much about that Bain guy? The one in Ops?"

Adie noticed Daylea smile and shoot a glance at Dannika. Dannika kept her eyes forward, her face hardened as she bit at the pierced loop in her lower lip. Finally, Daylea turned to Adie, barely having to breathe at all, and answered, "Sure. He's hot, right? Off limits, though. Guys in Ops and Recruitment aren't allowed to date. They're too on the move and their jobs are mostly above ground. Ivan says it would be too much of a distraction from their work. So it's in their contract. They basically sign up to be old bachelors."

Adie stopped running. "Wait. Recruitment?"

The other girls stopped and turned to her. Dannika smirked. "Yes, Adie. That means Jeff."

Adie looked up into the mountains. *Well, isn't he smooth.*

"Yep. Sucks for you," Dannika said.

"Dannika!" Daylea lightly punched her sister in the shoulder.

Adie placed her hands on her hips as she caught her breath. "No, it's okay. She's right. Guess I was kind of obvious. Sucks for me."

Dannika rolled her eyes and let the sarcasm roll off her tongue. "Kind of?"

"Like you're one to talk, Dannika." Adie perked at the sarcasm in Daylea's voice.

Adie glanced from one girl to the other, examining their reaction. It wouldn't surprise her if this routine with Jeff was common among the women here.

"You don't know anything." Dannika got in Adie's face. "Not Jeff, you hear me? That guy keeps me out of trouble, like a brother. He's a nice guy—which, by the way, is totally not my type."

"So it must be..."

"Enough." Dannika clinched her teeth until her jaw tensed. "I'm done." Dannika took off in a full sprint.

"Don't worry, Adie. She'll warm up to you eventually." Daylea started jogging again.

Adie barely heard her as she kept pace with Daylea. "But what about Lonie? She's married."

"They recruited Lonie and her husband as a team. I guess you could say she was grandfathered in. But she and her husband have an understanding. Lonie recruits young men and to lure them here, she's got to be a bit of a flirt. Jago's cool with it."

Adie's heart ripped. All that Jeff knew about her. The way he looked at her. Everything he said. The way he would touch her hand. It was all just a plan. Why would he accept a life like that? Why would anyone? Daylea sped up. "I better catch up to Dannika. I'm really sorry, Adie."

*

Adie continued her days in a fog, her mind bewildered. The meditation was the hardest. She could run and kick and box Jeff from her brain, but when it was time to slow down and meditate, his face was all she found behind her eyelids. His smile dominated her thoughts, and how they were last, dancing at the party. It was all she could do to try to tuck him away somewhere else. She hadn't even tried out that beautiful soccer field. Something about it reminded her of him.

The first day Adie gained 'official' partner status, she found Dannika in their closet with a half empty bottle of vodka, kicking at the walls. Black mascara ran down Dannika's cheeks. When Adie peeked around the closet door, Dannika hugged her knees with her palms balled into fists. The finger with the red garnet ring was scraped up and smeared with blood, as if it had come into contact with something hard. The wall, maybe.

"Um, Dannika? You gonna be okay?"

"Go away. I want to be alone."

"Yeah, sure. Okay, but um, I'm thinking I should get that bottle from you. Maybe get it back to the Dance Hall bar before someone notices it's gone."

A moment past before Dannika held the bottle up to Adie. Adie took it slowly, securing the twist top. She could see Dannika's finger a little better. The cut looked deep beneath the red stone. "Are you sure you don't need—"

"Go." Dannika's voice sounded hoarse and tired.

This was just the first of a series of incidents between Adie and Dannika that gave Adie a real sense of Dannika's volatility. Adie treaded lightly, as if in a dark tunnel where a train could come charging through any minute.

Not once did Adie go to Bethie or Daylea. Not once did Adie give Dannika away. Instead, she would just be there. When Dannika pounded down on a bookshelf so hard it cracked in half and a shelf full of books tumbled onto Dannika's toes causing her to fold over in pain, Adie called maintenance and told them that she had 'stupidly' tried to climb up the shelves in a hurry to get a book up towards the top, causing the books to fall on her partner's foot. As the maintenance man hauled out his tools after a quick fix to the shelf, Adie locked eyes with Dannika, and for the first time, Dannika nodded, acknowledging what Adie had done. This was the moment Adie knew that something shifted. Adie had earned Dannika's trust, and maybe that ·was what Dannika needed before she spent even one night in the sleep room with Adie. Dannika had demons—no doubt—and Adie finally understood that to share those with another Visionary must have been a threat of its own.

*

Though she had yet to have a murder revealed to her, Adie still wrote reports on her dreams as trial runs, to learn to capture details. Unless the dream was about Jeff. In that case, she'd just say there was nothing worthwhile to record.

Dannika would go down at 6 p.m. and sleep until 1 a.m., then Adie from 1 a.m. to 8 a.m. In their first two weeks, Dannika opened up two cases, and Adie took ferocious notes on how everything Dannika did after she woke, from her reporting, to the conference room meetings with the Analysts and Tech, until the night of the event when they would huddle up in the Ops room to witness their hard work in action.

Five weeks into their partnership, Dannika had a run of thirteen nights straight where she slept in peace. Adie noticed Dannika's hands shook as she typed her morning report. Adie yawned and stretched her arms.

"Are you okay, Dannika? You took your pills, right?"

Dannika rubbed at her forehead, snagging her sleeve on her eyebrow ring. "Yeah, um, I'm good. It's just..." She turned to Adie with a deep breath and tapped a pencil against her knee. "It's just that I never go this long without any visuals on The Ram case. He's too quiet. It feels weird, Adie. Like maybe he's messing with me?"

"Are your dreams with the Ram worse than the others?" Adie sank into the bedcovers next to Dannika.

"It's not the dreams that frighten me. It's...it's just that the Ram, he seems so unstoppable in my dreams. Like nothing could touch him. I just worry about Bain, you know?" Dannika hugged her knees and leaned her chin on top of them.

"Why are you worried about Bain? He's amazing. Talk about unstoppable."

Dannika looked Adie in the eye. "I don't know what I would do if I lost him."

"Oh. So, you and Bain?"

Dannika shook her head. "He's off limits, remember?" She paused. "He's just been on all my cases. I don't want to do this anymore unless I work with him. And before the Ram, I've never been afraid that I would. But now, I don't know. Things just don't *feel* the same. Almost like maybe The Ram is playing me, like he has a strategy or something and I'm part of it. I can't really explain it, but I've never felt this way about any perpetrator before."

Adie wrapped an arm around Dannika's shoulders and pulled her close.

"I know it's silly. I mean, I've never even met Bain face to face. Analysts say he has some condition that keeps him from coming down here." Dannika grinned a little and her cheeks grew a little rosy. "It's just so unfair, Adie, that I can't even meet him. You know, just maybe shake his hand."

"Is there anybody else down here that catches your eye? Someone in Tech, or Architecture and Construction, maybe? Some of the Analysts are pretty cute."

Dannika pulled away. "Ha. Analysts, are you kidding me? They're nuts. And they think I'm the one whacked out." She paused. "But no, there's no one. Just Bain."

"Yeah, I kind of know how you feel."

"I know you do."

Adie stood. "Why don't you grab some coffee before I fall asleep? Better hurry though."

Adie's head hit the pillow, and immediately she found herself in the middle of a forest so thick she had to keep pushing branches out of her way. She kept walking until she came upon a wooden door attached to nothing but air. Adie knocked but got no answer. She slowly turned the knob and the door opened onto a tropical beach.

A man stood knee high in the mellow waves with his back to her. When she was within twenty feet of the man, she could feel he was familiar. After one more step, her body rushed with excitement. It was Jeff.

He turned around and locked eyes with her. Adie smiled and ran to him. He grabbed her and pulled his lips to hers. A moment later, he stepped back and dove into the ocean. Adie put her hand to her forehead to block the sun as she looked for him, but a dense cloud rolled through and there was nothing but a bright white fog around her.

When the cloud passed, Adie was standing on a sidewalk at the entrance to a bank. Three employees exited the bank with briefcases and folders, waving goodbye to one another: it was closing time. Adie watched as a security guard entered the bank. A chill blew over her and she knew — this was the real thing, and she was nothing but an invisible witness. She followed the security officer into the bank. No one was in the lobby, but she saw a tall man with a receding hairline through a large picture window. A plaque beside the door to the large office read *Jim Noder, CEO.*

The security guard tipped his hat to Noder and fumbled through a ring of keys for the one that opened a door behind the main teller desk. As he disappeared through the door, Adie sprinted to reach it, but it had closed.

She glanced back at Noder to make sure he couldn't see her. Adie's shoulder's dropped. How could she screw up her first case? She squeezed her eyes shut and focused on removing everything from her thoughts. When she opened her eyes, she was in the corner of a room full of safety deposit boxes. The security officer was typing in codes on a big rolling money box, probably to transfer the money from a vault. A yellow blur whizzed by Adie's peripheral vision on her left. She jumped back into the wall of boxes and froze. Rens had the security officer in a head lock and looked ready to twist his head right off. He grabbed the officer's gun and put it to the man's head.

Adie watched every move Rens made to be sure she had them in the right order. After questioning the security guard, Rens removed a strange weapon from an inside coat pocket — like a small pistol with a bulb-like sphere on the end — and shot the security officer between the eyes without a sound. The officer dropped to the ground, half-hidden behind the money box. Rens removed the silencer and wiped down the gun, placed it back in his pocket, and disappeared. Adie watched the blood pool around the officer's head. Then as always, she became stuck on the victim's eyes, but this time, they weren't blank. They were completely gone.

Adie woke when a strong force shook her body.

"Adie! Adie, wake up. C'mon! Wake up!" It was Dannika.

Adie sat up, gasping hard.

Dannika stared at her, and Bethie stood behind her. Adie flopped back down onto the bed and rubbed her eyes. "That was the worst one ever." Her mouth was dry.

Bethie sat next to her and placed a hand on hers. Dannika had a cup of coffee in her shaking hands.

"What time is it?" Adie asked.

"It's only 3:30 a.m.," Dannika said. "You were totally freaking, man. Like, I've never seen any Visionary tear up like that."

"Look who's talking." Adie said.

Dannika grinned and nodded. "You get cooler every

day, girl."

Bethie helped Adie sit up. "So, this is good, honey. Your first case. Dannika and I will lead you through your reports, and we need to get on that right away since we aren't sure of your memory capacity yet."

Adie nodded, moved into a wheeled chair, and rolled up to the computer. "Um, there's one thing I think I better tell you right off." Adie paused until Bethie and Dannika gave her their complete attention.

"What's that, dear?"

"The murderer. It was Rens. It was the Ram's guy."

Dannika fell back into her viewing chair, her arms limp at her sides. Low and slow she said, "No freaking way."

CHAPTER EIGHT

Daylea was squatting with a hundred pounds on either side of the bar that lay across her shoulders.

"Hey." Adie picked up a small exercise ball and dribbled it around with her feet, then kicked it up with her toe to bounce it a few times back and forth between her knees. "That all you can do?"

Daylea set the bar on the rack with a smile. "Taking it light today. You been out at the field?"

Adie plopped onto a weight bench, setting her right foot on top of the ball. "No, I can't seem to get into it down there."

Daylea's eyes softened. "I thought soccer was your life."

Adie sighed. "It was—I mean, it is. I don't know. Guess I'm just distracted with everything."

"Hmm." Daylea retied the rubber band around her loose ponytail. "So, what's up?"

Adie twisted the blue garnet around her finger. "How does Dannika handle it? You know, when the dreams get more intense?"

"You call how Dannika behaves 'handling it'?" Daylea raised an eyebrow. "Anyway, I'm a little more concerned about how Dannika is handling you." Daylea removed the weights and placed them on a rack.

"What do you mean?"

"It took Dannika at least two years to have the kind of attention to detail you've acquired in only weeks here. And tagging in on her case in your dream? So crazy. I just know how she is. She really likes you, but she'll al-

ways want to be on top, if you know what I mean."
Daylea pumped out a few bicep curls. "But, of course,
now you guys are like, the 'dream team,' literally."
Daylea lowered into a leg stretch.

Adie rubbed her foot on a dumbbell. "I just feel bad
for her. It was the worse one I've ever had. Are hers always that way? Usually, in the dreams I feel like a bystander, and it all seems indifferent. But this time, I had
this awful guilty feeling, like I was involved somehow."
Adie shook her head. "It's probably how we take in so
much more detail for the reports, but I think I see why it
drove Dannika over the edge."

Daylea reached for the dumbbell under Adie's foot
and handed it to her. "Might as well use that." She sat
next to Adie, her elbow on her thigh as the dumbbell
rose and fell. Adie didn't' feel much like training, but
she imitated the motion to humor Daylea. "Anyway, it's
not just the dreams that have caused Dannika's illness.
It's likely that it's genetic in some form. But we have no
way of knowing." Daylea set the dumbbell to the floor
and stretched out her arm. "We were adopted."

Adie sat the dumbbell on her lap, just rolling it
around. "Oh. And where are your parents now?"

Daylea wiped at her forehead. "Lost them in a private plane accident. It was the biggie that brought Bethie
to Dannika. Dannika dreamt about the wreck. They were
good parents. Did a good job not trying to make me and
Dannika be 'identical,' since clearly we are not." She
shook her head. "Anyway, Dannika wouldn't come here
without me, but she was freaking out about dreaming
her parents' death, and she wanted to do something
about it. So here we are. I guess I kind of did it for her.

"Believe it or not, since you've been here, she's been
happier than I've seen her in a long time. She hated you

at first, but she hates everybody at first. You have a way with her. Something not even I have." Daylea wiped a towel across her forehead and pulled on a pair of bright yellow sweatpants. Two other sets of Visionary partners entered the studio and waved a hello. Daylea smiled at them and sat opposite Adie, with her back to the other ladies and keeping her voice now to a whisper. "But be prepared, because she'll be envious of you, too, the way she is with me, and all of us. We lost our parents to that plane accident, and with no identified family in the city, they don't let Dannika go up there. It would be too dangerous, even if someone were with her. We all get to visit every now and then, but not Dannika. She only gets the retreat. She kind of resents us sometimes."

"Isn't there anything they can do? I mean, is that really a life for Dannika, to never get to go up to the city at all?"

Daylea shrugged. "Not my rules. I gotta get going. You could probably use a round of circuit training before you go." She winked.

"No, thanks. But I'll throw in a few extra push-ups just for you at Aikido tonight." Adie smirked. "Besides, I have to meet in the Ops room in an hour."

Daylea leaned back from the doorway. "From what I hear, you're about to see why it's all worthwhile. Why the Visionaries keep at it. Good luck."

*

Adie strolled the hallway, conflicted by her feelings about her first experience watching Ops run interference on intel from her own dream. Maimey was wandering toward her, one hand following along on the wall, her feet dragging.

"Hey Maimey. What's up?" Adie stopped, glad for the distraction.

Maimey shrugged. "Just bored, I guess."

"Yeah? Well, um, why don't you go up and have Joe take you for a horseback ride?"

Maimey rolled her eyes. "I already did that today."

"Oh." Maimey's expression hit Adie hard. She knew Steph likely had her reasons for working with IPA, but kids didn't belong down here.

"Are you headed to watch an Ops interference?" Maimey's eyes perked.

"Yep. First time it's one of mine."

"Can I come?"

Adie knelt beside her. "I wish you could. I really do. I'm sure when you're ready, they'll put you to work around here."

Maimey kicked at the wall and used her lower lip to blow at her bangs.

"Hey." Adie stood and placed a hand on Maimey's shoulder. "If you want, I'll take you out to that soccer field later. Teach you some moves."

"Really?" Maimey's smile melted Adie's heart a little. Somehow, the thought of teaching Maimey seemed like an entirely different type of gift to offer. Not to mention it could technically qualify to lessen the lie to her parents a bit. "Awesome. Come and find me?"

"The second I'm done."

Adie descended down the steep stairway into the Ops room. Dannika was sunken into a beanbag on the floor, crunching on an apple. Demry's arms flailed around the large monitor switches as he typed in commands and pointed wireless remotes at the walls until all screens were up. Bain appeared on Screen Two. Jago flipped through a stack of papers four inches thick: the

Ram file.

Adie plopped onto a chair next to Dannika. "Hey."

Dannika kept her eyes on the screen. "Hey," she said through her mouthful of apple.

Adie rubbed her hands together, then leaned forward on her thighs, fingers entwined. Her stomach churned, and acid rose to the back of her throat. What if it didn't work? What if she didn't tell them enough, or the right time, or place? What if her first interference was a total failure? Would Dannika be disappointed in her? Would they have to start at square one? Would Bethie think she was incompetent? Would they send her home? Did she kind of want them to? If she went home, would she be free to see Jeff? Would Jeff even want to see her?

Dannika leaned toward Adie and grinned. "Hey, girl. Chill out. It's all good."

"So, you're not worried anymore?"

"Oh, yeah, I still am. But I feel like we have a one up on the Ram now, you know, with you dreaming on Rens. It's kind of like you're my assistant now." Dannika winked at Adie.

Yep, still has to be on top.

Dannika continued, "I'm feeling a little better about it. Besides, you're right, Bain is amazing." Dannika leaned back into the beanbag and crossed one leg over the other.

Bain's face grew bigger on the middle screen and Dannika became still. Bain looked past Jago and Demry to Dannika. Adie knew better than to turn her head completely, but from the corner of her eye she saw Dannika's face light up. Dannika gave the screen a small wave, and Bain nodded back to her. They seemed to hold one another's stare until Demry broke the silence.

"Okay, Bain, Adie caught the clock at 5:14 p.m. when the security guard entered the door to the safety deposit boxes, and then at 5:23 p.m. when Rens entered. The gunshot went off shortly after, at 5:28 p.m. We are going to try to get on tape what Rens says to the security officer for the DEA. But that alarm has to go at 5:28 p.m. sharp or that officer is toast. Triple the volume on that sucker so it really throws him. It's gotta be enough to make him run."

Bain's voice came through loud and low. "We've already got our watches matched to bank clocks, cameras on the money box and the wall trim, the wires and timer set, with an extension out to me for backup. If I don't hear the alarm the second my watch clicks over to 5:28 p.m., I push a button and she goes off. If I still don't hear, I'm busting in."

Demry punched coordinates into the computer as he talked. "Also, DEA wants to tail him this time, so back them up until they get to the location."

Adie glanced at the clock. 5:11 p.m.

"We're moving into position. Signing off," Bain said, with one last glance over Demry to Dannika. Adie was sure she saw him grin.

Demry started talking to himself out loud through each camera. "Satellites, check. Bank cameras, check. IPA van camera's, check. Street camera's, check. Collar minis, check. Watches, check." He went on and on until Adie thought for sure the entire world could be visible on those screens with the push of a button. Maybe it could.

Screen one showed the bank employees leaving and the security officer walking through the front bank door. Adie took a deep breath and rubbed her sweaty palms on her jeans.

Jago talked into his headset, and Demry moved back and forth along the switchboard, to change screen angles to keep up with the officer's movements and Ops locations. Dannika sat perfectly still, her eyes wide.

The security officer tipped his hat to a man in a large office — Noder — and shuffled through the keys to unlock the door. The camera on the left followed him down the stairs and into the basement safety deposit box room. Then the screen went blank.

Demry moaned and typed like a madman at three different keyboards.

Dannika stood up. Jago pulled the headset microphone to the side and yelled over to Demry. "What's going on?"

"I don't know."

Screen two still showed Bain and two other guys sitting quietly in their green floral company van. They all stared at their watches.

Jago pulled his microphone back to his mouth. "Bain. We've lost visuals on the deposit box room. Stand by with caution."

Bain looked to the camera that appeared to be implanted into the rear view mirror of the van and nodded, as if this information didn't faze him a bit. Adie saw him grip a switch with a large red button at the end of it.

Screen three showed the outside of the bank, where an occasional car drove by. Adie watched the clock tick by, the armpits of her shirt soaked through with sweat. Dannika paced behind her.

5:23 p.m.

Jago spoke through his headset. "Okay, guys. We can't see him, but according to our clock, Rens just entered." Then Jago turned to Demry. "Can't we at least get some damn audio in there?"

Demry's rubbed at his receding hairline, making what was left stand up all crazy, and kept punching at keys. "C'mon, c'mon, c'mon!"

5:27 p.m.

"Here we go," Jago warned everyone.

5:28 pm.

An alarm rang through the speakers so loud Adie and Dannika curled back and covered their ears. Rens busted through the door on screen three and darted off through the first alleyway.

"Copy that," Jago said into his headset. He turned to Demry. "DEA's on him. Focus on screen three."

Demry kept the screen on Rens, who dodged fences and garbage cans until the black Ram truck was in sight, parked on a side street in a quiet residential neighborhood. The passenger door flew open and Rens jumped in. The truck squealed off before the door had closed behind him. Jago called out street names and directions into his headset, and moments later an old car holding undercover DEA agents was discreetly following every turn of the truck. The middle screen zoomed in on Bain's face as he navigated the green van behind the DEA car.

Dannika continued to pace and looked up every few steps. Adie sat back in her chair and hugged her knees.

On screen three, the black truck pulled up to a large industrial brick building, where an oversized garage door lifted just enough for the truck to slip in and closed tightly behind it.

Jago yelled to Demry, "At least make sure you get the coordinates on that place. Get us what we need to get inside."

Demry nodded and sat before one of the smaller computers that still had a swirling green grid, various dots blinking randomly.

Bain looked into the camera. "I take it you guys got that. DEA's got their checkpoint now, so I'm headed back to check in at the bank."

Jago tipped his head. "Right. Good work, man."

Jago took a deep breath, glared at Demry as he threw his headset down on his keyboard, and stormed out.

Sweat poured down the sides of Demry's face as he locked in on the brick building and began to download building and spec reports. Adie watched as he captured images of the Earth far beneath the building and miles into the sky. Another computer listed characteristics of the building, such as the materials, wiring, phone lines, networks, wireless, satellite signals, any electronic devices, plumbing and pipes, venting systems, security systems, lock and key systems as well as keyless entries, watch animals, and all appliances. Not a single thing about that place was left unnoted.

Demry compiled an electronic report and waited for Bain to receive it on a square handheld device the size of Bain's palm. When Bain gave the thumbs-up, Demry wiped his forehead with his sleeve, then headed out of the room. "Sorry about that, girls. I need a drink."

Adie stared at screen three, a plain brick building that now appeared to hold nothing. Bain's face occupied the screen in the middle. He looked at Adie, making the first eye contact with her she could recall. "Nice job, Adie. Your recall reports were perfect."

"Thanks." Adie glanced over at Dannika.

Dannika raised her brows at Adie, then did a quick jerk of her head toward the door. "Do you mind?"

"Oh, yeah. No problem. Catch up to you later?"

Dannika held out her fist, the pink garnet rock protruding. Adie put her fist to Dannika's and their rings collided. Adie felt like some goofy fourth grader with a secret handshake, yet she knew that to Dannika, this meant something. But Adie wasn't one to ask.

Dannika winked at Adie, causing her brow ring to flutter. "You rock, girl."

Adie smiled. "You too." Then she glanced one more time at Bain on screen, who had allowed a small smile to run across his lips. Adie exited to leave the two alone and keep her promise to Maimey.

*

Adie and Dannika sat in Bethie's office, sipping coffee. Bethie entered carrying an armful of files. She clicked at her computer and Ivan showed up on her screen, sitting at a table piled high with Belgian waffles.

"Ugh! That man!" She turned toward them. "Anyway. You girls are outstanding. Your performance is to be commended." Bethie shook hands with Dannika and Adie. "We are making great progress on this Ram case." She turned to Adie. "I don't know how you did it — jumping into Dannika's case like that. But it's only happened once before. Pretty incredible. Nice work."

Bethie motioned for them to sit and poured herself a cup of coffee. "So, I thought you both could use a little time off."

Dannika looked down at her cup and swirled it around. "That's okay, we're good," she mumbled.

Adie stiffened. "Wait. No, I would love that. I want to visit my family. I'll take it. When can I go?"

Adie felt Dannika's eyes on her. She glanced to the side and could see that it was more of a glare. Adie thought about what Daylea had said and sighed. But she had to go, whether Dannika understood or not.

Dannika set her cup down and huffed out of the

room.

Bethie placed a hand on Adie's shoulder. "Don't worry, dear. She'll be all right."

"I just feel bad for her. I've watched her, um…" Adie sat silent for a moment and tried to choose the right words. "I've just been trying to help her, so it's hard. That's all."

Bethie took in a deep breath. "You're a good friend, Adie. But with Dannika's mental concerns, we only let her go out to the wilderness retreat. Her situation is unfortunate. See, you have to pass loyalty and confidentiality tests in order to go up for a visit to the city. We can't afford for anyone to make a mistake or leak any information. Dannika just never passes."

Adie tilted her head in thought. "Even on her meds, she doesn't pass?"

Bethie shook her head. "Even on her meds. She just forgets certain things she cannot say. Under certain types of stress, she can't keep her mind on an even keel. So, even with Daylea at her side," Bethie paused, as if she knew what Adie was thinking, "even with *you* at there every single moment, she's too much of a risk."

"Geez," Adie whispered. Then she took a deep breath. "Well, I need to go. Just a few days maybe. So what do I need to do?"

Bethie pulled out a machine and hooked it up to Adie's wrists and temples. She felt a small electrical current moving through the wires that aggravated her skin slightly.

"This is called the Purger," Bethie explained. "It will bring out every piece of information about a particular subject that you hold and that your brain feels is necessary. If your brain is trained enough to only purge non-sensitive information, you pass. An untrained brain will purge everything you know about your life at this moment, which would of course expose us, and you would fail." Bethie gave her a small smile. "Don't worry, it doesn't hurt."

Bethie began to ask her a series of questions regarding IPA. A electronic pen recorded what she said, while other parts of the equipment recorded her body heat, the dips in her voice, her heartbeat, and whether her eyes dilated or twitched. She asked what Adie would tell her family and friends to ensure it complied with the information they had been sent about her being in Spain. She asked her how she intended to spend her week, and she quizzed her on where she could and could not go and could and could not say.

Bethie scooted forward to remove the electrodes and wires from Adie's body. "Well, my dear, have a nice vacation."

"Really?" Adie's voice rose. "When?"

"You'll go first thing in the morning. Better get packed."

CHAPTER NINE

Joe adjusted the stirrups, pulling Dannika's leg around to lie on the horse's round belly. "Now you know where you're going, right?"

"Seriously, Joe." Dannika rolled her eyes and grinned. "Don't worry. Got my map. Not that I need it. I'll be fine. If I'm out more than three days, I give you permission to come looking for me."

Joe smiled and shook his head. He pointed to her pack. "Should I double check you've got everything you need?"

Dannika jerked her hand over her pack, as if it were full of diamonds. "No! I mean, it's okay." She'd reacted too quickly. "C'mon, Joe. How many times have I done this little trek?" Dannika reached down to give Painter a pat on the withers. "Me and ol' Painter, here, you know we're good to go. We'll be fine. Three days, Joe. See you then." And she headed toward the trailhead.

When she glanced over her shoulder, Joe was still watching her. He tipped his hat, a gesture she returned. It was then she suspected Joe must know she was up to something. Joe was the closest thing she had to a grandpa. He had taught her how to ride, to set up camp, to build a fire, and how best to navigate the wilderness on her own. The nice thing about Joe, though, was that no matter what he thought about her at that moment, he knew well enough to just let her be. Lord knows, no one else could seem to — except Adie.

Dannika had thought that little miss goodie was going to be one huge pain in her rear, but it turned out that Adie was kind of cool. Cooler even than Dannika's own twin. Definitely more than her parents had been. She gave Dannika something Dannika needed and no one seemed to want her to have. Space.

Despite her fetish with those ridiculous ballet flats, Dannika was beginning to feel like Adie just might have the potential to be more than a partner. Like maybe a friend. And if she could talk her into a tattoo, then they could really bond. She smirked, knowing the city above would fall through the Earth before Adie would put permanent ink to her perfectly porcelain skin. Still, Adie made Dannika's IPA imprisonment bearable again — almost.

The spring runoff trickled through the streams running alongside the trail. Every now and then, Painter would step off path to sip some of the icy water, and Dannika would take the moment to wet her whistle as well with a lovely bottle of potato vodka freshly stolen from the dance hall's neglected stash. Each long pull of the clear liquor gave her more courage to follow her plan.

Her pack was full of thin wool and mid-weight polyester. She wore a knit cap and leather gloves and chaps. Her sleeping bag was guaranteed to forty below, plus she had an extra bivvy sack. She had a stove, lighter fluid and matches, plenty of food, and most importantly, this time she had a companion. The liquid kind.

Dannika had tried sneak a gun from the safes in the gearhouse, but they never let her have access to the guns, which she thought was idiotic, since it was her best protection against the animals wandering about in the wilderness. But she knew what that was about. That she wasn't likely to use it to end an animal's life. Now her own — that was a different story. As if she would. All she could find was a switch butterknife.

She could admit she had issues — mostly because of all the damn rules around that place that seemed to only apply to her. Dannika knew she was a little different from most girls — hell, most people — but she wasn't completely crazy, no matter what all those arrogant psychologists thought.

After all this time, her own sister still just let it in one ear and out the other, all the while trying shove that worthless medication down Dannika's throat. It sure was a lot easier on everyone else when Dannika wasn't 'acting out.' But Adie would let it slide, let Dannika work it out on her own. Yeah, Adie was cool.

Dannika hit the fork in the trail where it veered to the left into the twenty thousand acres of unknown that no one at IPA was allowed to travel. They'd never admit it, but Dannika was sure that Joe headed out there every once in a while, and IPA seemed to just look the other way. But, of course, they'd never give her that same small dose of freedom.

She had never strayed into that backcountry, despite the nearly unconquerable temptation. They'd probably lock her up in some solitary cell. She took a long pull on the bottle, letting Painter graze a few moments. The consequences of disobeying were ugly. They'd take her off the job for at least two weeks and she wouldn't get to attend any of the fun events. Sometimes it was so hard to make the choice that kept her life normal — if normal was living as a supposed crazy woman in the deep unknown of the world.

The job itself was like superhero stuff to the unknowing people in the city. Dannika loved that part. Her best days were watching Bain — well, simply watching him would be enough—but to see him carry out a mission that her dreams had initiated was most fulfilling. Each time, their connection deepened, as if their souls were winding around one another. Like this joint venture to save innocent people was an intense aphrodisiac between them. Only IPA and their idiotic rules kept them apart.

If she took that path now, the one off limits to everyone at IPA, she surely would be making a life-changing decision. But what was her life anymore? No one could carry out the rest of their days the way she was required to, crazy or not. Getting to the city would have dire consequences, but she missed it: buildings that reached to the sky, rooftop gardens that overlooked a crowded city, live music that seeped from the alleys, traffic and horns and sirens that blared. She longed for all of it. Screw all this nature crap, man. She'd had enough. She would rather die than never be free to live, or to love.

One more long pull left the vodka only three-quarters full, and she knew that if she could just take that path and keep going, surely it would lead somewhere, possibly even the city. She could handle it there. A concrete jungle couldn't be anything by comparison.

"It's time for a little more adventure," Dannika whispered to Painter. Painter snorted and pawed at the ground. Dannika knew Painter could feel her tension right through the saddle. Kept pulling at the bit to the right, as if Painter knew the stakes of making a wrong choice, helping to give her one last chance to carry on as they always had. But she pulled Painter to the left and gave her a swift kick in the belly.

"Here we come, you lions and tigers and bears," Dannika called out with a smile. She peered out over her shoulder at the vast land filled with her past dreams, adventures, and everything she had known for the last five years. If she were caught, she'd be done. Every last privilege taken from her. Bethie and Ivan's already dwindling trust would shrink to nothing. But watching Adie pack and get all giddy to visit her family had been too much for Dannika. It was worth the risk. She sighed, tucked the bottle firmly in her saddlebag, and never looked back.

CHAPTER TEN

Adie lay on her bed as she enjoyed the gentle feeling the pale yellow walls gave her. Her mother hadn't changed a thing, which surprised Adie, since her mother tended to redecorate the rest of the house on a monthly basis. Surely, her mother would have found a new use for Adie's room now that she'd be off to college soon. Maybe a greenhouse for starting seeds — it had good lighting.

She wondered if her mother would even realize how much she had changed since going to 'Spain.' Could she really keep this secret? But then, she had kept her dreams to herself all those years, regardless of the fear and confusion and terror. There would just have to be a part of her that her family would never know.

The first day home had been fun, trying to imitate the Spanish accent that Steph had prepared for her, just for kicks. She felt confident she had her façade down pat: the location of the camps in Spain, the host family mother and father, brother and sister, the friends she had there, the kids ("Oh, they're just so cute and sweet; and some are really good soccer players, too."), a potential love interest — a fact Adie knew Steph had added just in case Adie might need a really good excuse to go back to Spain someday. The loyalty test included a lie-detector test, which had made her heart beat faster simply to think about it. But deep down, she knew that IPA was locked within her tightly, and her new life would be one that, to most people, did not exist.

Her mother was all engrossed in her new worldly daughter. The kitchen and living room had assumed the décor of Madrid, and everything they ate had garlic and onions in it — even at breakfast.

"Dad's home for dinner, dear!" Adie heard her mother call up.

Adie could smell the tapas. She took one last moment to look around her room. Maybe it was time for her to take down the posters of the USA women's soccer teams, the photos of Adie and Payton at the state championship, and the sweat-stained old cleats and shin guards Adie had sworn had sentimental value. Adie knew the only way for her mother to really let go would be to let go of this room.

Adie threw a light gray cardigan around her shoulders and checked her face in the mirror. She tried to think what she might be doing if Jeff had never approached her that day. Would she be going through the motions of just trying get through the summer, the thought of her first year at U of C the only thing to keep her going? Dreaming of murderers, never knowing she had the power to stop them? Would it have been better to just endure the nightmares and live a normal life? Or could that life be considered normal either? Definitely not.

She touched her lips and closed her eyes. Jeff's faced appeared and his grin sent shivers through every muscle, every tendon. Why did he just leave like that? And nothing since? Did Recruitment have to always lay low, separated from everyone else? She'd spot Lonie at the occasional meal, or strolling down the halls now and then? She'd even made excuses to wander down to Recruitment, just pass by the open doors and sneak a peek inside, but he didn't seem to be around. Did he just want to avoid her? Did he have other women who he knew wouldn't have the trouble of commitment? Would he want her, even if he could have her? Was this idea that he felt something for her just all in her head to begin with?

Adie opened her eyes. She was still so young. There would probably be someone else someday. There would have to be.

"Adie?"

"Coming, Mom!"

She followed the sweet and spicy scent of fresh cilantro into the kitchen, where her dad stood with a handsome young man in khaki pants and a blue and red plaid button-down shirt. His sleeves were rolled up and his pants slightly wrinkled. His dark hair was longer on top, swept to the side to reveal deep chocolate eyes. Adie stopped and took in his smile. Her cheeks filled with heat and she could feel her mother's joy radiating at her side.

"We have a dinner guest?"

Adie's father gave her a hug. "Yes, Adie, this is Witt Trudeau. He is my teacher's assistant, working towards his doctorate in Clinical Psych."

Adie offered Witt a firm handshake. She felt her lips peel away into a large smile. "Nice to meet you."

Witt grinned. "My pleasure. I've heard about you. Pretty cool, working in Spain. And congratulations on your soccer scholarship. That's a big deal."

Adie nodded. "Gracias." She looked away as a wave of embarrassment fell over her. She was trying way too hard without even trying.

Her mother reached for Witt's coat. "Let's go ahead and sit. Dinner is on the table."

"Isn't Payton coming?" Adie asked her mother.

"We told her we had guests tonight. You can call her later."

"Okay. I'm just going to use the restroom first." Adie moved past Witt slowly and their shoulders brushed. Her chest tightened as she closed the door behind her. She stared into the mirror again and shook her head. She blew a big breath out and tried to calm her heartbeat.

She leaned into the mirror and whispered. "I can predict people being shot by a gun, but I can't see this guy coming?"

Collecting herself, Adie joined them at the table, where, of course, she'd been instructed to sit directly across from Witt. Dinner conversation revolved around Adie's adventures in Spain, and Witt's sky-high ambition, according to Adie's father, to help bridge the opposing definitions between biology and psychology as to what was the underlying cause of human thought and behavior. Witt often used words Adie didn't understand, but she couldn't bear the thought that Witt should find her not up to his academic standards—which she wasn't.

She was careful to slowly sip the single glass of wine her parents had offered her, so as to not let the alcohol speak for her. Every now and then, Witt would whip his head to the side to get the bangs out of his eyes, and nearly every time, he'd focus on Adie and smile. She'd never found a napkin in her lap so interesting. She knew her parents were trying to set her up, and she hated them for that. She didn't want to like Witt for that reason—didn't want it to be the guy her parents set her up with. But her cheeks tired from smiling, and her chest filled with warmth.

As Witt put his coat on and said his thank-yous to Adie's parents, Adie could feel his eyes on her.

"Could I talk to you outside for a minute?" he said.

Adie's mother smiled and gave Adie a side nod.

"Sure." Adie moved toward the door.

The early summer evening air was crisp, causing Adie to wrap her arms around her shoulders. Witt leaned against the deck rail. "Kind of awkward, wasn't it?"

Adie looked down at her feet, nodding. "Yeah. I expect that from my mother, but my dad?" She smiled up at Witt, then looked down again. "Anyway, it was nice to meet you."

Witt paused. Adie could feel the tension in the silence. She looked up and waited for him to speak.

Witt scratched his head. He looked nervous. "Would you like to go to lunch? I mean, I know you only have a few more days before you have to go back to Spain, but, um, I don't know, maybe tomorrow?"

Adie felt her face light up. "Yeah. Sure. I'd like that."

Witt started to back down the steps to the walkway. "Great. I have class till noon. Pick you up after that?"

"Sure." Adie waved. "See you then."

"Tell your parents thanks again. Bye." As Witt walked to his '92 diesel Volvo, he turned to wave again before he stepped into the ancient-looking vehicle and drove off.

When Adie shut the door behind her, her parents were standing at the sink pretending to wash dishes together, odd since her father never helped with dishes. Adie turned to them, "Nice. Real nice."

"I know. Isn't he?" Her mother threw her towel over her shoulder and lifted a brow at Adie.

"No," Adie continued. "I mean, yes, he is nice, but that's not the point. Since when have I ever given you the idea that I would want a set up? And by my parents of all people." Adie rolled her eyes and started for the table. She carried a large platter of leftover enchiladas and a bottle of half-empty salad dressing into the kitchen.

Her mother took the platter from her. "Oh, c'mon honey. He's such a nice guy. We couldn't resist."

"Well, I am going back to Spain, by the way, if you thought some heartthrob might stop me." Adie went back to the table to retrieve empty wine glasses.

"We know. Your dad just thought he might be interesting to you. You've always been so...picky." Her mother turned back to the sink to rinse the wine glasses. "Your dad and I will take care of this, honey. You go relax."

Now her poor dad was roped into the one household duty he just couldn't stand — dishes. Adie was sure he now thought his bold move to bring home a guy was a mistake. It cost him precious post-dinner relaxation time. He smiled and nodded at Adie, though he surely knew exactly what she was thinking.

"Actually," Adie gathered up the remaining empty water glasses and unused silverware and brought it to the kitchen, "I will take you up on that. Dad deserves the abuse." She winked at her dad, then sunk into the deep leather couch and opened up a random book from the side table. She turned her head over her shoulder. "We are having lunch tomorrow, in case you were wondering." Adie peeked over her shoulder to see her mother and father give each other a discreet high five beneath the running water.

*

Adie lay in her bed and thought of Witt. Her heart hadn't fluttered so much since she'd met Jeff. In fact, she was pretty sure that those were the only two instances in her entire life when she'd met someone and felt so silly from the start. She thought back to the first time she'd seen Jeff—the supposed Mr. Palley—and giggled. She never could have predicted all that would happen. It seemed like years ago.

She wondered if Witt would have such a fascinating story. Something so incredibly unusual in his life that she couldn't help but to want to know more. He was probably just handsome and eccentric, yet predictable, like her father.

Her cell phone ID lit up with Payton's name.

"Hey, Payt. What's up?"

"Your mother dissing me on dinner, that's what. What gives?" Payton's voice sounded groggy and irritated.

"Sorry. My dad brought home some guy that teaches with him. I think they were setting me up."

"Oh, that's so gross. You're kidding me, right? Well, you survived." Adie could hear Payton chomping gum.

"He's actually kind of cute," Adie whispered. She didn't doubt her mother's ear was at her door.

"Oh!" Payton's voice rose. "Then next time I am crashing dinner."

Adie laughed. "Anytime. See you in the morning?"

"What? You aren't coming out tonight? Huge party at Jake's house." Payton's yawn vibrated through the phone. Adie imagined Payton spent her summer nights out a little too much.

"No. Sounds fun, but I'm tired. I'm sure I'll be up before you. Call me."

*

Adie's eyes were heavy. She let them close and began to think that a few days might not be enough. She did miss IPA after being away a couple of days. She really missed Dannika. But to meet someone like Witt—it made her feel different about that world. What if she would never meet anyone that she could share that life with? If not Jeff, would someone else come along? She remembered the interference. To watch an operation that was based on her visions was terrifying, yet the most thrilling adventure she'd ever encountered. But was all that enough, if the risk was to never have love?

Her breathing deepened and her body relaxed.

Adie could see Jeff clearly. His face was vivid, though it was dark. He was walking in a dark alley. Behind him was a street that looked oddly familiar. His hands in his pockets, his pace slow and lacking purpose.

She'd never seen him look this way, so drained of confidence, of positive stride. He swayed a little, like he might have had one too many drinks. She focused in on his face—tired eyes, blackened bags beneath them. He didn't smile and his hair was a mess.

*

He approached the end of the alley and turned right. Smack in front of him, a tall, stout blond man blocked his way. Jeff looked up, seemed to excuse himself, and attempted to slide out into the street to pass. The man's eyes squinted and his mouth tensed as he stepped in front of Jeff.

"Can I help you?" Jeff asked.

"Yes, you can," the blond man said. "You can take

me to where that Adie girl is."

Jeff tried to move forward again. "I don't know what you're talking about."

The man put a hand to Jeff's chest and took a knife out of his belt with the other. "Oh, yes, you do. She's working for you now, right? Young little sweet thing? You bring her to me, you can go."

"I'm sorry." Jeff's words seemed to slur. "I just can't help you. You've got the wrong guy."

The knife moved up to Jeff's neck as the stranger's thick arms wrapped around him. The face came into focus. It was Rens. He'd cut his hair, and he looked different—heavier, stronger, fiercer.

"Please, just let me go. I just want to go home and go to bed. I have nothing to tell you."

Rens ran the knife from Jeff's neck to his jaw line, drawing blood.

Jeff's eyes closed, his face scrunched up in pain, then Jeff raised a knee into Rens's crotch.

Rens folded forward, a face of agony, and Jeff took a fist to his temple. Rens hit the ground but kept the knife in his hand. Rens stabbed the knife into Jeff's thigh then pulled it right back out. Jeff winced and grabbed his thigh and lifted his other foot to plant a heel into Rens's forehead.

Rens flew onto his back, his face now bright under the street light. Jeff dove for the knife, but Rens pulled it away, took a swipe at Jeff's abdomen, but missed. Jeff gave him three strong kicks into his side and once again tried for the knife, but Rens swung his legs beneath Jeff and knocked Jeff off balance, causing Jeff to lose his stance. When Jeff hit the ground, his shoulder and hip took the blow of the concrete.

Rens rolled on top of him, the knife to his throat, and

said through bloody teeth, "One last chance. Where's the girl?"

Jeff just shook his head.

"Too bad. We will find her. I know you guys keep your people all tucked away. But she's gone too far. You can bet we'll find her. Your life, though, you could have saved."

Jeff's body went limp. He leaned back into the street, his shirt clutched tightly in Rens's hand, his throat completely exposed. His face went blank. On the verge of surrender.

A loud giggling pierced the air. Rens glanced up. A pack of six young women and two young men were strolling down the sidewalk.

Jeff's eyes opened, but he couldn't look behind him. He just watched Rens as conflict crossed his face. The giggling and chatter got louder as the group neared Rens and Jeff.

Adie was following the pack behind a tall guy with broad shoulders and peeked around him to see Rens and Jeff.

"What's going on there?" someone said. Footsteps quickened. It sounded like a herd of elephants on the quiet street.

"You lucked out this time, 'Palley'." Rens jumped up and ran in the opposite direction.

"Hey, you! Stop! We're calling the police!"

The group had reached Jeff and leaned over him. He heard a low male voice. "Oh man, he's hurt bad. Someone call 911."

One woman placed her hands beneath Jeff's head and looked over his cheek, then instructed one of the men to tie her scarf around his thigh.

Jeff reached up to a man who'd taken out his cell

phone. "Please, just call an ambulance. The police will follow." Jeff looked out in the direction Rens had run. "He's gone, man. Trust me, he's gone." Jeff laid his head back on the sidewalk.

*

Adie shot up in bed, her hair and t-shirt soaked in sweat. Her whole body trembled. She closed her eyes as she tried to see the street names. Edith Street, right in front of Cornell's Corner Market. She ran to her desk. Her hands shook so rapidly she could barely write it down. She squeezed her eyes tight and forced herself to narrow down a timeline. But she couldn't. It had felt too real. Everything told her there was no time. She glanced at the clock. Midnight.

Adie threw on her coat and boots, dug through her mother's purse for the keys, and slipped out the door to her mother's 1968 faded turquoise Chevy truck—the one used specifically and solely to pick up shrubs and flowers. She drove to Edith Street, less than a mile away, and parked in front of Cornell's. No one in sight. Only stillness. She stepped out onto the sidewalk where she saw smears of blood. She put a shaky finger down to the burgundy liquid, fresh and moist as it soaked into the tiny bits of gravel that cars had spewed to the side of the road.

"Oh my gosh, this really happened." Adie looked all around—still no sign of anyone. She could feel her heart throb like thunder. She hopped in her car and headed to St. Peter's Hospital. Three blocks from the accident, she passed three police cars, red and blue lights flashing in every direction.

Adie sprinted into the hospital. The emergency room

admission desk was surrounded by a family of five—two kids appeared to have head wounds and the mother held her arm. Perhaps a minor car accident. Adie tried to wait patiently until she couldn't stand it any longer.

She leaned over the now seated family, who was spitting out information to the admission clerk. Adie thought she could smell liquor on the father's breath. "Excuse me. I just need to know if a Jeff, um—" she searched for the words as she considered which name he might use. "Palley, Jeff Palley checked in."

The admissions clerk frowned, "Have a seat. I'll be with you in a moment."

Adie backed up, looking around for any door she might bust through. Her moment came when a nurse with a cart holding vital-signs monitor opened the door next to the admissions clerk and pushed it toward the seated family. Just as the door was shutting, Adie squeezed through. She looked at the names on doors and opened those without names.

Over the loud speaker, Adie could hear her fate. A very disturbed admissions clerk announced, "An unauthorized person has entered Wing A. I repeat, an unauthorized person has entered Wing A."

Adie heard footsteps that were surely about to round the corner when she saw the name on the door. *Jeff Palley*.

Adie busted the door open. "Well, hello there!" Jeff looked up, eyes wide. Adie shut the door behind her as a thunder of knocks banged against the other side.

"Adie, what are you doing here?"

Adie held the door closed. "So sorry, Jeff. I just had to know. And they were making me wait."

Finally, the force was too much and the door flew open, and pushed Adie towards the bed. Two security officers and three nurses flooded the room.

"It's okay," Jeff said, loudly and firmly. "It's okay." Jeff reached for Adie's hand, placed it in his own. "She's my girlfriend. She was just a little concerned. I told her my room number." Jeff pulled her hand to his lips and gave it a light kiss.

Adie's heart flipped over as she leaned her weight onto the bed and rested her hip next to Jeff's shoulder.

"So sorry," Adie said to the officers. "I know it was wrong, but the admissions lady wouldn't answer me." Adie let tears stream down her cheeks. She watched as the faces of the officers and the nurses softened.

"You'll need to fill out the visitor form," one of the nurses said.

Jeff left Adie's hand in his. "Could you bring it here for her? She's a bit startled."

Adie wiped her cheeks and sniffled.

The nurse nodded, and the rest of the staff followed her out of the office.

Adie stiffened. "Girlfriend, huh?"

Jeff grinned and blushed as he dropped her hand. Adie wished she hadn't said it. Maybe he wouldn't have let go. "Well, you weren't gonna get yourself off on those tears alone," he said. "Nice acting, though."

"Probably wouldn't win me an Oscar, huh?" Adie said through more tears. He reached up to wipe her cheek. It gave Adie a shiver and she dropped her gaze to the ground.

"But you're still crying." Jeff spoke softly.

"I know."

Jeff tipped her chin up and forced her eyes on his. "Thanks for coming, Adie."

"Are you okay?"

Jeff nodded. "It hurts, but I'll survive."

"I saw it, Jeff. The whole thing, in my dream, only an hour ago. I saw it in real time, Jeff." Her voice shook. "And I was there. With those kids that found you."

Jeff frowned. "Wow. That's... amazing. I don't think anyone has been able to do that."

"What does it mean? I mean, if it's in real time, we can't stop it, right? Isn't this a bad thing?" Adie felt a little panicked, as if things were slipping out of control.

"Woah, girl. Take it easy. It's okay. Something did stop it, right?"

"Yeah, a pack of college kids who luckily were heading home from the bars. They asked me directions in my dream, and I sent them your way. I just... I just don't understand."

"You stopped it in real time, Adie. That's really rare, you know that?"

Adie's mind raced, her eyes locked to his.

Without thought, she grabbed his hand again and squeezed it gently. "He almost got you. How do they know, Jeff? "

"He asked about you, Adie. Something's not right, for him to know your name."

Adie dropped his hand, turned away, and placed her face in her hands. "Oh my gosh. It's all my fault. If the dreams would have stayed with Dannika alone, no one would know." She turned to Jeff. "It's me, Jeff. Someone knew about me. How could that be?"

"I don't know, Adie. But we'll find out." He paused. "It's not your fault. What is going on with you and Dannika—your dreams colliding—it's a big deal, Adie. It'll take our work so much further."

"What?" Adie face froze. "How is that even possible?"

"Anything is possible, Adie." He stared at her with

gentle eyes.

Adie wondered if there was a double message to that statement. She thought quickly to change the subject. "So, what'd they say? About your wounds?" Adie pulled a seat to his bedside.

Jeff rubbed his hand over his thigh. Adie could see stitches in his cheek. She wondered if he felt self-conscious about them. She thought he'd never looked more handsome. "They said I'm going to be just fine." He put his hands to his sides, used them as a crutch to push himself up straighter, and looked Adie in the eye.

Adie felt weak, as if she might collapse if she didn't look away. "Can't I be of any help up here, Jeff, with you in here? What can I do?"

Jeff eyes narrowed. "No. You can only make things worse. Stay out of it, Adie. Just being here is dangerous enough."

"So, I just go back home, as if nothing's happened?"

"Yes." Jeff leaned his back on his pillow. "Everything will need to go back exactly as it was. It's the only way."

Adie paused in thought, anger rising up in her. All of this, and they go back to normal? First there was that *Anything is possible, Adie* baloney and now they'll just pretend neither of them feel anything? He'd almost died, and yet that wasn't enough for either of them to admit their feelings? Was she reading too much into all of this? Only one way to find out. She straightened up into her seat. "Well, I suppose that shouldn't be too hard. I met someone." She watched Jeff's reaction closely.

Jeff hesitated, didn't look her way. He closed his eyes and sucked in a deep breath. Adie watched his chest rise, and imagined her head there, her cheek warm against his skin, rising and falling with his breath.

Jeff spoke without looking at her. "That's really

great, Adie. Just make sure you're prepared to, you know, have to be dishonest with him."

"Yeah, well, apparently part of being with IPA means keeping things to ourselves." She watched him, hoped to find a sign, anything that might give her a glimpse of what he was thinking.

"It's your business," Jeff said shortly. "Just remember your vow to IPA."

"I can keep a secret, Jeff."

"I know you say that now, but trust me." Jeff turned to her, his eyes intense. "You get in deep and keeping your secret will be hard. If you decide to stick with IPA, you're better off with someone in IPA."

"Who? Like you?" Adie grit her teeth, her lips firmly pressed together.

Jeff's head dropped. He closed his eyes gently, then looked back up to her. "You know I can't, Adie." He inhaled a deep breath, seemed to hesitate. "If I could be with anyone, it would be you. But I can't."

Adie's heart dropped. Her glance dropped to the floor and she felt like that white linoleum might just slap her right back. After all of that, she wasn't sure if it was better to think he was off-limits or uninterested. Now that she knew, all that was between them was his signature on a piece of paper.

Her eyes rose to meet his. "You would?"

"Yes."

"Well, I'm sorry that's the life you've chosen," Adie's said in something that resembled a whisper.

"Yeah, me, too."

Adie felt her heart was full of daggers, and the seconds of silence felt like hours. "I better go. Will you *please* actually find me and say hello next time you're down at IPA headquarters, let me know you're all right?

I'm tired of all this you-avoiding-me garbage."

"Sure thing," Jeff said. "You understand why I had to do all that 'avoiding-you garbage,' right?"

Adie stood, leaned over Jeff's forehead and softly placed a kiss just above his brow line. He reached for her chin and pulled her mouth to his. Adie's whole body filled up with his kiss, as if she'd burst from her skin. Jeff moaned and backed off. He winced and held his cheek. His eyes squinted in pain.

"I'm so sorry. Did I hurt you?"

Jeff let out a deep breath, slid down into his pillow, and closed his eyes. "You could never hurt me, Adie."

CHAPTER ELEVEN

Dannika's heavy head fell to the soft make-shift pillow created with fleece wrapped into her cotton tee. The light breeze felt nice against her skin, and the quiet of the campground brought her a peace she hadn't felt in a long time. Even if she had just this one night, these short hours to be alone, to enjoy that delicacy of drink she was so often refused back at the agency. She reached over, taking in one more pull from the bottle, closing her eyes to savor that slight burn in her throat. She tilted her head back, feeling as if the liquid could run right through her, as if her core were empty. As if her soul had escaped her. She pulled the sleeping bag up over her shoulder and let her eyes rest.

She found herself moving slowly down a busy side-walk, arms linked with a beautiful older woman who had pulled her long silver hair into a low ponytail and wore only the slightest bit of mascara. Dannika's biological mother. It was Christmas, and the strip full of re-tail stores was lit up in colorful displays of toy elves and stuffed reindeer and fake Santas. Dannika and her mother stopped to window shop and laughed at an old holiday memory. Her mother pointed in admiration at a cashmere sweater in the window before they turned to continue on their evening stroll. When they turned, a masked man put his gloved hand over Dannika's mouth, and a gun to her mother's head.

Dannika woke rapidly and sat up, the only sound her heart beating too quickly for the slight rippling of the stream beside her camp. Her ears pumped with each beat and her veins felt thick, as if her blood were made of syrup. Her forehead pored of sweat. She glanced at her surroundings: the wooded forest, the narrow channel of water, the remains of a campfire, the items of her backpack strewn around her, Painter tied up to the nearest tree, a nearly empty bottle of vodka next to her pillow. Just a dream.

*

Her chest fell as she blew out a deep breath, and wiped at a tear on her cheek. This particular dream haunted her occasionally, kept things hidden from her. She would try to nail down a timeline, but Christmases would go by and the dream would return. Every time she would know that what she witnessed in this dream was years into the future, and that their real mother was out there somewhere, alive. She had a love/hate relationship with this dream; love because it meant her mother was most likely still alive, hate because she wasn't sure she would ever really know for certain.

Dehydrated and head pounding, she rubbed her hand along the ground, fumbling for her flashlight. She checked her watch; only four in the morning. She sat in the silence as the gleam of the moon reflected off the bottle beside her.

Something began building inside of her, her core filled up, moving into her chest, up her throat, until her head felt so tight it might explode. She reached for the bottle and slung it at the nearest rock, watching as the shards shot off in every direction. How long would she have to live this way? Why can't they let her seek the one person who might have the answers she needs? The one person who could love her unconditionally. Or who should.

Dannika shined the flashlight in every direction but only saw darkness among the treed shadows. She drank a half a quart of water and plopped back down onto her pillow. Her head was still a little hazy, but at least she wasn't spinning anymore. Tears built up, and the more she tried to contain them, the faster they came. She curled her knees into her chest and allowed herself to sob. She could never control her anger, but sadness, that was different. She wasn't the girl to cry. Not even if no one was around. But now, her body shook with each wailing sound that erupted from her throat. She no longer had the strength to fight what her body had been battling to release.

When she'd settled enough to hear the rippling of the stream over her own breath, she let her eyes slowly drift shut.

A slight breeze rolled over her exposed face. Dannika could hear leaves crunching to the south. Her eyes opened. She held her breath, her muscles on alert. Another rustling sound and her body tensed more tightly. Was she dreaming again? She couldn't be sure. She slowly turned her head to the side and caught a sparkle of the moon's glare off the stream. Another crunch of the leaves and she couldn't take it anymore.

Dannika sat up. "Who's there?"

She looked into the shadows to the south. Only the outline of empty branches filled the spaces. Then a form moved ever so slightly behind a tree only ten yards away. She grabbed her butter knife, pressed the smooth end which transformed the knife to a spear, and slithered her way out of the sleeping bag, her eyes on the dark form behind the tree. The only way to have the upper hand was to make the first move.

She charged the tree and a human shadow darted left, hopped the stream and knelt on the other side behind a large stump. Dannika held the small spear in her hand and willed her legs to move faster. Dannika cleared the stream and the black lump began backing up slowly. The dark figure held up a hand and screamed for Dannika to 'just hold on a minute' but Dannika had gained too much ground. Dannika pulled back her empty fist and lodged it into the jaw of the invader. Her next shot was to the gut.

The figure attempted to swing back, but Dannika ducked, grabbed the arm, and pulled the body over her own flat onto its back. She hopped on top and placed the spear to the person's neck. "Who are you?"

The invader moaned. Dannika grew impatient. "Tell me who you are or I'm going to remove your esophagus."

A hoarse, barely audible female voice spoke. "Please. Please, Dannika. Just, please, hold on."

Hearing her name only heightened Dannika's anxiety. "You better tell me who the hell you are before I slice you to pieces."

"Dannika, I'm with IPA. Just, please, I can explain."

Dannika pulled the spear away and clicked it back to the form of a butter knife. She eased her grip on the young woman's skinny arms. The woman pushed Dannika to the side and sat up, putting a hand to her face to feel her jaw. She had short, spikey hair, a sharp chin, and a tiny frame. But that was all Dannika could make out in the slim slits of light breaking through the tree branches. The woman looked up at Dannika. "That's your survival kit out here? A butter knife?"

Dannika narrowed her eyes. "It's a switchspear butter knife. It's all I could get a hold of. And I'll use it too, if you don't start talking."

The woman touched her jaw lightly. "No you won't."

"Yes, I will. Just try me."

The woman shot Dannika a firm look. "Dannika, we both know that you will never use a knife or a spear on anyone." She squinted up at Dannika. "So why don't you put it down and we'll go over and make a fire? I'll explain everything."

"No way. You talk now." Dannika could feel her hands shaking, unsure if was from dehydration or withdrawal or fear.

"Look, Dannika. I'm on a break. Just like you. I'm freezing and am not anywhere near as prepared as you are. So, please, can we go make a fire?"

Dannika stared at her for a moment. "Okay. You first."

*

Dannika followed the woman over to her camp. The woman sat next to the ashes from Dannika's fire and began to throw some sticks on the ashes at random.

"You don't know how to start a fire, do you?"

The woman shook her head.

Dannika piled tiny sticks into the form of a teepee, threw a few drops of gasoline on the top and lit a fire. With the glow of the rising flames, Dannika could see the woman more clearly. She was older than Dannika. Thirty, maybe. Beneath her sorry excuse for outdoor clothing of skinny jeans and a tweed blazer over a tank top, the woman's body appeared lean and limber. The woman opened and closed her jaw to test where Dannika had laid the blow.

Without looking up at Dannika, she introduced herself. "Name's Jocelyn. You got anything to eat?"

Dannika threw her a bag of beef jerky. "Continue."

Jocelyn opened the bag and ripped through a piece of jerky with her teeth. She winced and touched her jaw again. Dannika thought about apologizing but not yet. Not until this Jocelyn person spilled on why she was watching her.

"Like I said, I'm with IPA, too. Years ago, I was a Visionary. Like you." Jocelyn looked up. Dannika sat still, tense. She switched the butter knife to a spear and back again, and tilted her head to indicate she was listening.

"About five years ago, they told me I was going to be promoted. I thought maybe Leadership or something that involved above ground. But they told me that after all the years of hard work, I would be moved to Research. Sounded good to me, but it is not at all what I expected. I work long hours and they just mess with my head all day.

"The actual trail on our edge of the wilderness is a smaller loop than yours, and I got bored. Probably like you. They promised me three extra weeks in the city per year, but so far that hasn't been granted. So I sneak up here way more than I'm supposed to. Anyway, then I recognized you."

"Really. And how would you recognize me?"

"They talk about you—and that Adie girl—back at Research. She's your partner, right?" Jocelyn grit her teeth to pull at a piece of jerky.

"Yes." Dannika poked around at the fire. "She's my partner. Why do they talk about us?"

Jocelyn looked out over the stream. "Mostly because of that Ram case. You girls are all the rage, you know.

Everybody knows about it since that big article and photo layout in the interoffice newsletter. But with Adie, I think she's like me. I think they'll probably want her over in Research at some point."

"What do you mean, 'like you'? What exactly are they doing with you over there?"

Jocelyn sucked in a big breath and blew it out. "I don't know, Dannika. At first, they told me that they were just trying to figure out ways for Visionaries to have more vivid details when writing up reports. After they developed the memory scan, they realized that if they've reconfigured the short-term memory compartment of the brain, they can probably figure out how to actually retrieve our dreams from our subconscious. Then we wouldn't have to write reports, they would just scan us and the dream would appear on the screen. Like a movie or something. I know it is much more complicated than the memory scan, but they think it will be more effective for the Analysts to be able to see exactly what the Visionary sees."

Dannika threw another log on the fire. "Go on."

"So, it's just me right now. I'm the first Visionary for this pilot project. I have an extra lobe in my brain that has a network of about two hundred thousand extra neurotransmitters. I had an MRI when I was eight years old after a horseback riding accident. Totally got bucked off. Anyway, in the MRI, the doctors noticed I had this extra lobe. They monitored me each year, but it never seemed to have any negative symptoms.

"Until I hit seventeen and the dreams began. I actually couldn't handle it, so I started some, um, extracurricular activities to try to make it go away, you know? But, I just became a junkie, might even have died if it weren't for Bethie and Ivan. I guess that's why I stick it out. I feel like I owe them, you know?"

Dannika's thoughts ran through her own issues, her illness, how if she ever went up to the city, she'd probably be institutionalized or something. "Yeah, I do know."

Jocelyn sniffled and then looked up at Dannika. "I'm sorry. I'm just so glad to see you... I'm not around young people much. I know it's silly. Kind of lonely at Research, it being a new program and all."

Dannika rummaged through the forest and found two medium-sized logs and set them gently on the fading flames. "So how do these extra neurotransmitters make you such a valuable resource?"

"I'm not really sure. They don't tell us everything, you know." Jocelyn hugged her knees and rested her chin on top.

"No kidding. Drives me nuts. Obviously." Dannika smiled as she scooped some water from the stream into a small teakettle. "Coffee?"

"Sure. Thanks." Jocelyn rocked back and forth a bit.

Dannika lit a small camp stove and set the teakettle on top. Her muscles were still tight, and she certainly wasn't ready to trust Jocelyn. But the whole Research thing was fascinating. Maybe if they took her off the front lines, she wouldn't be such a threat. Maybe they'd allow her a visit to the city, just to hang out with Bain. She started to feel a little dizzy and rehydrated with her water bottle. She tried to kick the bottle of vodka under her sleeping bag.

"I saw you drinking, Dannika. It's okay," Jocelyn said. "I'm not gonna tell anyone."

Dannika just nodded. "So, about Adie. You think she's got this same extra lobe in her brain?"

"I guess." Jocelyn shrugged. "Gotta be something

like that to be so interested in her. And since you guys are dreaming on the same case, they'll want to determine if our condition is linked to that ability."

"So did you just get off work?" Dannika put a hand over the teakettle to see if the steam was rising.

Jocelyn picked up a stone and threw it into the stream. "Yeah. Suppose I could hang out with you for a bit?"

Dannika lit a cigarette and nodded.

Jocelyn straightened up. "Where'd you get that?"

Dannika held out the pack to Jocelyn. "My sister brings it back for me when she goes out on her one-week vacations. I don't get to go, since apparently I'm a lunatic and all that lame nonsense." Dannika rolled her eyes and waved her hands around her head. "Anyway, it's kind of my little treat when I go out alone in the wilderness."

Jocelyn took a cigarette and held it out for a light.

"I'm not supposed to be out here, though. They'd kill me if they knew I'd strayed from our own little backyard."

Jocelyn took in a big breath, blew the smoke out, and folded over into a coughing fit.

Dannika laughed. "Been a while, huh?"

Jocelyn laughed and held her chest. "Yeah, like never."

"What?" Dannika reached over and grabbed it out of her mouth, putting the ash out on the ground. "Sorry, but I can't be the one to let you start."

Dannika poured the steamy water over the black crystals, stirring with a plastic spoon. "You can have the first cup of coffee, though."

Jocelyn reached out and wrapped her hands around the warmth of the cup. "Thanks. So, when you going back?"

"Probably should head back tomorrow, I guess. It's about a day's ride. I'll be in a world of hurt if I'm late."

Dannika felt her body loosen. Jocelyn seemed cool. Cool like Adie, only in an older, wiser sort of way. And this Research stuff, it made life a little more interesting. And Lord knew Dannika could use a little more excitement.

Dannika poured her own coffee and blew on the steam rising from her cup.

"So, why do you take the risk? Why not just hang out in your backyard?" Jocelyn asked after she sipped the hot liquid.

"It's boring, that's why. I could navigate our back-yard loop with my eyes shut. I just needed something different. To get away."

"To drink." Jocelyn locked her gaze on Dannika.

Dannika smiled and put out her cigarette. Picked up her cup and took a sip. Then nodded slightly, "Yep, and to have a night where no one bothers me about having a couple of drinks."

"It's kind of invasive, huh, being a Visionary?"

Dannika peered into the sky. Wasn't it supposed to be the most rewarding job there was? Saving people from certain death? Wasn't it exciting to watch your dream go to work with Analysts and Technology and Operations?

"Maybe not." Dannika turned to Jocelyn. "Bethie says it's is our duty. That God doesn't give everyone this gift, you know. I guess I believe her. It just makes sense that when you're given something special, you should do something with it. Even though it sucks sometimes, I guess deep down, I know that people like us weren't supposed to use our talents for personal matters.

"Besides, Visionaries in the city that go undiscovered, or that refuse to join IPA, they only go crazy up there. Having to watch their dreams carried out in the media, like automatic replay. Unless they go to the police, but the police will just send them to IPA anyway." Dannika paused. "Wait a minute." Then she shook her head.

Jocelyn's eyes widened. "What?"

Dannika nodded. "Automatic replay. I bet that's what they are trying to achieve with you, Jocelyn. They are trying to configure your brain to produce a replay of your dream." Dannika sat up, excited. "Or maybe, that extra lobe stores a replay, and they're trying to find a way to extract it. It's brilliant." Dannika fell to her back and her arms flopped to the side. "Now wouldn't that be something."

Dannika sat back up. "So many times, we get there to write out that report, but even if it was only seconds after we woke up, we forget minor details — the color of the eyes, or the hair, or the exact spot or time just before it happens. But more importantly, the surroundings. Ninety-nine percent of the time, when we fail on interference, it is because of an inaccurate description of the resources available in the incident environment." Dannika lay back down. "I bet that's it, Jocelyn. I bet you and Adie have the brain capacity for automatic replay." Her belly rippled in small bursts of laughter. She took an enormous pull from the cigarette. "So cool."

Jocelyn seemed less excited about the idea. "Yeah, maybe."

Dannika noticed Jocelyn's solemnness, the way Jocelyn just scraped at the ground with a stick, numb to the power and success this discovery would offer IPA and the world. So why wasn't Jocelyn excited about being part of such a major breakthrough?

"Hey, at least you still get to go up to the city every now and then," Dannika said, softly.

Jocelyn shrugged. "Yeah. I guess I still got that."

Dannika stood up to pull out some dehydrated eggs. Out of the corner of her eye, some branches stirred. She glanced over her shoulder, but saw nothing but the wind weaving through leafless limbs, about twenty yards away. She whispered, "Jocelyn."

Jocelyn just kept stirring the dirt around with her stick.

Dannika whispered a little louder. "Jocelyn!"

Jocelyn looked up. Dannika put her finger to her lips, then motioned with her index finger for Jocelyn to move closer. Jocelyn crept over to Dannika.

Dannika leaned into Jocelyn's ear. "We're being stalked."

"By who?"

Ten yards ahead of the swaying branches, a small bush rattled. Dannika whipped her head around. "More like by what."

*

The light tan tail of an animal made its appearance, tucked behind the trunk of a birch tree. Jocelyn tried to step closer, as if to have a look, but Dannika reached out and put her arm across Jocelyn's chest.

"Be still."

"I just need to see it."

Dannika grabbed her arm. "Are you crazy?"

"But..." Jocelyn started to speak, but the animal had made its move. The mountain lion leapt from its hidden perch among the thick pine branches and tall grasses toward the camp.

Dannika turned and yelled, "Run!"

Jocelyn paused, then followed Dannika. She passed Dannika, grabbed her elbow, and screamed, "Follow me!"

Jocelyn and Dannika dodged spikey needles and sharp-edged rocks. Jocelyn stopped once to pick up a rock the size of her palm and slung it at the mountain lion, which had gained ground and was less than twenty yards away. The rock hit the mountain lion in the side of the face and sent it sideways, which bought them a few more seconds, until the lion regained its bearings. The lion peered in the direction Dannika and Jocelyn had gone, then continued forward at a more rigorous and purposeful pace.

"Where can we go?" Dannika screamed ahead.

"Just follow me!"

Ahead, Dannika could see the entrance to a cave in the hillside, a patch of tall, wheat-like grass surrounding it.

The mountain lion was within ten yards, gaining ground quicker than they could run.

"That's one of our portals!" Jocelyn said.

Dannika was by her side now as they dove for the cave. Then she heard Jocelyn squeal. The mountain lion had caught Jocelyn's heel. The lion tore its head from side to side, Jocelyn's leg swinging with the motion. Jocelyn grabbed at her hip, her face contorted in pain. Dannika reached into her sock, where the butter knife had survived the chase. She pulled it out and clicked it to a spear simultaneously, reached over Jocelyn and stabbed the lion in the neck. Blood poured out over her hand. The lion winced. It squeezed its eyes shut, but didn't release Jocelyn's foot.

"Hit the release, above your head. Just go, Dannika.

It will take you to Research. Go!"

"I'm not leaving you!"

The lion started to paw at the spear, and his jaws slowly let go of Jocelyn's heel. Just beyond the lion, another figure was slowly making its way toward the cave.

"Jocelyn! There's another one. How could that be? Lions don't hunt in packs." Dannika hoped Jocelyn had some kind of miracle advice. Like a lion treat that you could toss out and send them away. But Dannika knew they were no match for one lion, and two lions was certain death.

"Scoot back to the Ramp and I'll hit the release." Dannika pulled on Jocelyn's shoulder.

Jocelyn just leaned forward and squinted. "Wait! That's one of ours!"

Dannika glanced up at the second mountain lion slowly creeping up, eyeing his fellow species.

"One of our what?"

Jocelyn scooted back, her hand on her ankle. "The lion. She's one of ours."

CHAPTER TWELVE

Adie added an extra layer of mascara to her already clumping lashes. She wasn't so good at the makeup thing. The box had promised a 'smoky' look, but when she gazed in the mirror, the word 'scorched' came to mind. She washed it all off and reapplied a small bit of blush and one light layer of her older, dried-up mascara. She took a deep breath, trying to imagine how she would go about lunch with someone as amazing as Witt without thinking of Jeff. Witt deserved all of her attention, but Adie already knew he wasn't going to get it. She felt badly, but she reminded herself of Jeff's contract. He would never be hers. He was already married — to IPA.

She closed her eyes and tried to recall details of her dream about Jeff. Anything at all that might help the Analysts place it. Determine what caused her to be off, to dream in real time leaving no chance for a planned interference. Why wouldn't she have received that dream days prior like usual? What would have happened if that group of strangers hadn't been strolling on the same street as she'd been, and she hadn't given them directions that led them right to Jeff and Rens? Was she failing? Was something in her shifting? Would all of her dreams become real time and potentially ineffective? How would they possibly stop something she could only see within seconds of it actually happening?

She had never given a thought to having it all end, to placing that memory scan over her temples and leaving that life behind her. That might be her fate if she proved no longer of any value.

Most disturbing was that she had been working with the Analysts to master an important skill, the one that only opens its channels in the 'office.' She thought she'd made some progress on opening and shutting the stream of consciousness that allowed the dreams in. But clearly, she wasn't quite there yet.

She took a moment to record every detail of the dream. The first time Ops had caught Rens on tape, in the garage of Noder's assistant, Rens was scrawny, missing teeth, and had a dark, greasy pony tail. Either he had a Hercules of a twin, or he had gone through some major transformation. Adie's gut told her it was him. The one detail she could pick out from her dream was the eagle tattoo on Rens's arm. Jeff could make out the course of the fight, the thickness of his attacker's arms—not to mention the strength. But of the face, he wasn't sure.

Faces were the clearest part in Visionary dreams. Faces stuck in their heads like a poster on their bedroom ceiling. It was for this reason many Visionaries would become haunted by these faces. Every now and then, a Visionary would lose perspective, and Bethie had no choice but to put them under the memory scan, and send them back up to the city where a life counselor helped them begin again.

But Adie's life was finally on the right track. A soccer scholarship awaited her, and she had IPA in summers as an outlet for her gift. Taking the memory scan and starting over sounded more terrorizing than watching sixty thousand murders.

Adie ran her fingers over her calendar, unsure how she would survive two more days in the city when all she wanted to do was get back to Dannika and get to work on this case. If Rens could find Jeff, it was quite possible he could find her too. They would have to create a new plan to get intelligence on the Ram and Noder. If this real time stuff happened again, they needed to be ready for it. Bain needed a private investigator on the inside. An informant even. The stakes had just gotten higher. Too high.

*

Adie's head was spinning. It wasn't her job to devise a plan, to give Ops any kind of instruction, to indicate that the Analysts couldn't develop the best possible strategy. Somehow, the Ram knew who Jeff and Adie both worked for, and the only thing Adie could figure were dirty DEA cops. The Ram had made it clear he wasn't interested in backing down. He wanted to play the game.

The doorbell shook Adie from her daze. She thanked God for Witt, such a lovely distraction. Witt might get her through the day.

She stood and straightened out her jeans, slid into her tall brown boots, and pulled on a hunter green cardigan. She took a deep breath and practiced an easy smile in the mirror.

"Witt's here, honey!" her mother yelled up.

"Coming!"

When Adie's foot hit the last stair, she caught Witt's eyes and her stomach leapt into her throat. He was so handsome. In a completely different way than Jeff was. Even the way Witt made her feel by simply looking at him was different than she felt with Jeff. With Jeff, she just felt—happy. And safe.

Witt made her swoon.

Witt smiled, and Adie's cheeks reddened more than

the blush ever could make them. She faked needing to go the bathroom for one last look into the mirror.

"Have a nice time!" Adie's mother closed the door behind them, and she watched her mother in the window, pretending to wash dishes, until they drove away.

*

"I thought maybe Chimmies for lunch? They have great Mexican." Witt whipped his head to brush aside those long bangs.

"Sounds great," Adie said.

Witt's cell phone vibrated on the console between them. Adie couldn't help herself, dying to know if some other girl's name might appear. But only a number showed on the caller ID. Adie looked away for a moment and realized she recognized the rare area code. It should have meant nothing. But something told her it did. She glanced at the screen on the cell phone as it kept vibrating and tried to place the number.

"You can get that," Adie said. "It doesn't bother me."

"That's okay. I'm sure they'll leave a message."

Then Adie's heart froze. She was almost sure that the area code was the one on all cell phones used by IPA leadership. She forced herself to take deep breaths as she talked herself out of the possibility. Surely the area code was just a coincidence. Some rare one that Ivan chose because of its uniqueness or large availability of numbers.

Three little beeps indicated that a message had been left.

"Sure that wasn't important?"

"I don't recognize the number, so I'll just check into

it later." Witt smiled at Adie. "I just want to focus on our date for now."

Date? Adie felt a shiver flow from the top of her neck to her feet. The word tossed her insides around. She looked back to him and smiled, felt her entire core light up and her brain go tingly.

She must have had the number wrong, or maybe the number wasn't exclusive to IPA. Either way, she could feel nothing but honesty and sincerity radiate from Witt.

Adie ordered a black bean burrito with a side of rice and refried beans. The waiter placed the hot plate in front of her and sizzling fajitas for Witt.

"So, how's working with my dad?" Adie asked as she covered her mouth with her hand.

Witt chuckled. "Your dad is really cool. The students really like him."

"Yeah." Adie smiled, picking through her burrito with her fork. "I've always found him to be pretty cool, too."

"You're lucky, you know." Witt's face drooped into a more serious, unfamiliar expression. "To have parents like that."

"Yeah, I am." Adie paused. "What about yours? I mean, as long as we're on the subject."

Witt looked away. She wished she hadn't asked and stabbed a big bite onto her fork and shoved it into her mouth. By the time she chewed and swallowed, Witt still hadn't answered.

Adie leaned toward him. "I'm sorry. I should have let you bring it up."

Witt nearly cut her off. "No, it's okay. My parents are just very, um, well, first of all, they're divorced. They just fight with one another, so they don't pay much attention to me. I'm not sure either of them even knows

I'm applying to graduate school. Or what I'm studying. The conversation always just turns to their issues. So I don't see them much."

"I'm so sorry. Any brothers or sisters?"

Witt shook his head. "Only child."

Witt gazed at her for a moment, as her tongue twisted into knots and her brain filing through what to say next. He began piling fajita fixings into a tortilla. "Anyway, I'm pretty sure my interest in psychology stems from trying to figure them out all my life." He chuckled.

Adie smiled, relieved. Her father always said that same thing about his own family. That they were all so weird and screwy that he chose psychology so that he wouldn't have to die without understanding how being a part of that shaped his own life. No wonder Witt felt a connection to her dad. No wonder everybody did. Her dad worked hard to understand each and every person individually. It was his life's work, and it would never end.

"So, what do you hope to do with your degree? Or should I say, degrees?"

Witt took a sip of iced tea. "I want to go the science route. There is no doubt a connection between how the brain is wired and how we behave. But I also believe in the theory that our environment and surroundings and influences determine our behavior and guide our thoughts. I would like to be a leader in bringing those two together and figuring out treatments that integrate both sides." He took a deep breath. "It's a long road. Gotta get a doctorate, probably some med school, too. There's no quick route to being a successful researcher. Or then there's funding. Research will always need funding."

"Well, I think it's wonderful. I know you can do it." Adie smiled. Her purse vibrated and her cell phone rang way too loud.

She apologized as she pulled her phone from her purse. Glancing at the screen, she saw it was Jeff's number. She flashed back to the numbers that had popped up onWitt's cell phone screen. Yes, those first three numbers had been the same. But the rest were different. She sighed in relief and laughed silently at herself for even having the idea that Jeff would call Witt.

She pushed her chair from the table. "Excuse me, Witt. I apologize, but I do need to get this. It's my boss in Spain. So it must be important."

"Absolutely. I'll be here." Witt scooped a spoonful of rice into his mouth.

Adie slipped around the corner of the building and flipped open her phone. "Jeff! How are you?"

"I'm okay. I should be out of here in a few days. I've got some bad news, Adie." His voice was somber. Worse. It was sad. Adie braced herself. In this new world of hers, bad news could be just about anything.

"Okay. I'm ready." Adie leaned her back against the wall, clamped her eyes shut.

Adie heard a deep sigh on the other end. "So, there are a couple of things that have happened since my accident. The first is that after what happened with me, DEA and Ivan agreed to put an informant in the bank and schmooze Noder for information. She's already been compromised."

Adie gasped. "What? Like kidnapped?"

"Much worse."

"You mean dead?"

"Yes. She got into that basement vault, and she found the drugs, but she found much more than that.

Demry will brief you on it when you get back. Obviously, this is connected to the Ram case."

The salsa-tinged air stung Adie's nostrils. "That's bad. Really, really bad. Do I even want to know the second thing?"

"It's Dannika. She's missing. Bethie is very upset. She's got Joe out looking for her. We don't know if Dannika's disappearance is related to the Ram or not."

Adie put her hand to her forehead. "Of course it is, Jeff. After what happened to you? It has to be. I gotta get back there."

"That's what scares me. The only place Dannika could go on her own would be the wilderness. So if the Ram has kidnapped her, then this guy's a lot cozier with IPA than we thought."

Adie's hands were shaking. She could barely hold the phone. "How do I bail on my vacation without my parents catching on?" Her voice quivered.

"You'll receive a call from Steph in about ten minutes. Where are you?"

Adie suddenly felt guilty. She'd assumed that when he called her his "girlfriend," it hadn't meant anything. But at this moment, to answer honestly made her feel like a coward.

"I'm at a restaurant. With a friend."

There was silence at the other end. Then Jeff's voice was soft. "The friend you told me about?"

Adie cleared her throat. For a split second, she was prepared to lie. But the simple truth came out instead. "Yes."

Adie waited patiently through another brief pause. "When Steph calls you, say it's from your boss in Spain."

"That's who you are right now, Jeff." Adie smirked.

"Well, then say he is going to call you back," Jeff

said, "You'll need to excuse yourself from the lunch, and tell your 'friend' and your parents that your plane leaves tonight. A car will pick you up at five o'clock. The driver will be a woman in her fifties. She is DEA agent Brent Knox's secretary. Name's Beatrice but I'm pretty sure she goes by Bea. You'll need to say she's a U.S. liaison for the company you work for. Give her a big hug when you hop into the car, then turn to your parents and wave goodbye."

Adie sat back down across from Witt, tucked her hair behind her ears. She willed every nerve inside of her in order to keep her cool.

"Everything okay?"

"Yes. Just work stuff." She set the phone next to her plate, and immediately asked him about his classroom work. She noticed her voice was shaky and cleared her throat.

Ten minutes later, her phone rang. She stood and excused herself again. "So sorry."

She peeked around the building and noticed Witt scrolling on his own phone, already bored. Surely this first date would be their last.

Adie approached the table. Witt looked up and his brown eyes swallowed her.

"That was my boss again. He just had a coach bail on him. I'm gonna have to get back early." Witt set his phone back to the standard screen and looked over his shoulder, motioning to the waitress for the check. Adie continued, uncomfortable with the silence. "I'm so sorry."

Witt handed the waitress his credit card. Adie began reaching for her wallet. Witt placed a hand over her purse. "No. I got it."

"Thank you."

The car ride home held an eerie silence. Witt's phone vibrated on the console again. Adie slid her eyeballs sideways, without moving her head, and noticed it was the same number as before. Again, he didn't answer, but she didn't feel she had any leverage to ask questions.

Witt pulled up to her parents' front door and Adie sat back, conflicted by a feeling that she could melt into that seat forever.

Witt pulled her into an unexpected and awkward hug. "This is kind of unfortunate. I really like you."

Adie's heart tightened as she gently pulled away. "I'll be back. Soon."

Witt nodded, and Adie turned to walk away. As Witt was stepping into his car, she turned around and yelled, "Witt?"

He peered over the hood of the car. "Yeah?"

Adie smiled. "I like you, too."

*

Four hours later, Adie's bags were packed and in the hallway. Adie propped herself on a seat and leaned her head against the wall to look out the window, but all she could see was Witt's last smile. The look he gave her before he drove away. The one that proved they parted with what he'd wanted to hear. She let her eyes close and relaxed, and wondered when she might see him again.

Adie's mom was pacing when the silver Town and Country drove up. Adie kissed her mother goodbye, threw her backpack on, and grabbed her suitcase with each hand.

Just as promised, a fifty-something woman sat behind the wheel, but as Adie got closer, her expression didn't look too welcoming. She seemed to force a smile and waved Adie closer. The woman popped the trunk and Adie placed her luggage inside and slammed it shut. The back of the car was full of all kinds of random stuff, papers and files, blankets and pillows, bags of food. The front seat was empty, so Adie hopped inside.

Adie smiled at Bea, then reached her arms around the stranger. A few strands of Bea's stringy red hair stuck inside of Adie's mouth. "I was instructed to hug you, you know, like I've known you forever." Bea's arms tugged a bit at Adie's sides but didn't embrace her fully.

Adie looked back at her mother, who stood at the window waving with one hand over her mouth. She was sad for her mom, but all parents have to let go sometime.

Adie looked back at Bea. Her fists were wrapped so tightly around the steering wheel her knuckles were white. She began to drive, not looking at Adie, eyes wide and her breathing unsteady.

When they pulled around the first corner, Adie felt something sharp against her temple. Bea shrieked, and out of the corner of her eye, Adie saw the gun that had been at her temple move to the driver's. Adie swallowed hard and bit down on the inside of her cheek.

A voice behind her, low and cruel, spoke as the gun moved back to her temple. "Don't move, sunshine." The gun moved again to the driver. "And you. I told you exactly where to go. One wrong turn and BAM."

Adie jumped, and the man moved the gun back to her temple.

Adie turned slightly toward Bea. A stream of tears rolled down Bea's cheek.

"Look straight ahead!" The voice behind her shouted.

Adie squeezed her eyes tight, then opened them again. *It's gotta be a dream.* Yet, nothing had changed. A gun still stuck to her temple and that burley voice became recognizable. Rens.

The car squealed into a parking spot behind some old industrial building. Old brick buildings, fences, big semi-trucks. Adie didn't recognize any of it. Bea threw her head onto the steering wheel and exhaled enormous sobs, her mop of fire-red hair all around her.

"Shut it or I'll take care of it for you!" Ren's breath was hot on the back of Adie's neck.

Adie sat still and even willed her chest not to rise with her breath. In the back, Adie heard Rens digging through the blankets and food and Adie quickly jerked her head around in time to see him produce another body. The body was much smaller, certainly not an adult. Scrawny arms with chewed fingernails. Skinny jeans with black and turquoise street shoes. As Rens sat the figure up against the door, long, straight brown hair swung across the face of the victim, who made a small squeak. Adie felt fire in her belly as it occurred to her this victim was a child. She whipped her head back around and clinched her jaw tight.

"Now, you each are going to do *exactly* what I tell you to do. *Got it?*"

Adie nodded with quick jerks of her head, and sucked in deep breaths. Bea wailed, and Adie could hear tiny whimpers escape from the young girl in back.

Rens rammed Bea in the cheek with the butt of the gun. He grabbed her hair, yanked her head back and moved the gun around to her mouth. "*Got it?*"

She nodded again.

While Rens was occupied with his threats to Bea, Adie moved her head around to take in a full glance at the young person in the back seat. Her hands and feet were bound by wire. Her mouth was stuffed with a large white cloth tied at the back. Through the strands of hair falling over her face, Adie could see that her eyes were covered up with duct tape.

That was it. Adie couldn't stand it. Not for anyone, but especially not for a child. She closed her eyes and thought of Dannika. What would she do? She visually scrolled across all of the Visionary women before her whose photos hung on the training wall. They had all been trained for a moment they may or may not have to face. For Adie, this was that moment.

Adie swung her elbow across her body and delivered a sharp blow to Rens right between the eyes. With her other hand, she punched his Adam's apple and managed to knock the gun out of his hand.

Bea started screaming, and tears welled up beneath the duct tape on the face of the little girl.

Rens screamed and jumped over the seat, landing on Adie's back. Adie could feel as he tried to secure her neck into a deadly position; all it would take was one yank.

Adie scooted down in her seat and rammed her knee up into his nose. His head flung back, and Adie grabbed onto his neck as tightly as possible, the warm sensation of blood on her hands, slowly rolling down her arms.

Rens took hold of her head with his hands and slammed it into the car window three times. The third time broke the skin just above her eyebrow. Rens felt around for the gun, but he couldn't find it in the mess in the back.

Adie turned herself around so she could kick a foot into Rens's head. After her foot made contact, she fell head first onto the floorboard, upside down, her arm stuck beneath the seat. Her head pounded and she could feel blood trickle onto her forehead and cheeks. As she tried to work her arm free, Rens moved on top of her, a knife in his right hand above her chest, ready to dig into her heart.

Adie squeezed her eyes tight. Prayed for her family. Let her body go limp. She waited for the knife. For the feeling of it piercing her skin and taking her life. But it never came.

Instead, a gunshot rang in her ears and Rens's body fell onto hers. Blood and brain tissue gushed from his head all over her shoulders and arms.

The impact of Rens's body jerked her arm free. She opened the car door and pushed him out.

The woman had lodged herself between the steering wheel and the driver side door, too shocked to move. Adie quickly pulled herself into the back seat. The young girl's body quivered uncontrollably, the gun held tightly between her tied hands.

"We're okay," Adie cried out. "He's dead." Then she leaned toward the little girl. "It's okay. That was a very brave thing you did. I'm going to help you now." Something inside of Adie churned as she realized she recognized the features on the small girl's face.

Adie carefully pulled the duct tape from the little girl's eyes. She stopped every time the girl winced from the pain. Once the duct tape was removed from one eye, Adie gasped. The little girl, beaten and scared, was Maimey.

CHAPTER THIRTEEN

As the lion crept closer, Dannika saw that it was much larger than the first lion. Also much darker in color, with a hint of gold in its thick coat. A thin white collar hung around its neck. With a paw the size of a basketball, it whapped the injured lion's face. The smaller lion landed fifteen feet from the cave.

"Jocelyn, what is going on?" Dannika kept her voice low, her body frozen by what she had seen. Jocelyn held up a hand.

"Zeneva!" Joceyln yelled out to the lion.

The large beast had an elegance about her that Dannika had not seen in the wild. Her unusual jade green eyes seemed transparent, as if the animal's soul bled through them. Her fur gleamed like silk. She turned slowly to Jocelyn.

Jocelyn held up her fists and banged them together twice in a quick motion.

Dannika tried to process all that was happening in front of her, stiff in shock.

"Thank you, Zeneva." Jocelyn scooted back to Dannika and gripped her foot tightly. The animal dipped its head, as if acknowledging Jocelyn, and crept toward the opposing lion, now unconscious.

"It's safe to go. You should go now if you need to get back. Zeneva is one of ours. She'll protect you." Jocelyn squeezed her foot and grimaced in pain.

Dannika removed her button-down shirt, her bare arms immediately getting goose bumps from the chill.

She wrapped the shirt around Jocelyn's foot and tied a knot. Jocelyn winced at the pressure.

"I need to get you some help," Dannika said. She turned to look at the silver-dollar-sized perfectly round crystal rock dangling from the ceiling of the cave. She pushed it with her finger. "Hold on tight."

The floor of the cave dropped, and Dannika and Jocelyn began to free fall. The air in this portal was much colder than back at Headquarters. The earth felt different. Darker. Damper.

They hit the floor softly, and Dannika could feel gravel beneath her feet. Jocelyn reached out to pull a long string, which triggered a wide warehouse garage door to open up to a huge, open space.

Light slowly drifted into the portal. Enormous oriental rugs covered the hard cement floor. A coffee station, with a long wooden counter top, was the focal point of the room. a shiny espresso machine on top. Syrup flavors lined the tan rock wall behind it, with cups and straws on the counter. In a corner two loveseats faced one another. A wooden coffee table between them matched the counter. Books and magazines were scattered randomly on the table. Light instrumental retro music accompanied the dim floor lighting, giving the whole room the feel of a groovy, downtown jazz club.

"No orientation room here," Jocelyn pointed out. "We all come from Headquarters, anyway. But this is our gathering room."

"It's amazing!"

Jocelyn moaned and reached for her foot.

"Where's the doctor?" Dannika placed Jocelyn's arm around her shoulder to help her to stand.

Jocelyn pointed toward the coffee station. "There. That door will take us to the nurse's office."

Dannika started in that direction. "I think you're gonna need stitches. There is a doctor, isn't there?"

Jocelyn shook her head. "No. We're transported to Headquarters if we have to. But they try to avoid that."

Dannika stopped. "No, Jocelyn. Let's get you to Headquarters. I'll take you. Just lead me to the portal."

Jocelyn started to shake. "Look, I'm really starting to feel sick. Please, just let the nurse handle it."

Dannika moved on, Jocelyn limping beside her. She pushed a round quartz button, and the door opened up into a long well-lit hallway. Dannika shivered. The ground was certainly colder here. They must have been much further from Headquarters than Dannika had imagined, and they were possibly not as deep. The rock walls were more reminiscent of limestone, not the dark amethyst back home. The space had the feel of a clinical setting, sterile and quiet with doors every twenty feet on either side. The hallway didn't appear to have an end. No corridors veering off in every direction as it did at Headquarters.

"This is the one." Jocelyn reached for the handle. But her hand was too shaky. Dannika began to worry an infection had set in. "Jocelyn, are you sure I can't get you to Headquarters?"

"No!"

They entered the small nurse's office and Dannika wondered if she had just time-traveled, like back to the 1940s.

A woman with short, kinky hair and an old-school war-time nurse's uniform sat behind an old oak desk. "Jocelyn!" she exclaimed as horror crossed her face.

"Hey, Mary. Lion got my foot." Jocelyn's voice was barely audible.

Mary quickly scooted to a big row of cabinets and

grabbed a long syringe full of clear liquid.

"Sit!"

Jocelyn sat down, and Mary jammed the syringe into her left arm. "Okay. That should keep away infection."

"Thank you." Jocelyn took a deep breath as the medication settled into her system.

"It wasn't..." Mary began.

"No. Zeneva actually took out the one that got me."

Mary nodded and handed Jocelyn some apple juice. Dannika reached out her hand, "I'm Dannika. I happened to be out in the woods on my vacation, so I was able to get her back here."

"I know who you are."

Jocelyn looked at Dannika and quickly looked away. Dannika thought better than to ask questions, despite how unnerving it was to endure the temperament of this woman.

"How you feeling?" Dannika put a hand on Jocelyn's shoulder.

"Better. Just want to lie down."

Mary started pulling ointments and bandages from the cabinets. "Let me clean that out, stitch it up. Then you can rest."

Behind the nurse's desk, a tall cabinet was filled with blinking cartridges—some sort of tablets or electronic file storage. Digital tickers ran across their sides with letters so tiny Dannika thought only an ant could read them. She stepped toward them and ran a hand over a few at eye level.

"Stop that this second," Mary said in a harsh tone.

Dannika jumped back, jerked her hand away. "Geez, woman. You scared me to death." Dannika started to back away slowly and tilted her head to decipher at least one word on the blinking files.

"Go on. Move along. And watch that attitude toward your elders."

"Sorry. It's just so…interesting. I've never seen anything like it." Dannika still had not moved. "How do they work?"

Mary pulled at Dannika's elbow and sat her down on the other side of the desk. "That is purely confidential."

Dannika glanced at Jocelyn, who kept her eyes glued to her bandaged foot. "Well, I better start my way home. They'll get all freaked out if I'm not back in the morning."

"You can't go now," Mary said. "It'll get dark out there."

"I'm okay. I've got some gear out there."

"But, dear, you've only just arrived. You should stay. We can notify Headquarters." Mary's voice was firm.

Dannika narrowed her eyes, unsure of the reason for Mary's persistence. "Well, first of all, they'd probably lock me away and give the key to that Zeneva for dinner. I can't risk it. So, I would appreciate it if you could zip your lips about my being here. Anyway, we've got a big case going and I'm the Visionary on the case, so I have to go back. I spend all of my vacations in the woods. I'll be okay."

Dannika noticed how carefully she was speaking. She did spend her vacations in the woods, but she was never allowed past the Headquarters' loop. The most she had run into were squirrels and rabbits. Thought she saw a fox once. But never the kind of wild things beyond the loop. And never lions that could communicate with humans.

"Let her go. She'll be fine," Jocelyn said to Mary.

Mary narrowed her eyes at Jocelyn. "I think she

should stay, now that she's here."

Jocelyn grit her teeth. "It's not her time, Mary. She's on an important case. She needs to get back."

Dannika stepped back toward the door. She wasn't sure what was behind all this tension over her going home. The already small space seeming to cave in and an awkward, uneasy feeling set in her gut. What did Jocelyn mean, 'not her time'? Dannika had no intention of finding out what Jocelyn meant by that. She had work to do, people she couldn't let down, one quarter of a bottle of vodka waiting, and consequences she had no intention of facing.

"Look. I don't know what's going on here, but if Jocelyn is okay, I need to get home. If this is about Zeneva, don't worry, I won't tell anyone. I get that if you want to enjoy your wilderness retreat, you need protection. We don't have the same wild animals roaming on our side of the woods. I'll keep your secret. You keep mine. Trust me, I'm not supposed to be there..." Dannika stopped. It was enough not to be able to experience life above ground on her vacation, but if the wilderness was taken away from her as well, she may as well be dead.

Jocelyn said quickly, "You keep our secret, we'll keep yours. Right, Mary?"

Mary was silent, pretended to put away supplies.

"Right, Mary?" Jocelyn's voice was firmer.

Mary turned on her heels, wrapped her hands together in front of her. "Yes, that's right, Dannika. We will keep your secret. And we appreciate your cooperation in return."

Jocelyn rolled her eyes. Dannika knew there was a hidden message in that statement, but this was her moment to get out. "Okay, then. Nice to meet you both, and

I wish you well with the good work you're doing here."

Mary nodded. "May you continue your excellent work as well."

Jocelyn kept her eyes on Dannika, who waited for her to respond. But Jocelyn remained speechless. Jocelyn must have also been watching her words.

Dannika reached for the door, then looked over her shoulder. "So, Zeneva. Now that she knows me, will she, you know, watch out for me?"

Mary and Jocelyn both nodded. "She will," Mary said.

Dannika fell into a sprint through the hallway where the quartz button sparkled brightly beneath the florescent lighting. Dannika walked through the coffeehouse, where out of the corner of her eye, she noticed a figure seated on the couch. She decided not to acknowledge anyone, pulled the warehouse door string, and entered the portal.

Cold air whooshed upward until her hair whizzed around her face and her body lifted. Once back at the cave, she saw that dawn was near. She peeked around the corner of the cave. No trace of either lion. Her butter knife sat at the entrance to the cave, clean, reflecting the dawn- tinted sky.

*

Dannika maneuvered her way back to camp by following the sound of gushing water. Next to the stream, her gear was scattered, food containers busted open. Prescription bottles now empty. She grinned. "There's a raccoon out there probably thinks it can fly. Better you than me, buster."

Painter was still tied to the tree, untouched. He

tugged at the rope to get to some tall grass just beyond his reach. How odd that lion didn't go for the easy target. But Dannika knew that the lion likely felt she was just as easy. Or maybe it was that they were more of a threat.

She rummaged through what was left of her things. Little was left intact. Her sleeping bag was ripped down the center, dehydrated food bags were strewn all alongside the stream, her extra clothing pulled from her backpack. Every speck of food gone, the vodka bottle shards spread around camp. "Little suckers are all drunk now, too." She sighed.

Dannika rolled what was left up into a ball and stuffed it into her now nearly useless backpack. She put the trash into the saddlebags and loaded them onto Painter. "We're gonna have to head back tonight, buddy. At least our flashlight works."

She tightened down the saddle and went back for one last look around where she had camped. Her heart thumped as she ran back to her backpack, unloaded it, tore everything out. No sign of her map and her compass cracked. She reopened every piece of trash in the saddlebags, hoping the map was there.

Back at the camp, she retraced her steps twenty yards in every direction. Her hands began to get a little shaky. She shook her head. "No. No. No!" She placed her hands on her head and tried to calm herself, but she felt it all spinning out of control. The anxiety engulfed her, growing unbearable, like shards of steel were flowing up through her legs into her core, seizing all of her senses.

She dropped to her knees and pawed the ground for any glimpse of one of her pills that might have been spared. She punched at the ground until her hand hurt.

Tears soaked the dirt beneath her.

She tucked the butter knife into her belt. If she didn't make it back, she'd be through with every last privilege she'd been given. And she couldn't live like that.

Her eyes began to leak tears, and she started to feel like the woods were closing in. The darkness between the trees crept closer and closer. Without her meds for over 24 hours, she was losing grip on emotion and balance, between reality and what might become hallucination or dream. She began to roll around on the ground, then sat up, hung her head between her knees. "What to do. What to do. What to do. Settle down, Dannika. Settle down." She started rocking back and forth and beat at her temples. "C'mon, think, think, think. What way did we come in?"

She jumped up and headed toward the cave, but the sun had dropped and she couldn't determine which way she'd come. She ran back to Painter and packed everything back up. "Why, Painter? Why did I leave the trail? I'm an idiot. Dannika, you're such an idiot!"

Her hands on her knees, she sucked in huge, gasping breaths, then used all her strength to let them out slowly. She felt the world settle around her.

Dannika untied Painter from the tree, launched herself onto her tall back, and turned the horse opposite from where she thought the cave was.

Fifty yards into the woods, Dannika's flashlight, held tightly in her shaky hands, caught the reflection of two bright eyes standing in their path. Painter started to spook and nearly lost Dannika on a quick sidestep. The set of eyes came straight toward them. Painter seemed to calm, and Dannika knew, without even having to see, that it was Zeneva. Once within ten feet, Dannika noticed the sleek white collar.

"Hey, girl," Dannika said softly. "Can you show us the way home?"

Zeneva walked up to Painter, stared Dannika in the eye, then began her swagger off to the west of where Dannika had been headed. Dannika held Painter back for moment as Zeneva stopped and looked over her tail.

Yes, she is leading us. Dannika gently pulled the reins, and Painter stepped in behind Zeneva. Dannika held the light high so she could see in front of Zeneva. Within a couple hundred yards, they were back on a trail. Zeneva made a sharp right and began to follow the trail, Painter still in step behind her.

For four hours of nothing but darkness and stillness, Painter followed Zeneva faithfully. They stopped only to sip from streams and for Dannika to filter water for herself. Her body felt relaxed, felt a surprising peace.

It hadn't been medicine that had calmed her this time. It had been hope. Hope of the most unique kind — one that offered something different. Mystery. Possiblity. But most of all, absolute trust.

They reached a fork in the trail, and Dannika could see the sign firmly planted in the ground. Nothing disturbed from when she'd made the decision two days ago to overstep her boundaries and open up a whole new world. Zeneva began to back up, obviously aware of her place. Wild animals didn't come within miles of the Headquarters' wilderness. They weren't welcome.

Dannika turned to Zeneva and tapped her fists together twice. "Thank you."

Zeneva nodded, then turned and leapt into a full sprint.

"Bye, girl." Dannika's whisper faded into the light breeze as she wondered if she would ever see the fascinating lion again.

CHAPTER FOURTEEN

Adie woke to a honking horn. She jumped at the sound and snagged her sweater on her suitcase. Her heart pounded so hard she thought it might break through her skin. She stretched out her right leg, and millions of needles poked at her foot. Rarely did she fall asleep in such an odd position, atop lumpy baggage and pokey books. She massaged her neck before she glanced out the window.

"They're here, sweetie. I wish you didn't have to go, dear," Adie's mother called out from the kitchen. "Next time you're back for good, though."

"And off to college." Adie wiped at the drool sliding down her chin and peeked out the window. She slowly became aware of her surroundings. A warm house. A safe house. A gold Chevy Impala waiting to take her back to IPA.

She wondered what that dream had meant. For her. For Maimey. For Rens.

She wondered if the woman in that Impala was Knox's secretary at all.

The woman in the car looked different. Her hair was a golden blond, cropped short at her chin.

Adie's mother opened the door and grabbed her backpack. Adie lugged her suitcase out to the parked vehicle.

The woman stepped out from the car to assist in loading Adie's things. Her smile was delightful. Not a single wrinkle surrounded her eyes or lips. But Adie could sense she'd been enhanced in more ways than one.

Adie glanced over the real Bea's shoulder and saw that the car was completely empty.

Adie offered a warm smile, and as instructed, leaned into Bea for an awkward hug. Bea returned the gesture, giving Adie a hint of confidence that all would go as it should. She turned back to her mother and wrapped her arms around her shoulders. "Bye, Mom. I'll call you when I get there. I love you."

Her mother gripped at her apron as she daintily jogged toward the car. Adie locked eyes with Bea. For her mom to walk her to the car required interaction with a woman Adie should know quite well. Adie's mind raced through a list of the right things to say.

By the grace of God, Bea reached out her right hand to Adie's mother. "I'm Bea. I help coordinate the overseas recruitment. It's so nice to meet you. Adie was able to get in on quite the opportunity. I'm sure she has shared so much with you."

"Yes. Yes, it sounds just wonderful." Her mother squeezed Adie's hand one last time. "We do miss her so." Adie's mom leaned in for a kiss on Adie's cheek, then let her daughter's hand fall to her side as she turned back to Bea. "It's a pleasure, really. Thank you for all you have done for her. Meeting you, I see that..." Adie's mother placed a hand to her mouth, tipped her head downward.

"Mom...I'll see you in three weeks." Adie grabbed her mother's hand.

"I know." Her mother smiled as she worked to hide a tear. She ran back up to the house and turned at the door to watch her only daughter leave two days earlier than planned. Maybe deep down her mother had hoped Witt might convince her not to leave again.

*

Adie hopped into the front seat of the car. She turned to her mother and waved goodbye. Adie peeked over her shoulder one last time to inspect the seats and floor. Spic and span.

"So, Adie dear," Bea said. "Knox told me I am supposed to drop you at the edge of the forest over by South Hills. He said you would know the right spot once we got over there."

Adie nodded. "Yes, the end of the unmarked lane about a mile past my favorite coffee shop." Speaking of that coffee shop made Adie smile. It was the first time that she had interacted with Jeff. She grinned as a buzz ran through her, and she began to pick at her cuticles. She started to understand what Jeff had to do as Recruiter. He had to charm. He had to make girls feel comfortable, special, desired. If he hadn't played it so smooth, she would never have followed him into such a crazy, unknown world.

Something about passing that coffee shop caused the pieces to begin to fit. He couldn't possibly make another girl feel the way he'd made her feel that day if he was in love with someone else. Adie likely couldn't turn the other cheek the way Jago did with Lonie. Jago and Lonie had a history before IPA. Adie's heart sunk as this realization became clearer than ever. He could never be with her.

Adie looked over at Bea. "So, you know about us, I take it?"

Bea nodded slightly. "Well, I know you do contract work for the government. And that you live deep in those woods." She gave Adie a huge smile. Red lipstick stuck to her teeth. "I also know you are really important, living like CIA or something. Must be some life."

The Impala veered off the freeway and a few turns later, they entered South Hills.

"Right up there," Adie instructed and the Impala pulled to a stop.

"You really have to pull that suitcase into those woods? No one to help you?" Bea asked with a tap of her fake fingernail on the window.

"Yep." Adie squeezed a bicep, surprisingly pleased at the little bump that wasn't there a few months ago. "We train pretty hard. You know, in case we're ever in danger."

"Anything else I can do for you?"

"Another hug?" Adie said. "I just really miss...people up here." She wanted to say *the innocent kind*. The kind that weren't emotionally scarred by the constant invasion of violence and crime. The kind that just went about their day getting manicures and haircuts and coffee and facelifts and paychecks and utility bills, and their worst nightmare was wearing the wrong dress to a dinner party. Or not having a dinner party to go to at all.

When Bea's arms folded around Adie, she collapsed, surprised by her own tears swelling up until they overflowed. Tears that seemed to question Adie's choice of ever joining IPA.

Bea squeezed more tightly and removed a lock of hair that had fallen over Adie's face. "You okay?"

Adie sobbed deeper.

Bea held her and began to sway. "It's okay, honey. I know it's sad about the informant that was killed. From time to time, this happens in our cases. We lose someone and it's awful and terrible and no one is sure what to do. But you can be sure of one thing." Bea pulled away and tilted Adie's chin up to meet her eyes. "Jora wanted to be there. She did that job for a reason, and she knew she put her life in danger as part of it. People like Jora, dear, they are willing to give it all up for justice. It is who they are, and they will die for it. She's okay, dear. I promise you. She has floated right up to heaven with a badge of honor all over her proud face, because she helped to crack one of the biggest DEA cases in years."

Adie nodded. Bea really didn't know anything about it all, but she had one part right. It was the reason Dannika was gone. It was the reason Adie would go to find her. It was one of the things they had in common that had bonded them tighter than super glue. They both would die for it, too.

*

Adie met with Demry, Jago, Jeff and Bethie back at the conference room. Jeff looked so different. He'd cut his hair and his face scarred over, but for Adie, every trigger still fired.

Adie couldn't help but notice that Dannika's twin sister was not in the conversation. "Where's Daylea?"

Bethie answered. "Still up in the city. She should be back tomorrow."

"What? You didn't even tell her sister?"

"It's in Dannika's and Daylea's best interest. Daylea isn't mentally tough the way you are," Bethie said. Adie knew she was right, but it still made her heart sink. If it were her sister, tough or not, she'd want to know.

"So, Dannika came back and left again the same day?" Adie asked.

"Or someone took her," Jeff added.

"No," Bethie said. "Joe couldn't find her in the Headquarters' wilderness, so he let us know. Then someone saw her outside the Visionary office briefly. It appears she left on her own. Joe saw her take off on Painter before he could check her out."

"And do you believe him?" Adie aimed the question mostly at Demry.

"I do," Jeff said.

Demry sat silent. Bethie watched him intensely.

"Demry, do you think Joe is telling the truth?"

Demry crossed his arms. "I don't know. I'm starting to feel like there's a lot around here that I don't know."

"No kidding," Jeff added and looked at Bethie.

"Am I missing something?" Adie asked.

Jeff looked at Bethie. She closed her eyes gently and nodded.

Jeff explained about the Research facility. "It's beyond our wilderness boundaries, apparently," Jeff continued. "Tech finally determined that the Ram was using our memory scan when things didn't go his way. Like it couldn't have been obvious."

Demry glared at Jeff. "He was careful. It would seem impossible for the Ram to have access to a memory scan."

Jeff ignored Demry and continued his train of thought. "Ivan thinks that the leak of the memory scan may be traced to someone in that department."

"Who works at this Research?" Adie asked.

Jeff turned to Bethie. "Bethie, so who's there? I mean, besides the department head. Surely that Mayer guy has some interns at the least to do the dirty work."

Bethie took a deep breath and set her shoulders back. "You guys know I don't like keeping anything from you, but the government grant we received stressed confidentiality. I'm sorry, but I just can't tell you. I can tell you that the memory scan was developed there. It became

our way to offer IPA employees a way back to the outside world, and some government agencies are in pur-
suit of their own licensing for it. Current projects at Research are focused on making interference more effi-
cient. But again, that's all I can say."

Adie laced her fingers together on the table. "Any
way Dannika could know about this?"

Bethie shook her head. "There's no way that I can
think of, but if she went off her meds, it's possible that
she didn't stay within the Headquarters' wilderness
boundaries. Jago checked into Dannika's meds, and it
looks like she's been taking them as prescribed. It's hard
to know with that girl. It could be that she found out
about Maimey."

"Wait," Adie frowned. "What about Maimey?"

As Jeff turned to Adie, she forced herself to lose any
suspicious expression. She didn't want them to know
about the dream. Not yet. Not until she could make
some sense of it.

Bethie wiped beneath her eye and answered. "No
one could find her one afternoon, and we thought
maybe she'd snuck off with Dannika. But Bain found her
outside of the Ram warehouse after we reported her
missing. She was tied up and her mouth and eyes bound
shut. Whoever put her in that condition didn't follow
through with something they were probably supposed
to do. We suspect Rens. They left her there, and we
aren't sure why.

"Ivan suspects that there must be something going
astray at Research, because no one else would know
about Jeff or Maimey or even you, Adie. Your identities
have somehow been compromised. Jora was quickly
discovered. And our most significant piece of psycho-
logical technology has found its way into the hands of

our perpetrator. It all speaks to an inside job. And Research seems the most probable."

Adie put her hand to her forehead, then rubbed at her eyes. The vision of Maimey in the car came to her mind. Of Maimey holding the gun. Killing Rens. Adie shook her head, then stood. "Has anyone checked the alcohol inventory lately? I used to keep tabs on what was available, to make sure Dannika wasn't sneaking into the dance hall and stealing from it."

Jeff leaned back into his chair. "What is it, Adie? What are you thinking?"

Adie looked into a far corner of the room as she tried to put her theory into words. "If Dannika got into the alcohol, then we know she might not make good decisions. Or if she's stopped taking her meds. Either way, it could make her extremely irrational and volatile." She paused. "I need to go after her."

Jeff's face went red. "No. We don't need to be on a goose chase looking for you, too. No one besides Ivan and those of us in this room know about Dannika's absence. Not even her sister. They all think she's been granted extra days in the wilderness, and we need to keep it that way. So just sit tight and play along, and Ivan will send out Ops to find her."

"I am the only one she'll listen to, Jeff. More than her sister. More than Bethie. More than you. It's me she trusts now. Joe can lead me. If we exhaust the entire wilderness, then we'll go up to the city. C'mon Jeff. Don't you see that I have to go?" Adie's body tensed, unsure how Bethie might feel about what she'd said.

Bethie put a hand over Jeff's. "She's right. Dannika has responded to Adie better than she has to anyone in all of her time here. If Dannika is out there, alone, searching for something that she'll never find, Adie might be the only one to bring her back."

"Then I'm going with her," Jeff said firmly. Adie wanted to smile. It felt good to hear he wanted to be there. To protect her? Maybe. Maybe not. It didn't matter. He wanted to be with her.

Bethie put a hand on Jeff's shoulder. "You sure that you are up for that?"

Jeff breathed deep, put a hand on his chest, and winced from the lingering pain. His face melted as he released a sigh. "No." He glanced up at Adie. "I'm sorry. I wish I could go, but I can't. I wouldn't be any help to you right now. I would slow you down and probably make us a target for whatever is out there."

Demry spoke up in a strong voice. "I'll go."

Bethie nodded to him. "Ivan is preparing to go to Research. I will let him know that you will need a map of the wilderness retreat at Research. Let's hope this is her own doing and not the Ram using her as bait."

"Then it's done." Adie nodded to each of them and exited the room.

*

Adie unpacked her suitcase and threw a few items into her backpack for her journey at the same time. She inhaled deeply. Rose hip perfume mixed with fig and aloe soap reminded her of Dannika. Dannika would talk about stuff that Adie could never imagine. How to act with boys, or what to do with power. Sometimes, they would lie next to each other, staring at the ceiling, and talk for hours. Dannika began to confide things in Adie that even her twin sister didn't know. Like that Dannika planned to find their real mom someday. And that she had often considered taking the memory scan and letting them place her up in one of those institutions in the city. At least she might have a crack at a normal life and wouldn't feel like such an outsider. But even so, the thought of that had scared Dannika too much. What if she did have a memory or two that didn't get removed? What if the dreams reminded her of what she used to do with them? Dannika knew herself well enough. Any hint of her past would only ruin any plans of a new future.

Beyond all of their laughter and their long talks about the different kinds of futures they could expect, one secret they shared bound them tight. They were both in love with men they would never have.

Adie put away her suitcase, zipped up her pack, and went to the sink to gather up a few toiletries to take with her. She opened the mirror above the sink, and a folded sheet of paper drifted slowly into the damp porcelain. Adie picked up the letter, and brought it to her nose. Dannika's rose-scented perfume. The letter had been folded into thirds and sealed with wax. She turned it over and saw the name written on the letter. Adie sighed.

She longed to open the letter, but it was not meant for her.

Now she knew. The Ram had not gotten to Dannika. Dannika had gotten to herself.

Adie tapped the letter against her hand. She owed it to Dannika to deliver the letter. In fact, it became clear that if she didn't deliver the letter, Dannika's life would be in danger. She took a deep breath and accepted what this meant. Whatever it was Dannika was after — revenge, freedom, answers — Adie knew she would be hell bent to get it. And anything Dannika might lose in that process, including her life, would be worth the price.

It wasn't Adie that Dannika would need on her mission, but someone else. Adie knew that whatever Dannika was doing, if she did it alone, it surely would end either incredibly good or incredibly bad. And Dannika needed proof that the good ending was worth it. She needed confirmation. From the one person who could make her feel whole. Feel sane. Feel safe to continue a life in her own skin, in her own head. Adie closed the mirror and threw her backpack on her bed, and pulled out the maps. "I'm never going to let you live this down, Dannika, for making me stay here and wait this out."

Adie opened the door to the Ops department and quickly went down the steps. In the dark, chilly room, she searched the boards and buttons and switches for his name. Finally, she saw the big blue switch labeled for Bain, and she pushed the lever. The large screen in front of her lit up, the man on the screen at a kitchen table reading a newspaper. Adie saw him put his hand to his ear as he caught the signal she had just sent to him. He looked up at the camera, a quizzical look on his face. He probably had never been contacted by a Visionary alone.

"Hey, Bain," Adie said nervously. She didn't know why, but he always made her muscles tighten, as if on guard. He had made Dannika calm, and he made Adie squirm. Maybe it was his size, or his serious demeanor. Or his accomplishments in the field. But at this moment, she had to work past that and follow Dannika's inferred instructions.

Bain stepped closer to the camera. "Hey, Adie. You alone?"

"Yes. I'm not supposed to tell you this, but Dannika is missing. She left something for you." Adie waved the letter in front of the camera.

Bain pointed to the left side of the screen. Adie

looked at the edge of the screen, and noticed a small slot. Blue tape wrapped around the handle. It matched the blue switch on the board. She pulled the lever and placed the letter in the opening. A loud suction sound rang through the room.

"Wow. So that's coming to you?"

Bain nodded. "I'll get it in a few minutes."

Adie folded the maps into fourths. "You're going to need these too. Maps of the wilderness beyond Headquarters. We believe that Dannika is out there somewhere, looking for...something." Adie opened the slot, placed them in and closed it.

Bain nodded. "I'm actually familiar with that part of the property. Ivan allowed me to wander out there, since I'm not bound to living at Headquarters."

Adie froze. Did this mean he knew about Research? "Really? Um, are there any other areas off limits to the rest of us?" Adie tried to sound disinterested, unspecific.

Bain's face was genuine. "Nope, just did a little hunting out there. There are a lot of mountain lions and moose. Ivan let me hunt, but he felt it was too dangerous for anyone else."

And he didn't want anyone to know about Research. But nothing in Bain's answer gave her any reason to believe that he knew.

"Don't worry, Adie. The good news is that I'm a hunter. I will find her, wherever she is." He scratched his head. "I'll keep Demry posted."

Adie put her hand to the screen. "No." She paused, inhaled deeply. "When you see the letter, you'll know why. You need to go alone. I'll handle Demry."

"What? You read the letter?" Bain asked, his cheeks flushed enough to be visible on the screen.

Adie smiled a little. "I don't have to. I've been listening to it for months."

Bain rubbed his eyes with his fingers. Adie wasn't sure if he was tearing up, or just trying to make himself more comfortable, but either way, it was enough to know that whatever chemistry Dannika had thought developed over the years working interference cases through that screen, she'd been right.

"Bain, she's my best friend. Please, bring her home."

Bain nodded. "She's mine, too."

CHAPTER FIFTEEN

Zeneva swiveled her head under Dannika's arm. They sat at the edge of a small creek, just at the edge of the Headquarters wilderness boundary. Dannika looked back over her shoulder, where Painter stood tied to a tree. The weight of the supersized lion pushed Dannika a foot to the right. Dannika lost her balance and fell over backwards, laughing. She sat up and hugged Zeneva, then pulled out of her back pocket the small flask of vodka.

She knew that they would come looking for her. But she would have time. She had checked back in after her allotted three days, and as far as everyone knew, she was preparing to go back to work. On her medication and in control. Adie would be back in a couple of days and everything would return to usual.

Except that Dannika knew she couldn't stay. Not after even such a small taste of freedom. The city was out there somewhere, and her mom, and Bain. She couldn't live at the will of those arrogant Analysts that frothed at the mouth whenever they got the chance to re-evaluate the best Visionary at the agency. They could take their overzealous diagnosis and constant hovering and shove it — anywhere but back in her face. Their obsession with her dreams and her illness surely constituted its own oddity. And they thought she was the crazy one.

Dannika took a swig of vodka and felt a sadness creep through her. She didn't want to have to leave Adie that way. Just a letter. A simple note with nothing more than a vague explanation. She was finished with this world of secrets.

That's why the letter she left was not for Adie. Adie wouldn't understand. She hadn't been with IPA long enough. She hadn't wilted beneath its pressure the way Dannika had.

Instead, she knew her only hope was to engage the support of the one person she knew she could no longer be without. And if he didn't choose her, then maybe her real mother would. And if neither of them wanted her, then she didn't want to have to live in that kind of misery, that kind of wanting with no hope of receiving.

She rubbed Zeneva behind the ears and thought of their childhood pet. A large yellow lab named Monster. Daylea was always scared of monsters, but Dannika knew the monsters under her bed, personally. And she also knew the monsters in her head. Neither of them ever touched her. So she was never afraid. She knew it was cruel, but she named the dog Monster to scare Daylea. It was mean and she knew it. But someone who was always that happy deserved to have something to fear.

A tear rolled down her cheek. She wasn't sad to leave her sister. Only Adie. What they had was special. But one day, Dannika would be too far gone anyway, and Adie would have to pull the load herself. Dannika was providing her own early intervention, or at least that was what the Analysts would say.

She sucked in the cool mountain air to fill up with the strength to follow Zeneva and move on. Turning back would be easy. Adie would not have found the letter yet. Not for another day or two. The image of herself at age thirteen flashed vividly. She closed her eyes and drank in the memory of herself as a teenager. Backpack full of food and clothes. Running away from home. That was the day she'd discovered that she and Daylea had been adopted. Her parents thought a graduation into their teenage years deserved a diploma of truth.

Her real mother had given them up, birthing them at an age too young to be rational or responsible, only sixteen. Dannika set out to find her a short ten minutes after learning about her. She made it as far as the local mall, only about ten blocks away, and realized she had nothing to go on.

It was her first real episode of destruction. Possibly, learning that her life had been a lie had been the trigger. She couldn't be sure. But whatever caused her to go mad, it consumed her wholly. She swung her backpack at the head of a security officer, and ran through the mall, stepping into stores screaming and pulling things from the shelves. When the police tried to grab her, she bit their wrists until they bled and kicked them in places men would prefer she didn't.

By the time her parents were notified, she'd been charged with enough misdemeanors to grant juvenile delinquent status. She fulfilled her community service, one minute happily picking up garbage, the next spitting in the van driver's face. She became completely unpredictable. Then came her 'mild bipolar' diagnosis and the medication began. So did the dreams. Something about all that stress must have been some kind of trigger, because the dreams were there to stay.

Zeneva led Dannika and Painter back to the cave. The forest was so thick and lush on the Research side. Like it was full of secrets, covered up by foliage and moss and spider webs.

Dannika hadn't stopped thinking about Jocelyn. About how lonely and unhappy she seemed. Dannika needed someone to lead her, to keep her head level, and if Jocelyn would want to escape, she would need someone brave.

Dannika gave Zeneva a good rub behind the ears. "Lead Painter back all the way to the edge. She'll know how to get home from there." Zeneva nodded as Dannika gave Painter a pat on the withers, rubbed her muscular shoulder and neck, then finally met her eyes. Painter whinnied. "It's okay, you're in good hands."

Dannika grabbed the reins and placed them in Zeneva's sharp teeth. "Go ahead, girl," she said to Zeneva. "Take her home." Dannika watched in amazement as Painter willingly allowed the big lion to lead her away from the cave, weaving through pine branches and birch trunks. After two minutes, Dannika could no longer see them.

She located the rocky knob beneath the ceiling of the damp cave. It was a bit of a game of hide and seek, and Dannika fumbled around until she felt that familiar circular formation. She pressed hard and braced herself.

*

Minutes later, the large garage door opened to the massive coffeehouse room. Dannika sighed in relief that the room was empty, and she quickly scooted across the room to the door to Research.

She tiptoed into the bright hallway, gently turning the knob of the door to the nurse's station. The electronic file cabinet against the south wall was still blinking. Dannika thought there might be enough light reflecting off the file boards to see something. The tiny red letters quickly sprinted across the side of the files, so fast and small Dannika could make out none of it. In the tall cabinet, she saw the electric file boards stacked in their individual compartments, piled to the ceiling twenty feet high. She ran her fingers along the edges of the file boards, the way she would spindles on a staircase as a kid. Some of the boards were blinking, others just black.

About two-thirds the way to the top, the brightest one blinked hard and fast. Dannika thought that this could provide some better light. She pulled a chair over, careful not to make a sound, climbed on top of it, and reached for the file board. As she pulled it out, the entire cabinet shifted, slid to the left, and revealed a dark empty space behind it. Dannika pulled the well-lit file board all the way out, too anxious about what lay beyond the cabinet to try to decode anything about the file itself.

She stuck her hand into the darkness, feeling nothing. She held the file board into the space and could see that it kept going. A tunnel. She reached out and touched both sides. The tunnel was narrow and only six feet tall. Cement walls on all four sides made it cool enough for to give her goose bumps.

She held the file board up for light and felt around for some knob or button to close the tunnel. Nothing was obvious. There were no alterations on the walls, but a small slit where the ceiling met the wall just to the left of the tunnel door caught her eye.

She stuck the board into the slit and the wall shifted back to close. In complete darkness, she felt her way forward. Finally, a sliver of light. She continued toward it and saw light seeping around the edges of a door. A door with a handle.

Dannika took a deep breath. Did she dare? Just open this random door? Yell out 'Surprise!' She nodded to herself. Yes. She didn't come this far to wimp out. She was created to help people, and right now, the person who needed her help was Jocelyn.

She slowly opened the door. Light fell across her shoulders and her face to reveal another large room. Similar to the coffeehouse room, but with a more institutionalized feel. White ceramic tile floors. White walls. White tables. White chairs. So different from the colorful underworld of Headquarters.

A sliding door opened. Dannika swallowed hard and dodged to the right. She found herself tucked between a white leather recliner and matching sofa. She peeked around. A line of elderly people, single file, walked through the room to a small window. When the first in line got close, the window flew open. Nurse Mary set small paper cups on the window ledge and placed pills into the cups. The elderly rotated through, took their pills with a swallow of water, then moved to the back of the line.

While the last elderly man was lobbying against taking his pills, Dannika heard a familiar voice. She peeked around a little further. Jocelyn's sweet smile was convincing the man to swallow the mammoth pill. Dannika watched as Jocelyn gently held the cup to the old man's mouth and urged him to give in. He crimped his mouth shut until finally Jocelyn poked her finger into the side of his mouth the same way Dannika would to get the bit into the mouth of her horse. The old man opened his mouth and Jocelyn stuffed the mammoth pill along with others into his mouth, squeezed his cheeks, and poured water in so he would get them down. She then escorted the line of shuffling old people out of the room, and led another group in.

This group was loud, sounds of banter and cussing and threats. Jocelyn limped her way to the window, apparently still sore from her lion attack, and held the first in line by both arms. Dannika could see they were all tied together, their faces screwed up in anger, their mouths pushing out profanity. Vivid insanity in their eyes.

Dannika took a deep breath as her chest tightened. Something in their body language felt familiar, their tension and anger resonated deeply with her. Even their demeanor seemed to resemble her own at times. Mary crushed up the medication and put them into a chocolate milk shake. Jocelyn helped each one of them slurp it up as quickly as possible and scooted them out of the room. They didn't want their meds either.

The medicine window shut and the room was silent. Dannika sat back on her heels and waited to be sure the room was empty. She felt a tap on her shoulder. Her stomach leapt into her throat as she whipped around to stare at Jocelyn.

"What are you doing here?" Jocelyn whispered. "Are you crazy?

Dannika smiled and crouched down behind the couch. "Actually, yes. Well, half-crazy, apparently. But I guess you already knew that."

Jocelyn stood. "Yes, of course. But you shouldn't be here. They'll want to keep you here."

Dannika stayed tucked back in her hiding place. "Actually, I'm going to make a run for it. I was in the neighborhood and figured I'd stop by to see if you want to join me."

Jocelyn shook her head. "No one will be coming here until dinner. You can stand."

Dannika stood, blushing. "So, what's with all the patients?"

Jocelyn's smile vanished. "I can't tell you that. Look,

I appreciate what you are trying to do, but they would find us. You need to get out of here and go back to Headquarters, Dannika. If our boss, Mayer, finds you, it won't be pretty."

Dannika jumped when an automatic air conditioning unit switched on. "But Jocelyn, you said that you were lonely and tired of being here. Don't you think it's worth a shot? We can make it in the city, I know we can."

"Dannika, you don't understand. Do you really think they'll just leave us be? They'll be on our tail in no time, and who knows what they'll do to us. Besides..." Jocelyn pointed to her foot. "I mean, hello. I'm not exactly in full-sprint condition. Trust me, Dannika. If I thought it was possible, I would go. It's not safe for either of us. This is the life we were meant to live. You need to accept that. Please."

Dannika's eyes began to tear up. "No, you don't understand. My life at Headquarters is done. I can't do it anymore. They drug me up and keep me hostage. I already can't go up to the city. I don't ever get more than one stupid glass of wine unless I steal it, and everyone treats me like some crazy witch, walking by me on eggshells, and eyeing me like I'm a freak. I will never get to leave there, I will never get to meet my real mom, and I will never get to be with the man I love. So why? Why does it even matter? Why does anything matter?"

She dropped to her knees. Her head fell into her hands, sobbing. She began punching the floor. Harder. And again, even harder. Her knuckles turned red and swelled instantly. Jocelyn reached out to stop her, but one last contact with the floor and they heard a snap. Dannika reeled back in pain, holding her hand. She could barely move her fourth and fifth fingers.

Jocelyn put a hand on her back and rubbed gently.

"Dannika, you've probably broken your hand. We need to get to the nurse. We'll think of an excuse why you're here. Don't worry."

Dannika sniffed hard with a nod and winced. Jocelyn led her through the door from which the patients had entered. They took a hard left and ended up back in the hallway. The lights were on in the nurse's office, and Mary was at her desk, scrolling through the touch screen of a file board.

As Jocelyn led Dannika up to the desk, Mary retracted the file and jammed it into its home in the electronic cabinet. "Hello there, Dannika. May I ask what you are doing here...again?" she said without looking up.

Dannika ran through the plan she and Jocelyn had devised in the two minutes it took them to get to Mary's office. "Um, Jocelyn was telling me how much she missed some stuff we have back at Headquarters that you guys don't get to have here that often." She smiled at Jocelyn. "Like chocolate. Why would you not get to have chocolate anyway? That's really lame. You must want your people to be miserable."

"Well, if you must know, the chemicals in the chocolate mess with our experiments with the brain. Same with alcohol, caffeine, salt, and sugar. So, yes, our subjects have limits here." Mary wrinkled her nose and pushed her glasses up.

"That sucks. Maybe I don't want to stick around here," Dannika said. "Doesn't that just suck, Jocelyn?"

"Actually, yeah. It does kind of suck." Jocelyn giggled under her breath.

Mary scowled at her. She removed her reading glasses and set them on the top of her head. "Do you really think you were discreet in the dining hall behind that couch?" Mary pulled her glasses back on. "Now, let me see that hand."

Dannika squeezed her eyes shut as Mary pinched near her wrist. "Just a sprain. We'll get it wrapped up."

"Well, it hurts like hell," Dannika said. "After all the pills I saw you pushing out the window, I'll bet you've got some seriously posh pain killers." Dannika twisted at one of the loops through the cartilage in her ear.

Mary just shook her head.

"Here, take these." Jocelyn handed some white and green pills to Dannika. Then she turned to the nurse. "Mary," Jocelyn said softly. "What about Mayer? If he knows she's here?"

Mary tilted her head down to look over her glasses, "You leave him to me, you got that?"

Jocelyn nodded.

While Mary put the supplies away, Dannika's eyes wandered up to the spot where she had removed the file board to use as a light. It was still empty. She grit her teeth hard and quickly looked back at her hand.

"You have no idea what you are getting yourself into, young lady. But you will need rest. And as soon as you feel up to it, you will head back to Headquarters immediately. I'm going to have to notify them. You know that, don't you?"

"Please don't." Dannika's voice softened. "I'll go back tomorrow, I promise. They'll never think to look for me here. I'll tell them I spent another night in the wilderness. Just please."

Mary stared hard at Dannika.

Jocelyn sat next to Dannika and put her arm around her shoulder. "Please, Mary. For me?"

"Very well. I have no idea why I am agreeing to this. Jocelyn, I will keep Mayer occupied for the night. You find Dannika a room."

Jocelyn led Dannika to a room with all white walls and a wrought iron bed. "I'll get you some sheets."

"This is it?" Dannika's skin crawled at the emptiness of the four walls.

"I know. It's lovely, right?" Jocelyn failed to hide her sarcasm.

Dannika pursed her lips. "It's fine. So you'll think about it? About coming with me?"

Jocelyn sat on the bed, pat the empty spot next to her.

Dannika sat down. She began to feel a familiar calmness fall over her. Every muscle in her body was relaxed. "Jocelyn, you gave me anti-anxiety meds instead of pain killers, didn't you?" Dannika felt lightheaded in an elated sort of way.

Jocelyn sighed. "I gave you both. Snuck it past Mary. We don't need you to punch out the beautiful white walls in here. You can thank me in the morning." She smiled. "I also gave you a sleeping pill. We need to hide you for a day or two until your hand heals enough to head back home."

Dannika rolled her eyes. Seemed like the solution to everything around here was a pill or two for a quick fix. "Jocelyn, please tell me. Now that I'm here. What's really going on here that everything has to be so secret and hidden from Headquarters?"

Jocelyn looked down. "I want to, Dannika. I really do. But I can't. I don't know everything anyway. I only know a little. I can tell you that you need to control yourself, or you will be placed in the compound with all those old and crazy people.

"There are two kinds of research here. The one I'm involved in. And the one they're involved in. Trust me, you don't want to be a part of the looney bin."

She walked over and cracked open the door, peeked left and right, then closed it again. She took a deep breath. "I'm not supposed to know what all of those patients are here for, but I have done a little snooping around. Mayer tries to tell us that those are old IPA employees that need protection, but I've done my homework, and that's not true. I have a hunch Mayer has some private projects going on, and I'm not so sure even Ivan and Bethie know about them.

"See, those old people, when they first came in, they were said to be IPA employees that were living in an elderly-assisted area at Headquarters. They were all happy, told the same stories over and over, laughed just as hard every time. They could never remember my name, and would tell me what a pleasure it was to meet me every time."

"Alzheimers?"

Jocelyn nodded. "Yes. Mayer took each one into surgery, claimed they needed a knee or hip replacement, but three weeks later, they all were walking like zombies."

"And the crazy people?"

"Well, so far, he's conducted surgery on a few of them too. But they come out way different. They're still angry and volatile, but they're, like, wicked smart. I'll give them a four-hundred-page novel to read and two hours later, they'll come out asking me for another. We'll play poker and they can recite every card that's been played.

"Once I caught onto it, I started my own little experiment. I placed a page full of nine digit numbers in front of those who have had surgery and those who haven't. They are allowed to view the page for one minute.

The ones who haven't had surgery can't make any sense of the numbers. But those who have can tell me every number and not miss a dang one." She raised her brows at Dannika.

Dannika shook her head in disbelief. "So, why are you willing to tell me all of this now?"

She leaned closer to Dannika, talking softer. "Dannika, when I met you, I probably would have run away with you that very second. But when we came back that day, while Mary fixed up my foot I snooped around her desk. I found some interesting articles, white papers, and really random technical specifications.

"There is definitely another side to Research. The side I'm on is doing good work, perfecting the interference process. In my heart, I feel like the other side has a different motive.

"Dannika, I'm going to need some help. And what you did for me was all I needed to know I could trust you. So if you're willing to trust me, you need to do exactly as I say."

"And the lions?"

"I don't know how they do that. Not yet. And I'm not sure why. But I know the lions are good. At least all of the ones I've met."

Dannika's eyes were drooping, her head lolling. Jocelyn helped her to lie down on the plain mattress, resting her head against the pillow. Dannika eased out the words, "So, Research is kind of like bipolar."

Jocelyn whispered, "I guess you could say that."

Jocelyn ran her fingers through Dannika's hair as Dannika's eyes closed, her breathing heavy. "Then maybe I'm exactly where I am supposed to be."

CHAPTER SIXTEEN

Adie wandered into the dining hall and poured a cup of tea. She was going to go crazy waiting around here for Dannika to turn up. She knew Bain would find her. She felt confident about that. But when? She had looked over the map of the outer wilderness, and it was enormous. Hundreds of thousands of acres. Dannika was a pine needle in a grove of spruce trees.

Lunch would be served in an hour, so Adie just sat, staring at the murals on the walls.

Each wall of the dining hall had a different mural painted by some of the employees on their down time. Each wall like a window, as if to suggest that the dining hall was a restaurant up in the city. One wall showed a row of retail stores, sandwiched by two coffee shops on either end of the block. Another wall displayed a park, sprinkled with tiny children climbing trees and kicking balls. On a third wall was a skyline of tall city buildings. The wall where they entered was brilliantly painted as a large stage curtain, as if when you walked into the dining hall, you could transform into whatever city dweller you might wish to be that day.

Sometimes Adie would look at the skyline and imagine Witt dining at the top of one of those buildings with some brilliant grad student. Other times, she would dream she was a famous author, heading into one of those coffee shops to write her next masterpiece. That skyline caught her attention today. It made her feel small. Helpless.

Jeff walked through the big curtain doors and pulled

up a chair beside her.

"Aren't you and Demry taking off soon?" he asked.

Adie twirled her cup of tea in a circle. "I'm not going."

She thought she heard a sigh of relief from Jeff. He sat up straighter and pulled his chair in closer. "Why not?"

"She doesn't want me to go after her. She wants someone else." Adie tried to hide her frown. She understood Dannika better than anyone, and she knew exactly why Dannika had needed Bain to go and not her, but it still sent a pain through her chest.

Jeff frowned. "I don't understand. How do you know what Dannika wants right now?"

"She left a letter." Adie paused. "For Bain. If anyone goes after her, she wants it to be Bain."

Jeff's face went blank as his mind churned and calculated. Jeff leaned back into his chair. His posture relaxed a bit. "Well, can't say I'm surprised." He seemed to shift the direction of his comment, as if calculating his words. "I mean, if she needs some back-up, he probably *is* her best option."

"That's not why." Adie tapped her nails on the cup. "She doesn't want protection. She wants validation."

"Validation of what?"

Men were so frustrating. She didn't want to answer that question, since Dannika's situation with Bain so closely paralleled her own with Jeff. But this was not the time to guard herself. Dannika was running around in the wilderness, most likely trying to play out some Romeo and Juliet scenario with Bain, while they desperately needed her back here with Adie, hard at work. After all those years saving lives, Adie knew Dannika had finally realized that she needed something to live for as well. And if she was wrong about Bain, she would not come back.

Adie blew out a deep breath and turned to look at Jeff. "That he could love her. You know, if he were allowed to."

Jeff eyed Adie. Finally, he spoke. "Of course. She loves him." Jeff slapped his hand lightly on the table as if he had come to some sort of realization.

"Yes. And it drives her madder than hell that she can't have him." Adie could no longer look at Jeff.

Jeff reached out for Adie's chin, tipping her head toward him. He gently stroked her cheek, ran his fingers softly across her lips. Adie closed her eyes, let the feeling radiate throughout her. His lips touched hers, warm and soft, and her eyes opened. After a simple kiss, Jeff sat back and held Adie's hand. "If I could do that every day, for the rest of my life, I would." His expression became somber, his eyes sad.

"Why did you do that?"

"In case you need validation."

Demry broke a long silence when he rushed through the curtain-painted entry. Jeff jumped from his seat, pulling his hand from Adie's quickly. "Okay, lovebirds, Bethie wants us in the conference room immediately. I guess Bain is going out instead of us?"

"Yes, he is," Adie answered. Demry cursed the air. As Jeff stood, she thought he looked concerned. She couldn't be sure what it meant. If maybe he would think she might be worth that risk someday.

*

Bethie sat at the head of the conference table, her face stern. She motioned for everyone to take a seat. A circle of stained-glass water goblets surrounded a large pitcher of water. Seated at the table were three supervisors from Tech and five from Analysis. Behind Bethie stood two guys from Ops. Bain's sidekicks. Adie shied away from them at first. She'd never seen anyone from Ops in person before. They were huge. A few poured themselves a glass of water and took a seat.

Bethie cleared her throat and took a sip from her goblet. "So, there are a number of things we need to cover. I can't seem to reach Ivan, so I suppose he's working through things over at Research, and therefore I will need to make some decisions myself." She leafed through a file of papers. "This Ram case has gotten quite ugly. Not only for the Feds, but for our company as well. Just to ensure everyone is on the same page, I'll give you an update on where we stand with all urgent issues, and we will need to make some action items.

"First, we've taken precautions to protect IPA HQ and all of its employees. Invisible electronic shields now surround all dry land portals to our underground offices. Anyone that steps within twenty feet of this shield will receive a high-voltage shock. No one can get through. Lonie has been out on recruitment, and Daylea is on vacation, along with about ten others, so they will be notified and Jago will deactivate the shield to allow them to enter, then reactivate it. This is temporary. Most likely we will have to implement a more permanent solution if we are to remain secure at Headquarters." She took another sip of water.

"Secondly, Dannika's absence is a priority. Her situation is quite dangerous, as we noticed that she has not taken her meds in days. Her brain is hypersensitive, and without those meds, the imbalance is certain to cause her much distress. We believe she has ventured beyond the

Headquarters' wilderness.

"Initially, we planned for Adie and Demry to set off after Dannika, but there have been some new developments, as there always seems to be with that girl. She has insisted that Bain be the one to come after her. This indicates she may have some very clear ultimatums. We are all deeply concerned for Dannika. But we're on top of the situation and we are confident Bain will find her."

Bethie paused. She flipped another page of the file and placed her hands on top of the pages. "Now, while we wait to hear from Bain, we still have the Ram case. Before our sweet informant Jora was taken from us, she discovered disturbing evidence. She found the drugs. That was a no brainer. But it turns out the drugs were just a cover up. By the time her killer had gotten there, she had dug deeper than simply an illegal amount of marijuana. The pot was an attempt to throw a curve ball, but to who? Apparently, Noder was coming unglued. He knew nothing about anything beyond the drugs. The Ram was using him to cover up something bigger."

Jeff shifted in his seat. "Bethie, what did she find?"

Bethie sighed, tapping her pen against the table. "Maps. Of hundreds of miles of hidden underground tunnels that attach to IPA Headquarters. Not even Ivan or I knew of these tunnels."

"You've got to be kidding." Jeff rubbed his forehead.

"That's not all. Jora was good. Really good. So based on how she was discovered and the shape in which that basement room was found, this is what we believe happened.

"The maps weren't enough for her. She wanted more. There were lots of random numbers on the maps. A three-digit code here, a five-digit code there. She wrote a list. Then she figured there must be some secret vault that these numbers opened. She pulled paper off the walls. She hammered at the brick and cement. Since it was after hours, she thought the noise wouldn't be an issue. She pulled out an entire wall of safe deposit boxes and low and behold, when she peeped through the holes where they had been, she saw a vault.

"Somehow that waif of a woman pulled the deposit box shelving from the wall, and found the keypad on the wall for the vault. It was ten lines long, each line varying in length of numbers. We have no idea what brilliant thought pattern she had that allowed her to figure out which numbers fit where, but she got into that vault. And you'll never believe what she found."

Adie looked around the room as Bethie paused. Everyone held a blank stare, eyes wide and torsos leaning forward as if her next words might jolt them from their seats.

"Brain parts. About fifty of them. Frozen and stored." Bethie's face nearly turned green.

"Ugh. Disgusting." Adie covered her mouth and put a hand to her gut.

"That evidence still sits in the vault in the basement of the bank. We confiscated the maps, but the other...um...the other items were left until the Ram is caught. Obviously, these were what were truly being hidden, and the only way we know how to catch the Ram is to leave them there. He'll surely be back for them.

"The bank is being watched by the FBI, but of course, they are not as familiar with the Ram as we are, so this will be tricky. Plus, we no longer have Dannika to give us hints and clues as to when the Ram may strike. And although we do have Adie to hopefully get some intel on Rens, as you can imagine, this complicates things.

"As you all now have learned, there is a Research department at IPA. It is located about sixty miles from here by underground, but the portal in the wilderness is only about fifteen miles from the edge of the Headquarters' wilderness boundaries. Ivan has gone to investigate how the memory scan, which was developed at Research, has been shared with the Ram. They are the only suppliers of this model and scale of a memory scan. Ivan had no record of any additional scans being produced, meaning that either the Ram has received the scan from a leak at Research or a leak at one of the government agencies.

"Ivan will hopefully sort this out with Research. Of course, anyone offering anything of ours, including information, to unauthorized people in the cities above will be arrested immediately. This leak *will* be found. Of that you can be sure."

Adie was not used to this body language from Bethie, this tone in her voice. She'd always been so bubbly, patient, and calm. Today, the worry-infused tension was apparent in the dark circles beneath her eyes, the shakiness in her voice, and the unusual way her mouth tilted into a tiny frown.

She continued. "The only way to truly discover how this is all connected is to catch the Ram and interrogate him. Or to catch the coward at IPA. Neither of these will be easy. And until Dannika returns, finding the Ram will be difficult unless he goes back to the bank, or Rens does something really stupid."

"So what do we do now?" Demry rocked back and forth in his seat with impatience.

"We wait until we get another lead. We continue our work. When we get Dannika back, we can hone in on the

Ram, but until then, we'll have to let the FBI handle it. And we wait to hear from Ivan, and hope he finds a trail of who might have revealed us and why."

Adie took a deep breath and clenched her fists. "No."

"What do you mean, 'No'?" Jeff asked.

Adie stood up and walked quickly over to the Ops guys standing at ease. "You guys get this, right? Doesn't anybody see? We can't wait. We don't have time to wait for Dannika to return and hope she'll spot the Ram in her dreams. We have to go after him. Does nobody agree?"

The Ops supervisor named Chaz with buzzed hair and a military stance raised his hand. "I absolutely agree. What do you propose, little angel?"

Adie caught Jeff's expression out of the corner of her eye. He glared at Chaz. Clearly he didn't approve of the nickname.

Adie stayed focused. "Without Dannika's dreams, we need somebody up there." She paused. "I'm going in. As an informant at the bank."

Chaz tipped his invisible hat to her. "Right on, girl."

Jeff stood. "Absolutely not!"

Adie stared at Jeff. "It's the only way. I was Dannika's partner. I know the way the Ram moves better than anyone second to Dannika. I get his thoughts. I know everything she saw. Every detail. Every spasm of his eye or jerk of his head. Dannika's dreams, they're...they're more intense than the rest of us. They streamline detail and snapshot critical items. She's the only Visionary I've met that retains a photographic memory of her dreams. Most of us write our reports immediately after our dream because the details slip away from us over time. Not Dannika. She remembers every crumb of food on the ground, every spec of dirt on his pants. And because I have been on that journey with her, so do I. Just tell me what to do, and I will lure him in. I know it."

Jeff gave Bethie a look of desperation. "She'll be killed. Quicker than Jora. She has no informant training."

"No," Bethie sat taller and narrowed her eyes at Adie. "She has something better."

A silent confusion filled the air, as everyone, including Adie, tried to sort out what Bethie was talking about.

Bethie glanced up at Adie with a smile. "You might be onto something. You just might be able to stop the Ram, even without Dannika."

"How?"

"The same way you stopped Rens from hurting Jeff."

Adie's dream of Jeff revisited her and she shuddered. "I don't understand."

Bethie nodded to Jago. Jago leaned into his elbows on the table. "Adie. When you told us about your dream with Jeff, it validated to us that you have a special gift among the Visionaries. Similar to how Dannika has the power to serial dream in that photographic detail, you have a power as well. Bethie suspected it, but after you saved Jeff, we were sure."

"What do you mean, saved Jeff?"

Bethie's voice was soft again. "That group of college kids that happened to be there, that wasn't chance, dear. You put them there."

"I did?"

"Yes. You possess a gift that occasionally brings dreams to you in real time, and when they do, you have the power to interfere in that moment. It's very rare and very powerful."

Adie face went blank. "I knew it! I knew something must be different about those dreams. That's remarkable." She tried to process what this meant. Her face must have given away her thoughts.

Jago turned to Adie. "Has it happened any other times that you are aware of, Adie?"

Adie lowered her head and fiddled with her hands in her lap. "Yes, it has. With Maimey." She looked to Bethie. "I'm so sorry I haven't had a chance to tell you."

"So it was Rens?"

"Yes." Adie answered. "I suppose I thought you all knew it was the Ram's doing."

"It's okay, dear. We did." Bethie assured her. "However, there may be some details in your dream that will help you, up in that bank." Bethie smiled.

"Really?" Adie lit up. "You're gonna let me go in?"

Bethie nodded at Jago, and he began to unload on Adie.

"It is critical that you understand in depth what we know of how your special asset works. Your brain contains an extra lobe. It's located just behind the frontal lobe, and it processes quickly and impulsively. It is called the Ignition lobe. It has a heightened sense of action, and it's tied into your personal emotional response. Under certain circumstances, it 'ignites' and you can actually run a 'live' interference in the dream itself.

"With Jeff's incident, you sent the crowd of twenty-somethings down that lonely street just in time to chase off Rens. And it seems that your dream with Maimey was a little trickier and actually quite amazing, because you sent yourself in to stop him. How you managed that will require further analysis."

Adie nodded, almost in a daze. "It's settled then. I go into the bank, and get into that vault. Just tell me how to stop the Ram in my dream."

"It's not that simple, Adie. Based on what we know of how this part of your brain operates, it is triggered by an emotional reaction. So, you only receive this live feed and become a part of it if the subject in danger is someone you care about. A lot."

Adie blushed as Jago had just revealed to the entire agency that she must *care about* Jeff.

Adie squeezed her eyes shut and held her head in her hands. "So it's much more complicated than me just being the bait?"

"She can't go in, Bethie," Jeff pleaded.

Adie sat tall, her face firm. She looked at Jeff and knew that everyone could see the longing in her eyes. For him. But she couldn't have him. And everyone in that room knew that too. So what, really, did she have to lose? "I'm sorry, Jeff. But I'm doing this. It's the only way to put an end to it. To all of it."

She turned to Jago. "What do I need to do?"

"You need to prepare. First, you'll pose as a bank customer. You'll need to spend a few days entering the bank, pretending to use your safety deposit box so that you can be comfortable with the environment. We'll have to bring the DEA back in to help you with details and planning to lure the Ram into the bank. It'll be intense, Adie. You sure you're up for it?"

Jeff threw his head into his hands. "This is insane!" He looked up at Bethie, his eyes strained and red. "Why are you willing to do this?"

"Because Ivan taught me a long time ago that we are given a gift by God, and it is our divine responsibility to use it. Because I believe in Adie. I believe in all of you. It's no coincidence that each and every one of you are here." She prompted Adie. "If you say you are ready, I trust you."

Bethie's words filled Adie with courage like never before. They gave her power, as if Bethie had just unzipped her and stuffed her full of bravery, confidence, and purpose, and zipped her right back up.

Adie smiled, walking over to place a hand on Jeff's shoulder. "Bethie is right. I need to go."

Jeff turned to her, his voice full of hopelessness. "So, who exactly, will be *your* bait, Adie? Who is going to be the person you care about so much that the dream interference will work? If you care about someone that much, are you really going to put them in a position where they could be killed?" His voice rose, his cheeks reddened. "Are you going to invite your dad to the bank? Your mom? Oh, wait, I know, how about your little brothers? That should do it." His hands moved wildly as he talked. His voice shook. "You heard them, Adie, you can't just pick some random stranger to fill those shoes. So who's it gonna be, Adie? Have you thought about that?"

"Yes." Adie locked eyes with Bethie, then turned back to Jeff. She put one hand on each of his shoulders and looked him straight in the eyes. "It's going to be you."

CHAPTER SEVENTEEN

Dannika woke to a buffet of breakfast food spread across a long card table on the opposite side of the room. Her eyes still felt heavy and her head fuzzy. She sat up and looked around as she regained understanding of where she was. Four white walls. A mattress and pillow, no sheets, just two large blankets spread over her.

She slowly eased out of bed, looked around for the few belongings she had brought along. The flask — gone. The pocket knife — gone. Her photo of Bain — gone.

The door slid open. "Good morning, sunshine. Or should I say, good evening?" Jocelyn said as she brought in yet another tray of fresh fruit and ice water.

"I think there's enough food here to feed me for days."

"Well, you've been sleeping that long, so I guess you might need it." Jocelyn made room on the table for the new tray.

Dannika frowned. "What do you mean?"

Jocelyn sat next to Dannika. "I gave you a sleeping pill that should have knocked you out for twelve hours. But you just slept for forty-eight hours straight."

"Wow." Dannika shook her head. "Mayer know I'm here?"

Jocelyn shook her head no. "Mary thought we should keep that secret. He's not always stable, doesn't handle change well." Jocelyn raised a brow. "He's hoarded up on some observation project right now, so after you eat up and get some strength back, you can be on your way." Jocelyn set her eyes firmly on Dannika. "To Headquarters, not some lame brain idea of escape. Got it?"

"Uh huh. Sure," Dannika answered as she munched on a banana. Jocelyn didn't know everything about Dannika's plans. Like that someone very important would be coming for her — that is, if her life meant anything at all.

Jocelyn sat in a plain wooden chair across from Dannika. "Look, there is something I need to tell you. Mary doesn't know I've found out about Research's long-term plans. Mayer — he watches people at Headquarters, the way he used to watch me. He keeps tabs on those he thinks might be useful in future projects. At least, that's how it happened with me.

But once I got here, I found out that if you don't turn out to be productive, well, he can't send you back to Headquarters, so you are forced to make a decision — take the memory scan and go back up to the city, or donate part of your brain to animal science. Either way, you lose yourself." Jocelyn's chest rose with a deep breath.

Dannika's eyes widened. "What? Like a lobotomy or something?" She shook her head. "That dude is whack." Then the pieces fell into place. "Wait. You mean like Zeneva?"

Jocelyn chomped on a strawberry. "How else do you think she understands you so well?"

Dannika leaned foreward. "This is actually kind of brilliant, you know."

"Yes, it is. It's also kind of evil. I don't blame the animals. They end up being quite helpful, guarding Research. But for the poor souls who don't truly understand that choice, it's sad. They just wander these halls, lifeless." Jocelyn shook her head. "Anyway, you and Adie...both on the list." Her eyes were serious.

Dannika picked at an orange peel. "No freaking way. Who in their right mind would put that lunatic—the real kind, I might add—at the helm of this gig?"

"The world ain't rosy anywhere, Dannika, not even down here."

Dannika put a hand on Jocelyn's knee. "Well, don't worry. If I ever end up here, I know I am useful. Besides, I'm blowing this joint."

Jocelyn locked eyes with Dannika. "Do you remember a single dream from that forty-eight-hour slumber just now?"

Dannika chuckled. "No, but I was heavily medicated. I'm not surprised."

Jocelyn nodded. "Yes, let's hope that's it. But over the next couple of days, be prepared for any lagging visuals that might come up. Mixing all that medication could trigger something."

Dannika dove into some pancakes. Jocelyn left to get Dannika some clean clothes. When she returned, she handed Dannika the photo of Bain. Dannika rubbed the face gently, then looked up at Jocelyn.

Jocelyn put a hand on her shoulder. "I always really liked him, too, back when I worked at Headquarters. I mean, not the way you do, but he was great to work with."

Dannika just nodded and tried to keep her lip from quivering.

Dannika filled up on French toast and bacon and then followed Jocelyn to an entertainment room. Four white walls enclosed three flat screen televisions, video games, two laptops, and tall bookshelves loaded with paperbacks.

"Just relax, okay? I've got a little work to do. Mary knows you're here so she'll keep anyone else out." Jocelyn locked eyes with Dannika. "Do not leave this room until I return. Then I'll help you get out of here. Got it?"

Dannika waved her off as she pulled the cover off a laptop. "Sure. You go figure out how to save the world. I'll be right here." Maybe Research wasn't so bad. Maybe it would do. A new home. A new start. A new friend. Dedicating herself to something even more meaningful than saving individuals one by one. Maybe this was what she was built for. No, what she was born for. Maybe she and Bain wouldn't have to put their lives on the line to be together. Maybe if she was tucked away at Research, she wouldn't be in the way of Bain's work. She could prove that their love for one another could be part of it instead.

*

Mary entered the room. "Hello there, sleepyhead." She handed Dannika a cup full of pills. Dannika slapped her hand, causing the pills to fall from the cup and land in the corner of the room.

"I've told you before, I don't need any of that!" Mary leaned down to gather up the colorful meds and placed them back into the Dixie cup. "If you want to me to allow you to leave Research—ever—then you will take those pills."

"Fine, but I know what meds I take. Show me the sample packages. So I know what I'm getting. I don't want you putting me under and trying to dig into my skull or anything. I don't trust you people."

Dannika looked back to her game of solitaire on the

laptop and froze. She wasn't supposed to know that, because Jocelyn wasn't supposed to know that. She sat still for moment and tried to keep her breath steady in Mary's silence.

"Very well, then. I'll be back with those samples, and I will witness you taking them."

Dannika shook her head, as something like steam rose through her chest, to her cheeks, and began to numb her brain. How dare that woman act like she her doctor? She didn't need any damn pills right now, and she was going to have to get out of there before that idiot of a nurse tried to pull rank on her. Dannika began to feel dizzy as a wave of hard anger trickled through her body.

Dannika sprinted to the door, quietly catching it before it slammed shut and locked from the other side. She slowly pulled it open, peeked her head out, and checked both sides. Mary wasn't in sight. No one was.

Dannika crept down the hallway in the opposite direction of the nurse's station. The bright white walls wound in all directions to form an endless maze. One hundred yards down the hall, she decided to take the first door she didn't recognize. Somehow, she would find her way out of there. She would get to the city, and Bain would find her. With him by her side, she would demand from IPA a life she deserved, or she would expose IPA, especially this whole creepy Research place. Take away whatever hope IPA had with all this techno-psychology stuff. The same way they had slowly chipped away at hers.

The door she chose opened up to another long white hallway. She closed it gently behind her and continued on tiptoe. She slid a finger against the wall to regain her balance every few steps.

With her eyes tightly closed, she placed her hand on her stomach. Just like during her deep meditation, she used her awareness of energy. She went in the direction she felt any type of pull without second guessing her motions. Her feet moved to the right, and she let them take her. She kept her hand on her gut and let her mind go blank.

She continued to take left and right turns as her body navigated the labyrinth instead of her mind. She finally hit a dead end where a large wooden door, painted bright white stopped her. She reached for the handle, sure it was locked. But it occurred to her that most of the doors in Research seemed to be locked from the outside, kept people in instead of out. She turned the knob, heard the small click of the lock, and the door opened up to a tiny white room.

At the back, in a plain white wooden chair, sat Ivan, his hands and feet bound to the chair by wire and his mouth gagged by a cloth. His eyes were huge and his breathing heavy. He squirmed wildly, but not even the chair would move.

"Ivan!" Dannika slammed the door behind her and rushed to him. She started to pull at the cloth at his mouth, tied behind his head. She cursed her bitten fingernails as she tried to dig into the tight knot. Her lips curled up in fury. She finally undid the knot and tossed the cloth to the floor.

"Dannika. You've got to get out of here. Please. The danger here is beyond my control. Please, just leave me. Go!" Ivan said in a harsh whisper.

"No way, Ivan. I'm getting you free." She started to work at the wire on his hands, but she had no tools and it was tightly secured. "Did that Mary lady do this? Or that Mayer guy? Who did this to you?"

"Dannika, just go. Before it's too late. Bethie and I have been fooled. We have been ignorant. This place is very dangerous, Dannika. However it is you got here, you need to go. Now!"

"I am getting you free, or I'm not going anywhere."

Dannika heard the door open behind her and she locked eyes with Ivan.

Ivan shook his head. "Just let her be, Mayer. This doesn't concern her."

Mayer walked toward them. Dannika stood still, contemplating her next move.

"Well, well, well. If it isn't our infamous serial dreamer. If she wasn't so full-bore crazy, she could have been useful to us long ago, don't you think, Ivan?" Mayer's voice sent a shiver down Dannika's spine.

She felt him move closer. Ivan begged. "Let her be, Mayer."

Dannika didn't like seeing Ivan's eyes that way. So full of uncertainty. He was the confident one. Never shaken. Everyone's rock. He had always had such control.

She could feel Mayer's heat. He was right behind her. She meant to speak, but her body responded first. She landed an elbow between his legs and sent him to the floor. She kicked a bare heel into his temple and put a fist into his jaw.

Mayer's glasses flew from his face. He tried to regain his stance, but she kneed him in the back. She gripped a handful of his thick dusty blond hair and rammed his head against the ground.

"Dannika, please just make a run for it. Get to the portal and just run. Please. This will not end nicely." Ivan yelled.

But Dannika could only see Mayer, and she wanted

more of him. She wanted to peel out his eyes.

"Why did you do this to him? Huh?" She said between gritted teeth.

Mayer just moaned as he rolled around on the white tile floor.

"You better start talking, you pansy jerk."

Every time he tried to stand, she laid him out again. A blow with the heel of her hand to his chest, a fist to the Adam's apple, an elbow to his temple, a foot to his abdomen. She let up when he failed to move from a fetal position for a good ten seconds. But she stood over him, on her guard.

"Dannika. That's enough. Just go." Ivan pleaded.

Dannika leaned over Mayer, her fists still pulled back and ready to spring. Her knees bent, each muscle in her leg tense.

For a moment, the room was quiet, the silence broken by the words behind her, 'not so fast.'

Ivan shifted in his seat and yelled out Dannika's name, but he was too late. As Dannika was just about to lean in for one more blow when the needle jammed into the back of her neck. The world went blank and fuzzy, and pins and needles flowed through her like a river.

Her body fell limp to the floor, and her head slammed against the speckled tile. She opened her eyes to a cloudy haze and saw a dark form over her. Just before her eyes closed, she made out the form. Mary.

CHAPTER EIGHTEEN

Dannika woke up on the floor of an unfamiliar house. She sat up on her elbows and looked around. Antique couches with worn-out colonial fabrics and mahogany frames surrounded her. She heard a noise to her right and saw a doorway that led to a kitchen. She scooted over to the edge of the doorway, leaned her head around the edge.

A woman chatted away with two teenage children, one girl with a younger brother. The children were laughing and eating breakfast. The woman was pretty, a blond ponytail pulled back with a headband to hold down the strays. She wore a tailored red and black dress with an apron over it. Her smile was gentle and full of admiration for her children.

A tear fell down Dannika's cheek. She sat in awe of the family going about their morning as if nothing could touch their perfect world. As if they lived in a world that was safe, and merciful, and good. Heavy footsteps rushed down the stairs, and a petite middle-school aged girl seemed hurried through the room. As the young girl passed, Dannika noticed a photograph of Noder on the wall.

She knew then she was in a dream. Noder was in jail, and she was invisible to the family. She took in the details around her. Open windows or doors. Movement. Anything.

Dannika felt her senses heighten. Something was about to happen. The air all around her felt thick, her chest heavy. It was coming. She braced herself for what she might see. She had seen a lot of awful things in her dreams, but she had been blessed enough to never have a vision of a child.

Minutes flew by as the children scurried upstairs, the footsteps on the ceiling heavy and fast. The woman stood by the door, looked out the window, and gathered up backpacks and lunchboxes. She yelled up to the children and reached out for the door. When it opened, Dannika's heart began to pound in her chest.

The Ram, tall and lanky, pushed by the woman and shut the door behind him.

Dannika was confused. Where was his sidekick? The one who always did the dirty work? Never had she dreamt about the Ram where Rens was not his puppet.

The Ram put a gun to the woman's head and fired. Her body fell to the floor into a pool of blood and gore, flesh and bone.

Dannika covered her eyes. She didn't want to see the rest. She began to rock back and forth, begged herself to wake up. She told herself it was clear what was happening, she could report on this, she didn't need to see what happened next.

Through three gunshots, she pleaded to be done. The third was the loudest, and she heard the thump of a limp body coming from the ceiling above her.

She had never been emotional in her dreams, even after all the violence and death she had seen, but now she sobbed uncontrollably. She heard footsteps travel down the stairs. She lifted her head, reminded herself it was her duty to capture any details that might make for a successful interference, any indication of a timeframe, or hint of a place for a distraction. She told herself she was still the brave one, the best Visionary, and she sat invisible in her dream to prepare the team at IPA to stop such madness.

She stood up, glanced all around her, and made a mental map of entries to the home, the way the rooms flowed, where furniture was placed, and where televisions, computers, and telephones were located. Anything that might help the team make a successful plan. But emotion rose up in her chest again, hot and strong.

She wasn't sleeping at Headquarters. In fact, she didn't know where she was sleeping at all. When she did wake up, who would she report to? Who would help her stop this horrible crime she has witnessed?

Slow, loud footsteps emerged from the stairway. She stood still, quieted her breath as she watched the Ram make his way to the front door. At the entrance, he turned and looked Dannika right into the eye.

Dannika jumped back. She looked around, rubbing her hands together. She felt her heart might explode. How could he see her? Her breathing doubled and she just began to shake her head. *It's just a dream. It's just a dream.*

His eyes narrowed at her. "Sorry, there sunshine. But you can't stop this one." He disappeared through the doorway and slammed it shut.

*

Dannika opened her eyes. Immediately she felt she couldn't move her arms or legs, or lift her neck. She rolled her eyes to the left and right but could only see white walls. She looked down toward her feet. Just over her toes she could see the door. Every limb of her body was strapped down tight. She thought to scream, but she knew that would be of no use.

Her dream flashed before her, and suddenly she could see Noder's wife's face on the ceiling. She saw the children smiling and laughing. She had to save them. She just had to. Then she thought of Ivan, and her heart sank. He was probably dead. And it was her fault. She should have just done as Jocelyn asked. But her dark side had erupted, her anger had stirred, and she had gotten out of control, and oh, dear God, why didn't she just take her meds like she was supposed to? Why couldn't she just have rational, logical thoughts? Why couldn't she just do as she was told?

She clenched her teeth. She couldn't control it because she was meant to be different, and she would defy all of the stereotypes society tried to label as the psychotic or even the slightly loony, and she would make this all right as soon as she could only get herself free.

The door opened quietly. Dannika gazed over her toes and recognized the figure, her face coming into view above her head. Jocelyn put her finger to her lips. This time, Dannika would listen. Jocelyn ran her fingers over Dannika's forehead, through her hair, then whispered, "You okay?"

Dannika nodded.

Jocelyn got down near her ear. "Just keep quiet. I'm going to get you out of here."

Dannika knew Jocelyn didn't want her to talk, but she had to know what had been going on. How long had she been asleep? "And Ivan?"

Jocelyn just shook her head. "Not sure. They aren't telling me anything. I'm doing my best to play along."

Dannika's eyes filled with tears. Guilt twisted through her. Her breath came hard and fast. Her cheeks got red and hot. She balled up her fists just as Jocelyn started to cut through the thick nylon straps around her wrists.

Jocelyn stopped. She grabbed Dannika's hand. "I know what you're thinking. You didn't do this, Dannika. This was all in motion well before you. If anyone should be blamed, it should be me. I've been totally blind. I've been living here with Mary and Mayer and haven't seen this coming. If we're going to get out of here, you have to do exactly as I say. Do you understand?"

Dannika chest rose and fell sharply. "Why do they want Ivan?"

"I don't know."

Dannika tightened her fists and beat them against the table.

Jocelyn shoved two pills into Dannika's mouth and held her mouth closed with her hands. "Swallow those. Dannika, swallow those now!" Her whisper was loud and her face intense. Dannika swallowed and the pills scraped against her throat.

"I'm sorry, Dannika, but there's no time to explain. We have to get out of here first. If I cut you free, can you listen to me this time? It's critical that you don't get your own ideas right now." Jocelyn hands gripped the table. "If Ivan is going to survive, we have to get to someone at IPA Headquarters. If you can't do as I say, I'll have to leave you here. But I don't want to do that. Do I have your word?"

Dannika nodded. Then her eyes went to the ceiling and she prayed. She prayed that she would be given the strength to do as she was told. To genuinely believe in someone other than herself.

Jocelyn began to cut at the nylon. "Okay, but the second you go off on your own, I'm going to have to leave you."

' They sprinted through the long white halls and crept into the nurse's station. Jocelyn ran her fingers up the file boards and stuck her hand in the one that was missing. She let out a huge sigh and pounded her fist on the file board cabinet.

"What is it?" •

"The one we need. It's missing." Jocelyn began to pace.

Dannika remembered where she had put that blinking file board. "I know where it is."

"You do?" Jocelyn turned to face her.

"That's how I got into the dining room where you found me. I figured out how to get through that tunnel. I left that blinking file board in there."

Jocelyn smiled and shook her head. "No way. That's incredible. I thought you had snuck in through the patient door. We have to get that file board. You can bet that Mayer has the main portal guarded. That tunnel has a secret portal. They don't know I'm aware of it. Let's go!"

They tiptoed out of the nurse's station, and followed the hallway to the dining room entrance. "Wait here." Jocelyn popped into the dining hall then back out. "It's clear."

They moved quickly across the room to the door to the tunnel. The handle of the door had a large round open center, like a hole. "Give me your thumb," Jocelyn said.

"What?" Dannika frowned. "What for?"

Jocelyn gave her a look that said, '*Just do as I say*.' Dannika stuck out her thumb. Jocelyn placed her thumb into the open hole. A light beam ran a circle around her thumb, and with a click, the door opened. The two snuck into the tunnel and closed the door behind them.

"What the—" Dannika whispered.

"Everything in this tunnel operates on the terms of the person associated with the file board. Fingerprints, movement, objects of possession. Right now, that person is you. That's all I can explain for now. So where is the file board?"

"Above the door at the other end."

They scurried to the other end. Dannika reached up and retrieved the still blinking file board, handed it to Jocelyn, then followed along the wall. Jocelyn stopped and wedged the file board into a crack in the wall.

"This is it. Once I push this file board all the way in, the portal will open, and we'll need to move into it immediately. The opening lasts for five seconds, then it shuts. We'll be transferred to the surface. The portal exits at the bottom of a lake. It's the emergency exit so it doesn't get shielded in lock downs." Jocelyn turned to Dannika. "You can swim, right?"

Dannika thought about the last time she swam. It was at the country club pool with her adoptive mother. She'd been seven years old. She'd still been afraid to be completely submerged, and some lame bully kid jumped in the water and pushed her under and held her there. She squirmed and punched at his stomach but he didn't let up.

Finally, he let her go and she reached the surface, scrambling for breath. She looked around to see if anyone had noticed, but Daylea was water wrestling with some stupid boy from their soccer team, and her mother was sipping a martini in her bikini, talking with friends. She never went underwater again. Not even in the bathtub.

She swallowed hard. Fear engulfed her like a swarm of bees. But this was no time to be a coward. This was a time to be brave. "Yes, I can swim."

Jocelyn jammed the file board into the wall and the crack opened. "Quick! Step in!"

They both jumped through the crack, and it slammed behind them. In pitch dark, the floor rose and Dannika felt like her stomach was left behind. Light-headed and nervous, she looked up and braced herself for the water. The portal elevator was shaky and seemed to last for hours, but minutes later, it stopped. Although still dark, Dannika could see a circular opening above them. Water rippled across the clear thick plastic.

"Okay, so let the water fill up the elevator, then we'll be able to push ourselves up through the opening. Then it's swim faster than you have in your whole life. Got it?" Jocelyn seemed so confident. Like the thought of a surge of water on top of them and then hoping you could hold your breath forever wasn't absolutely frightening.

"Got it." Dannika assured her, while not so sure herself.

Jocelyn grabbed her hand and pressed a button on the portal wall. The plastic began slowly folding back, and water rushed over them. Jocelyn squeezed Dannika's hand tight.

Dannika closed her eyes and sucked in a deep breath. The portal elevator filled to where Dannika and Jocelyn could begin swimming upward. Dannika felt panic fall over her. She started squirming and kicking. She felt vertigo and lost all control. She flailed under the water and tried to bat it away from her face.

Jocelyn tried to pull her upward, but she punched at Jocelyn's stomach. Jocelyn's hand gripped her head tightly. She opened her eyes and could barely see the outline of Jocelyn's face, inches from her own. Jocelyn nodded, then did a quick jerk with her chin toward the surface.

Dannika kicked her feet, faster and faster. Jocelyn was right in front of her with every stroke until they surfaced. They swam to shore and pulled themselves onto the rocks. Dannika's wet clothes brought on a chill within seconds, her breath heavy.

"So after all that, we're gonna freeze to death." Dannika's teeth chattered.

Jocelyn put her thumb and finger up to her mouth and whistled loudly. Through the woods, the sound of crackling branches grew nearer. Zeneva ran up to Jocelyn. Jocelyn scratched her behind the ears and said, "We need warmth."

Zeneva turned and ran off.

"What, she understood that?" Dannika asked as she hugged her knees.

Jocelyn snuggled up next to her, hugged her own knees, and placed her chin between them. "I've been snooping, remember? Mayer has done all kinds of crazy experimental work with the brain. Some successful, some not so much. But one major success has been in his animal experiments. He has removed parts of the temporal lobe of some of his human patients and placed them in our lions. This lobe processes language. He developed a microchip that connects the human temporal lobe to the animal one, and in turn, it translates for them. Crazy, huh?"

Dannika's jaw dropped. "Un-freaking-belie-vable."

Zeneva returned with two large bear skins, still thick with fur, in her teeth.

"Nice work, Zeneva. Now we need to find some shelter and build a fire." Jocelyn got up and wrapped the bear skin around her body.

Dannika followed Jocelyn to a small cave. A fire pit was already dug out, and Zeneva brought in mouthfuls of sticks and small logs. Jocelyn pulled back a rock and revealed a pack of matches.

"You've been here before, I take it?" Dannika wrapped her bear skin more tightly around her.

"Well, like you, I don't get to go up to the city much, so I come out here a lot. It's been okay, though. From time to time, I have company." Jocelyn looked up at Dannika.

Dannika pursed her lips together. "Really? Who do you bring up here with you?"

"I don't. It's actually one of your guys that works for Headquarters." Jocelyn watched as Dannika formed a teepee with the sticks. She lit a match and the sticks took to flame.

"But we aren't allowed to come over here. No one is," Dannika stated, confused.

"One person is." Jocelyn stopped blowing at the fire and leaned back on her heels. "Bain is allowed. He hunts out here. Where do you think these skins came from?"

Dannika's heart sank. So there was her answer. Bain didn't ever want her. He came out to the forest to play Tarzan and Jane with Jocelyn. She bit her lip hard enough to refer pain to her belly. Tried to combat the twinge of rage mixed with disappointment. "Why didn't you tell me? You know, after you found the photo."

Jocelyn moved next to Dannika. Dannika scooted away from her. Jocelyn placed a hand on Dannika's knee. Dannika pushed it off.

"Dannika, it's not like that. We hung out by the fire sometimes, and all he could talk about… was you."

Dannika looked up at Jocelyn. She loathed the sincerity in her eyes. "Really?"

Jocelyn smiled. "Really."

Jocelyn moved back to the fire and placed small logs on top of it. They held their hands up to the fire.

Jocelyn spoke. "We have to move fast. Our clothes won't dry out here. Zeneva will lead us back to Headquarters, and we'll—"

Dannika interrupted. "No. I'm not going back there. I have to get to the city. I had a dream. About Noder's family. We don't have time for all the policies and procedures at Headquarters. The first thing they'll do is lock me up and try to psychoanalyze me from head to toe. The Ram is going for them. I have to save them."

There was silence, and Dannika looked up at Jocelyn. Jocelyn's face went blank. "Jocelyn?"

She didn't answer.

"Jocelyn?"

Jocelyn looked up at her. "Does he get all of them?"

"Yes, he does. And I have always been invisible in my dreams. But this time, the Ram saw me. He said I wouldn't stop him this time."

Jocelyn's face froze. "He said what?"

"He looked me in the eye, in my dream, and he told me I couldn't stop it this time. Something is really wrong. And I'm afraid that Headquarters will get too bogged down with analysis and planning and the Ram will be right. I messed up with Ivan, and I don't want to mess up again. There were kids, innocent children. I need to save them, Jocelyn."

As Dannika's eyes filled with angry tears, she noticed Jocelyn's eyes grow wet as she squeezed them tight. Maybe Jocelyn felt the same way. That too much had gone wrong, and this was their chance to make it right. Saving a whole family and capturing the Ram, that would be the end to all of this.

Jocelyn began to weep louder. Dannika crouched by her side. "It's gonna be okay. Ivan is going to be okay."

Jocelyn rubbed her nose with a wet sleeve. "Dannika, did the woman, you know, in your dream, Noder's wife, did she seem happy?"

Dannika sat back on her heels. "Yeah. She did. Why do you ask?"

"Because she's my mother."

CHAPTER NINETEEN

Jocelyn held a finger to her lips and pointed to the cave entrance. Dannika had heard it too. Footsteps. And it sounded to be from more than one being. Dannika felt her eyes widen. She knew that kind of danger out in the wilderness. She wondered if the bear skin around her would fool another bear into thinking she was one of them. Fear seeped up her throat as she eyed Jocelyn. She would know what to do.

Zeneva crept to the cave entrance and peeked around the wall of the cave. Dried residue on the forest floor crackled more loudly as the footsteps approached. Zeneva slowly backed into the cave. Dannika braced herself and prayed that Zeneva could fight whatever might be coming. Another lion rounded the entrance to the cave, slightly larger than Zeneva and with tones of auburn woven through its coat.

Jocelyn jumped up and dashed to the large animal. "Tred!" She snuggled into him and scratched beneath his neck.

Dannika was grateful that the lump in her throat could subside. "What? There are two of them?"

Jocelyn smiled back toward her. "Actually, there are four. This is Tred." She rubbed the enormous animal down its back. "Hey buddy," she said. "Bain with you?" Jocelyn turned to Dannika. "I usually only see Tred when I see Bain."

Dannika's jaw tensed. Did he find the letter? Was he here for her or to play forest games with Jocelyn? Did he know everything that had happened?

Bain peeked into the cave. "Jocelyn?"

"Yeah, Bain. In here."

He slowly walked into the cave and stopped abruptly at the sight of Dannika. Dannika gasped. Her chest tightened. She had never seen him in person, but he was even more magnificent than on screen. He looked twice as tall and wide. His eyes and chin were sharper and his mouth more defined. He seemed to look her over silently.

"You gals okay?"

Dannika opened her mouth, but no word formed. Jocelyn stood. "Yes, we are. We're wet and cold, but managed to escape. There's a lot we need to tell you. Ivan's in trouble."

He let his chin fall to his chest and closed his eyes. But he didn't ask questions. Dannika thought for sure any normal person would fire away questions, demand answers, and quickly sort through them to determine a course of action. But Bain was Ops. And he was killer at Ops. Ops took orders and formulated a plan. They didn't ask questions.

"We have to get you girls back to Headquarters so you don't freeze to death." Bain locked eyes with Dannika. She looked away.

Dannika knew Jocelyn was waiting for her to explain, but she couldn't even move, like she was star struck. Love struck. Jocelyn stepped closer to the fire. With a jerk of her head to Dannika, she explained. "She won't go to Headquarters. She's had another Ram dream; he killed Noder's family. She's afraid they'll get in a tizzy over her leaving and won't act fast enough." Dannika couldn't help but notice Jocelyn's cheeks quiver. Like she was trying to be so strong, but deep down Dannika knew what that was like. To stay strong when all you want to do is curl up and cry, or put your fist through a wall.

"I think she is probably right. I've been working with Dannika's team long enough to know how they will approach this case after she's run off like this." Bain squatted next to Dannika, his knees cracking. "Did it feel real? Like the others? Or could it possibly be one of those, you know, when you aren't quite…right?"

Dannika appreciated what he was trying to do. To soft-pedal her illness. But this was serious. And yes, dammit, it was real. She stood and gazed at him. "They will be dead in twenty-four hours if we don't go to them. Bain, I wasn't even invisible to the Ram this time in my dream. This case is falling away from me. We have to go. Please."

Bain stood, wiped a wet lock of hair from her cheek. Dannika thought her entire body might explode. Bain seemed somewhat conflicted, but all he did was stare at Dannika. He rubbed his finger over her cheek as she stood perfectly still, and the blood pulsed through her veins like a dam had just been released. Bain turned to Jocelyn.

"Please, Bain."

He backed up to Tred. "Here's what we'll have to do. There's a portal from this wilderness to the city. It's how I travel here to hunt. Jocelyn doesn't know where it is because we have always stayed firm on our agreement that she won't show me the portal to Research, and I won't show her the portal to the city, and that way, neither of us risks getting into trouble." He scratched under Tred's chin.

"So Tred will take you. But it's not exactly warm out there, so you'll need to grip tightly to the lions' necks and let them carry you. Keep the bear skin on top of you. They are fast and powerful travelers, so hang on tight. It will take twenty minutes for them to get you to the portal. They have to go around a couple of small rivers, so the route they take is longer. But I can't keep up with them and they can cross the crevasses and rivers, so you two just get to that portal. Tred knows the combination.

*

"The portal comes out into the city just behind a large steel-sided warehouse. On the north side of the warehouse, there is a door." He walked over to Jocelyn and handed her the key. With that simple action, Dannika's heart sunk. Of course he trusted Jocelyn with the key. She wasn't crazy and unpredictable.

"Go down and change into some of my clothes. Wait for me there. I'll bring you something more appropriate. At least you'll be warm."

"Got it," Jocelyn said.

"Bain?" Dannika finally spoke. "Just don't forget. We don't have much time."

He nodded. "I know. Don't worry, I'll find Noder's address. My guys and I will stake it."

"And Ivan?"

"I'll notify Bethie." He paused, seemed to fight some internal conflict. "Ivan would want us to tend to this first."

Jocelyn put out the fire and hurled herself on top of Tred. Dannika rubbed her fingers through Zeneva's ears and pulled herself onto the lion. It was the first time she realized just how large these animals truly were. Her feet didn't even touch the ground. The size of a small pony.

As the large lions traveled beneath them, Dannika's body drew in the chill of the air that seeped under the bear skin, but she just gritted her teeth. She could tell Jocelyn was struggling with the cold as well. They reached a bare spot beneath a circle of birch trees. Tred walked over to the one with the largest trunk and began to place his paw strategically on certain areas of the trunk. Each spot would light up as his paw engaged.

The forest floor began to pull away from itself, and a bamboo cage rose around the two girls. Neither of them had been in a portal to the outside for so long. They gripped one another tightly. Dannika buried her head into Jocelyn's neck. Dannika looked up and caught the gaze of Zeneva. "Bye, girl."

*

This portal seem to weave and spin like a roller coaster, and made Dannika nauseous and pale. Just as the bile was rising in her throat, it stopped and light spread above them. A steel cylinder raised them upward to a concrete parking lot. The red brick warehouse sat directly to their left. Being in the outside world again restored something to Dannika's soul, something deep and healing. It made her heart fill with a courage she didn't remember having for a very long time.

She grabbed Jocelyn's hand and sprinted for the north side. At the door, Jocelyn's hands shook as she forced the key into the lock. They slipped down a narrow chute of stairs and let the door slam shut behind them.

They found themselves in Bain's private world. There were only two rooms besides the main den, which doubled as a kitchen. Jocelyn ran into one, discovered it was a bathroom and directed Dannika to the other. They raided his dresser and quickly stripped themselves of the damp clothing that clung to their frigid skin. They both pulled on extra-large long sleeve tees and sweats that would have fallen to their knees if they didn't hold up the waist.

They snuggled under a blanket on the couch, and Jocelyn grabbed a book that sat on a table. As she turned to the first page, Dannika rested her head against Jocelyn's shoulder and lost herself in sleep.

Dannika woke to Jocelyn and Bain shaking her and telling her it was okay. She propped herself up on her elbows and looked at them in shock.

Jocelyn rubbed her forehead. "Sorry, but you were tossing around and yelling 'No!' over and over. Are you okay?"

Bain watched her intensely. She hated that he saw her this way. The way everyone had surely told him that she was. Crazy. She closed her eyes and tried to remember her dream. Then it came to her. The Ram was holding her by the neck, strangling her, yelling at her, 'You can't stop it. Not this time.'

But she was too afraid to tell them. Two dreams like that might cause Bain to think it dangerous to go after the Ram without Analysis, and they didn't have time to wait.

"I'm fine." She sat up straighter. "I don't remember what it was. But I'm okay." Jocelyn hugged her, and Bain's look told her he didn't believe a word. But he didn't pursue it. He just handed her a pair of women's jeans and a small orange and blue t-shirt that said, 'Go Broncos!' Dannika looked over the outfit and rolled her eyes before slipping into the bathroom to change. When she stepped out in her new god-awful attire, Bain and

Jocelyn were talking quietly on the couch.

Bain stood and stepped over to his bedroom door. "Dannika, can we talk?"

Dannika thought she would die. Really die. Everything down to her toes felt too fearful of what this might mean. Yet, wasn't this what she had dreamed about? Of being alone with him?

Bain held out a hand to her. "Please excuse us, Jocelyn."

Dannika caught Jocelyn give her a thumbs-up and sneak over to the couch with her book. Dannika entered his bedroom and closed the door.

"Sit." He ordered.

If there was one thing Dannika did know about Bain through all those years of working with him, it was his bluntness. She sat on the bed. He sat next to her, his weight causing her to shift toward him. She nervously scooted away again.

He reached under his mattress and pulled out her letter. Dannika waited. For criticism. For rejection. But then she saw that it wasn't opened. The wax still sealed it. She shook her head, her eyebrows furrowed.

"Why didn't you open it?"

Bain rubbed the wax with his finger. "Fear."

"Of what?"

He didn't answer. He just looked at her. "I have to tell them I found you, Dannika. They're all worried. So I need to let them know immediately."

"I understand." She lowered her head. "But why didn't you open it?"

"Dannika, you are the one constant that gives my life meaning. Your gift, it gives me a job. I'm head of Ops, and I could have chosen any other Visionaries to work with, but I always request your cases. You're so...right on…and the details. You make my job so…easy. Have you ever thought of it that way? That you provide something extremely meaningful to someone else…like me?"

She shook her head. "No, I guess not."

"I didn't think so." He sighed. "But I was afraid this letter would tell me you were gone. Forever. I've heard it all about you ditching your meds and you know, how you can be so volatile. I was just scared of—of what you might be capable of."

Dannika rubbed at tired eyes, then started to grab for the letter. Bain pulled it away. "No. Someday, when this is all over, I will read it. And you and I will discuss it. But we need to think of more than ourselves right now."

Suddenly, Dannika couldn't believe she had written the letter. She felt like she'd just shot herself in the foot. It had been selfish. And would only make him scared for her. It would only clarify how crazy she really was. But he was right. First things first and the Ram was preparing his deadliest yet. Maybe she would sneak in and steal the letter. Maybe then he'd never read it.

He grabbed her hand and led her out of the room. Jocelyn raised her eyebrows as they exited the room. Bain spoke firmly. "Not what you think, Jocelyn."

Dannika saw her face drop and had to grin. She crossed her legs on the couch next to Jocelyn. Bain walked over to a plain wall in his kitchen and hit a code on a keypad on the wall. The wall lifted and revealed a large monitor and a panel full of buttons, microphones, cameras, and more keypads. He pushed a series of buttons, and they could hear other Ops guys, their breathing loud, as if they were hovering over a microphone.

"580 Thundering Lane. Stake it. Probably within a day. New interference protocol. This time it has to end. It's gone too far. The Ram will be brought in, alive or dead."

Dannika and Jocelyn looked at one another. Interference had never been about killing the killer. It had been about detouring the event from happening. Dannika bit down hard on the inside of her cheek. She knew why Bain was doing it. For Ivan. Just like her. They were even more alike than she thought.

CHAPTER TWENTY

To save time, Adie would have to rely on Jago's short version of *Informants for Dummies* and Demry's technical expertise to learn her way around the bank. After four days of intense surveillance, Adie had her one shot to go into the bank basement vault and get her bearings. She memorized every crease in the wallpaper, every dent in the file cabinets, and the full range of motion of the security cameras.

If the Ram knew Jeff was snooping around the bank basement, Jago and Bethie had no doubt that he'd go after him. To make sure, they piggybacked their plan with another theory. There were only three people that the Ram would suspect knew anything about what he had hidden in those vaults, due to flow of information: Jeff, the lead DEA agent, and Noder.

With one exception. Pillow talk.

If the Ram suspected that Noder knew anything about what was hidden in those vaults besides the dope, then he'd suspect Noder's wife, Samantha, might know as well. If Samantha began making frequent trips to the bank's deposit box area, they were sure the Ram would notice. After a few fake calls to Samantha from Headquarters where they insisted all customers had to double check their boxes every few days for security purposes after the recent incident, she had done as requested. 'The bank' requested Samantha come again, and Demry had confirmed the phone was tapped. The Ram would know when she came to the bank. Jago's tremendous experience with criminal forensics proved that with both Jeff and Samantha inside that vault, the Ram could never resist the opportunity to nail them both at once.

Jeff brought copies of the maps that had been confiscated when their informant was killed to the bank vault. He would take out a deposit box and pretend to examine documents while he waited for Samantha to get there and the games to begin.

If he was going to sit around and wait for Adie to sleep for a couple of hours, he might as well see if he could make out the numbers. Adie thought that wise, as the maps would surely entice the Ram even more. The more intense the attack, the better chance she had to stop it.

When Demry gave the signal that both Jeff and Noder's wife had entered the basement deposit box room, Adie popped two prescription sleeping pills that IPA had formulated. She lay back on the soft velvet of her work station bed. Bethie punched buttons on a device at her side to help record Adie's emotions and brain activity while she slept. This would allow Bethie and Demry to keep Jeff up to date on Adie's heightened senses, which would indicate something was about to happen.

Within minutes of swallowing the pills, Adie's eyes felt heavy.

She was sitting on a sofa in a house. She noticed the antique décor of the home, so different than that of her own parents' house. Mixed antiques and modern pieces of furniture placed together with an eye for detail. A blond woman hurried down the stairs, quick feet in ballet flats. Adie quickly jumped behind the couch.

She couldn't help but notice how beautiful the woman was. Adie glanced up at the wall leading up the stairway and saw the family pictures. She squinted to see a photo of a family of six and focused on the familiar face of the man. One she knew she'd seen, but not in person. Only in photos. In studies. At IPA. The name that matched the photo smacked her like a blow to the gut. It was Noder. This was his house. His family. This woman was Noder's wife.

Wait. Wasn't she supposed to be at the bank?

"Let's go, kids!" The woman yelled out. "We have to get to the bank before the basketball game!"

They were too early.

Her plan to plant the family in the bank hadn't worked. Instead, she had been planted here.

Adie panicked. How was she supposed to interfere with the Ram's plan in her dream if Jeff wasn't there? And how were they going to catch the Ram if the authorities weren't there to get him? Her heart sped up. She ran up to the woman, but the woman walked right through her. She got in her face and tried to scream at her. About the danger she was in. But the woman just walked rapidly around the house and gathered up her things, humming an unfamiliar tune. It must not be live. From everything Adie knew about her gift, if the dream were live, then she would be a part of it.

Adie put her hands to her head and tugged at her hair in frustration. Should she try to wake up? No, she needed to see what happened so she could report to Headquarters and run a physical interference with Ops. That was plan B.

She plopped on the couch, already saddened by what she'd have to see. She'd seen many a homicide, but she'd never had to watch any children die. She and Dannika had been lucky to be spared that kind of occupational hazard.

She gritted her teeth and waited for the action to

start. As always, she would be the invisible bystander, and plan B would be to run the interference as usual. But they would have to catch him, and they all knew that meant more room for error. More room for failure.

The door clicked and a large black boot stepped around the door. Rens held a pistol tightly in his right arm. He closed the door quietly behind him. Then he looked Adie in the eye, throwing her completely off guard. He put his finger to his lips and whispered "Shhhh."

*

Demry stormed into Adie and Dannika's office. Bethie's eyes widened at his forceful entrance.

"Bain found Dannika. She met Jocelyn. Anyway, details later, but she had a dream about Noder's family, in his house. The Ram got them. Dannika predicted a timeline of twenty-four hours so Bain is getting an Ops team out there."

Bethie nodded. "No Rens? Wait a minute. So you think Rens and the Ram might split up, one at the bank, one at Noder's house?"

Demry shook his head. "Don't know. I'll call in for Fed backup at the bank in case Adie does get a live feed. But I'm guessing the live gig isn't going to go down, and Dannika is probably on target with the Ram going after Noder's family."

*

Dannika and Jocelyn glued themselves to the monitor in Bain's kitchen. They could see Bain and three Ops agents hidden in an old station wagon parked down the block from Noder's house. On the monitor, they watched the Ram walk up the sidewalk, like he was a regular visitor, and pick the lock on the front door. Bain focused on Rens, tucked away in the bushes. Bain and the Ops guys surrounded the house, and Dannika covered her eyes with her hands.

Jocelyn started to pace. "I have a really bad feeling."

Dannika kept her eyes on the screen. "Don't worry. Bain never loses."

Dannika could hear Jocelyn bite her nails, her footsteps loud and clunky across the linoleum.

A loud buzz echoed in their ears and they heard another voice. Demry was trying to contact Bain. Dannika and Jocelyn froze, let every word Demry and Bain exchanged seep right into them.

"Apparently, they've got Adie asleep to try to pull in a live feed at the bank. Obviously, the Ram had different plans. She used the Nomad sleeping pills, so you know what that means. Either way, she's going in."

Bain's voice came through louder. "Yeah, man. Got it. We'll watch for any course changes and keep you up to date."

Dannika turned to Jocelyn. "What's he talking about, the Nomad pills?"

"Same ones I gave you. They knock you out in minutes. And they allow you to travel into the dreams. Be present there. But Visionaries aren't supposed to be present. It's too dangerous. So IPA only uses them in special cases."

"That was probably how the Ram could see you in that dream of Noder's family. The pills had made you visible to him."

"Why are they so dangerous, I mean, aside from revealing our identity?"

Jocelyn stared at the monitor. "Because if you die in a Nomad dream, then you never wake up."

"So what does that mean for Adie?" Dannika's body tensed, scared for Adie.

Jocelyn tilted her head, squinted in thought. "Well, I'm guessing that they put her under so she could go in on a live dream, to run interference. They baited the Ram. But what I'm getting from all of this is that the Ram didn't take the bait. At least not in the form they planned."

"So?"

"So, since Adie's dreams tend to follow Rens, Adie will still travel in her dream to where Rens goes. And she will be visible and present there, but only to him."

Dannika's voice shook. "So why wouldn't it still work?"

"Because if her dream follows Rens and he goes off course from the bank, then the Ram isn't after anyone she cares about."

Dannika ran her fingers all over the panel. She frantically pushed buttons until Jeff's face popped up on the screen. "Jeff, where are you?"

Jeff's voice streamed through."The bank. We're reeling in the Ram using Noder's family. But before he gets to us down here, Adie is going to stop it."

Dannika's brain hurt. The whole room twisted around. "But she can't stop it."

Jeff frowned, seemed confused. "Why not?"

"Rens and the Ram are going after Noder's family at their house, not the bank. So she can't stop it, Jeff, because you aren't there."

Dannika pushed at the buttons wired to Bain. Jocelyn reached her hand to grip Dannika's forearm.

"I think I can stop it."

Tears filled Dannika's eyes. "No. No. This is all wrong. I just want him to come back. I just want Bain to come back and Adie to wake up. We should never have done this."

Jocelyn grabbed her arm and turned her around. "Dannika, I can stop it! Help me stop it."

Dannika froze.

"That is my mother. I'm the one that can stop it." She pulled two large florescent green pills from a pocket. "The new, unreleased version of Nomad pills. Stole them from Mary's office. I'm going in. Tell Bain to do *nothing* but wait."

She swallowed them whole, threw herself down on the couch, and closed her eyes. Her body went limp. Only her eyes rolled back and forth rapidly under closed lids.

*

Adie sat motionless on the couch. Watched the woman in the kitchen as she rummaged through her purse and pulled out a checkbook. Rens snuck around the stairs, where another room wrapped around, and entered the kitchen through a back entrance. Adie had never felt emotion in these dreams, but this time all she could feel was helplessness. Failure. The house was silent as she waited for a gunshot. She covered her eyes, not wanting to see the mess of a woman fall to the floor in the kitchen.

Then she remembered her dream with Maimey. If Rens could see her in the dream, then why did she need to be a bystander? She glanced all around the living room, searching for anything sharp. A letter opener held the place in a book on the table next to her. She quietly slipped it from the book and held it in front of her as she crept into the kitchen, past Noder's wife, still humming away, who didn't so much as flinch at her presence. Adie slipped behind a pantry door, letter opener gripped in her hand so tight her knuckles were white and the heel of her hand started to cramp.

She started to shake at the thought of what she would have to do. But it was just a dream. And all it would do is stop it. Then the Feds would nail the Ram and they could get some questions answered.

She heard a crack of the hardwood floor and saw Noder's wife turn her head toward the noise. Her face went blank. The checkbook hit the floor. The terrified woman gripped the counter, ready to scream, as Adie felt the heat of Rens just outside that pantry door. She opened the door, caught Rens's eye. Then she thought of Maimey holding that gun, and courage surged through her like wildfire. She jabbed the letter opener into Ren's gut and sent him to the floor.

Out of the corner of her eye, Adie saw the woman push the children out a back garage door.

The front door slammed.

"What's taking so long, you incompetent fool?" A loud boom of a voice.

Adie backed toward the garage door when a gloved hand grabbed her elbow.

"Well, what do we have here?" The Ram's cold, black eyes stared right into hers.

Adie's breath was short and unsteady as she held the letter opener tight against her side. "You can kill me. But you can bet that either way, they're gonna get you this time."

The Ram pulled her backwards. "I have a feeling this has not gone as planned for you. Am I right? Because it certainly has not gone as planned for me." He grinned. "How did you do it? We blocked all visual lines, even altered the timeline for your little psycho partner. So, this should have been easy."

Adie felt a round barrel press deep into her rib. *What did he mean we?* She tightened her grip the letter opener and jabbed it into the Ram's sternum.

The Ram threw his head back in laughter, dug the gun further into her side.

"You don't even understand your own powers, do you?" The Ram delivered with a low chuckle. "Your little lover boy would have to be here for you to get to me."

"How do you know that?"

The Ram rubbed the gun along her lips. "Aw, yes. I would want those lips too."

Adie neck tightened, "How do you know about Jeff?"

"Wouldn't you love to know? But sorry, I can't possibly let you live to be a tattle."

"You can't kill me in my dream, idiot."

"Oh, didn't that precious little Bethie tell you? Those pills that put you out so quickly, they make you a Nomad dreamer. You die in a Nomad dream, you never wake up."

Adie had no idea what he was talking about but it didn't matter. "Bethie knows I'd give my life in a second if it meant capturing evil losers like you."

He pulled her in closer. His disgusting breath made her nauseas. "However, you did stop Rens. How'd you do it? Lover boy isn't here, so how did you stop it?"

Adie had no idea how she'd gotten to Rens. She'd just acted out of impulse, and it had worked. She didn't have an answer, but she would need one or the Ram would find her useless.

"I...I..."

"She didn't stop it. I did."

Adie watched as the Ram jerked his head over his shoulder. Adie noticed the letter opener still sticking out from the Ram's chest like a costume piece. He hadn't even thought to remove it. A woman who looked in her early thirties with spikey blond hair stood with a gun pointed at his head.

The Ram let Adie's elbow drop. "Well, if it isn't Mayer's little lab rat."

"And what exactly are you, then? At least he valued me enough not to dig into my brain." She mocked.

"Not yet." The Ram eased his way toward her.

The woman cocked the gun and the Ram paused.

Adie just wanted to wake up. Try to make out what was going on. Who was this woman? How did the Ram know her? How did the Ram know so much about IPA?

Adie ducked her head back toward the kitchen—no sign of Rens. Somehow in the midst of the action, he'd escaped.

The woman kept the gun pointed at the Ram's head, which Adie noticed was uncomfortably close to her own. "Let her go, Ram."

"But then I wouldn't be doing my job, now, would I?"

"Do you even know what your job really is, Hank?"

Adie felt the Ram's grip lighten.

She continued. "You've been fooled. Brainwashed. You should let her go. We're the good ones, Hank. You're not even in control of yourself. Someone else plans your every move."

"It's not going to work. I'm the Ram now. Do you really think I would fall for any of *your* psycho-babble?

Need I remind you who I work for?" Adie felt his fingers tight again.

"You were a good man before, I can tell you that." The woman's voice was softer, her guard still up and her eyes sharp.

Adie swallowed deep. She knew any moment one of those guns would be released, she just couldn't be sure who would be first.

The kitchen door swung open and Rens wrapped Adie into a headlock, a knife held at the base of her neck.

Adie's eyes met the woman's as the woman's stare seemed to deliver a message. Sit tight.

The woman glared back at the Ram, who now had raised his gun for a standoff. She clenched her teeth. "What? Mayer not feel like you're good enough on your own? Gotta have some big bully to watch over you?"

The Ram snarled and looked over his shoulder at Rens, who still held tightly to Adie as if waiting for the Ram to give him the signal to slit her throat. The woman kicked up her right foot and his gun flew back into her hands. She flipped his gun around, then pointed both in their direction. She tilted her head and offered a teasing smile.

"Now, you tell your stooge over there to let my girl go, and you're free. Otherwise, cops are here in five. Seconds, that is."

The Ram spit at her feet, then motioned for Rens to follow him out the front door.

"What?" Adie screamed. "You're letting them go?"

The woman walked up to Adie and leaned toward her with a whisper. "Don't worry. They're not going anywhere. Bain's outside. Name's Jocelyn. Visionary from IPA Research."

"Wow," Adie said. "You're kind of tough, you know

that?"

Jocelyn smiled. "You're not so bad yourself."

Jocelyn walked up to the stairway wall and gently rubbed the photo of Noder's wife on the wall.

"So you know her?"

"My mom. She's why I'm here."

Adie woke up, her clothes soaked in sweat. Jeff held her hand to his cheek.

*

Dannika rubbed the thighs of her jeans until her hands were raw as she watched the monitor. She had done as Jocelyn said. Bain and Ops were just waiting. Jocelyn lay still as deer in headlights on the couch, barely made a sound with her breath. Everyone just waited.

The Ram walked out of the house, Rens on his heels. Bain crouched down, slowly moved toward him one foot at a time.

Dannika froze, covered her face with her hands. All she could hear was the buzz of the technology around her. She waited to hear a gunshot. Multiple gunshots. Sirens. Ambulances. But instead, she heard the screech of truck wheels and a huge thump followed by a crash. She spread her fingers open and saw Bain and the other Ops agents run out to the street where the Ram lay.

Bain put his gun to the Ram's head, poked at the body, but the body was lifeless. Chaz reached down to grab the Ram's wrist to check a pulse. As he grabbed one wrist, the Ram's other wrist bat away Bain's gun and the Ram put a heel into Chaz's gut. Chaz keeled over and the Ram grabbed at his weapon. Before the Ram got the gun free from Chaz, three more weapons pointed to his head and chest. The Ops team stood frozen prepared to fire.

Bain stood feet apart, arms crossed. "Really? You really thought you had a chance?" Bain asked while the Ram was getting cuffed.

The Ram simply snarled.

Bain turned and ran back into the house. Dannika peered over her shoulder. Jocelyn was still in a deep sleep. She started rubbing her jeans again, and winced at the pain. She didn't even breathe until Bain came back out the front door. He looked right into the camera and said, "There's nobody there."

CHAPTER TWENTY ONE

The conference room was packed with key personnel as well as all second in command and top specialists in each department. The room was large enough to hold a hundred people but that day the anxious thirty of them seem cramped.

Adie listened to the conversation flow through the room. The double edge of a success and a failure. An end to the Ram but a beginning of a new battle, the one against their own in Research. Not to mention Rens on the loose. With all the chaos when the Ram was hit, Rens had slipped off like a snake through the forest floor.

Jocelyn had overdosed on the experimental sleeping pills, and was being carefully watched in an intensive care unit down the hall. Adie had so many questions for her. The last time they had checked in with her, she was still foggy on details. She directed them to Dannika, insisted she had told Dannika all she knew about what was going on at Research. But Dannika had been too overwhelmed by the interference with the Ram and then her inability to wake Jocelyn. She'd managed to notify Bain about Jocelyn, but shortly after she'd raided Bain's liquor cabinet and had passed out on the green carpet of Bain's bedroom.

Adie tapped her fingers on the conference table. All eyes were on her as if she was the one with the most knowledge and understanding of this situation. She looked at Jeff as he scribbled notes on a piece of paper then crossed them out. Over and over. As if he would have an idea for what to do next when not one lucid person knew how to get to Research, or if the Ram was a solid subject for interrogation, or what to do about the secret vault in the bank. The only thing they could feel good about was that Noder's family had been encouraged to go on a glamorous vacation to some place where no one could find them, and maybe stay there. Noder wasn't getting out of jail any time soon.

Bethie was digging through Ivan's office, looking for any clues to how to get to a Research portal.

Adie turned to the large monitor on the far wall and watched Bain as he twirled a pencil on his fingers. He hadn't a clue what to do either. He knew the direction every tree root spun around in the Research wilderness but not a single portal.

After a half hour of mumbles from around the room, Jeff slammed his fist to the table. "The maps!"

"What about the maps?" Jago asked.

"They're maps to something. Maybe they lead to Research without a portal." Jeff ran over to a tall file cabinet, typed in a code, and sifted through the tall rolls of paper. Then he narrowed his eyes and pursed his lips. Adie knew he was holding back as that familiar vein in his neck began to pop. "The maps. They're gone."

"What about your copy?" Adie asked.

Jeff walked slowly back to her. His eyes passed over each individual face. "Yes, my copy will do fine. But who's missing here?"

Everyone glanced around and quietly took inventory. Adie looked straight ahead. How could she have not noticed? They were distracted, missed the largest detail. A top executive of IPA not in attendance. "It's Demry."

The room grew loud with speculation. Adie tuned it

all out and thought about Demry and what she knew about him. How he jumped on the Ram case the minute Dannika had her second consecutive dream. The way he hovered over Dannika, like he might miss something. Like she held the key, or the secret, and at any moment, it may be revealed. How the minute she went missing, he'd offered to go after her and had seemed upset when that plan had changed.

Adie glanced up at the monitor. Bain had already begun to assemble his firearms. He sat and placed his face into his hands.

"We'll send Daylea to watch over Dannika." Adie caught eyes with Daylea, and she wrapped her arms around her torso and nodded. "Bain, we'll wait until you get here to make a plan."

Bain started rocking back and forth.

"Bain?" Adie said.

He didn't answer. He just rocked.

"Bain, are you okay?"

Jeff grabbed Adie's elbow. "He's claustrophobic. Terrifyingly so. He's never done any work down here. I don't think he can come with us."

Adie turned to the monitor. "It's okay. We can do it. You stay with Dannika."

Bain stood, ran his fingers over his short hair, clamped his hands behind his neck, and rested his head there for a moment.

The room was silent, all eyes on that screen. Adie knew what everyone was thinking: they needed him. Bain and Demry were nearly inside one another's heads. Bain could anticipate Demry's thoughts and moves. And wasn't he the strong one? How could something as simple as a tunnel really do him in?

Bain turned to the screen. "I'm sorry."

Like the flick of a switch, it occurred to Adie how Bain and Demry had worked together. Never side by side, but via this exact type of scenario. Via the monitor. Audio. Anticipation and improvisation.

"You know what, Bain, you're going to be more helpful on the outside anyway. Right there in your comfort zone." Adie smiled at him, realizing that she had figured out a crucial detail, one that no one had likely thought of.

"What?" Bain looked up again, the self-doubt heavy on his shoulders and chest.

"You and Demry always worked via monitor and earpieces, right? Well, that's the way you know him best. You anticipate his orders through that camera, on your watch, and that earpiece. So you're going to lead us to Demry the way Demry used to lead you." Bain's face lit up.

Chaz stepped toward Adie, standing closer than she would ever want him to. "That's right on, girl."

Jeff stepped between them as Adie leaned back over the maps. She analyzed every corner, ran her fingers down each edge, pulled the maps out, and placed the sides together to make one large map.

Bethie excused everyone except Adie, Jago, Joe, and Chaz. The maps showed miles and miles of tunnels, most without any description of where they led to. The numbers at the top of each map seemed to have no correlation to anything at all, except in opening the hidden bank vault. There was no indication of a primary entrance, and the tunnels seemed to join back up and form continuous circles that went in several directions.

Chaz rubbed his forehead. "This is just crazy. It's a big maze that goes nowhere."

Adie followed each tunnel with her fingertips, hoping to find one that didn't link up to another circle or to a dead end. But her finger met up with repetitive flow or an obstacle every time. She felt Jeff place his hand at the small of her back. He gave her an uneasy look, as if in defeat. She memorized the feeling of the warmth of his hand on her back, but it only hurt her more to leave it there. She pushed his hand away, leaned back over the map, and focused on the outer edges.

"Do any of these borders resemble the shape of any of the rooms here at Headquarters?"

They moved the maps around, switched their placement until they matched like a puzzle. They sorted it all until everyone agreed the lines matched, the spacing was correct, and the tunnels looked like there was some sort of flow.

Joe placed his hand at the top of the map. "Right there. You guys see it?"

All heads bobbed and weaved over the spot where his hand was. No one answered.

"Are you all telling me that this seventy-year-old geezer can see that and all you young pups without glasses can't see it?"

They leaned in again, but no one answered. Adie thought she saw Jeff blush.

"The edge of that map right there, that shape on the other side of the wall of that tunnel, that's the gondola room. No doubt in my mind."

Adie leaned in further. She traced the lines with her forefinger and her garnet ring followed the rhythm. He was right. The gondola room where they caught their portal to the wilderness had a very unique shape, like a pentagon, with deep corners and large benches cut back into the walls. No other room at Headquarters had this shape.

Jeff slapped Joe on the back gently. "Nice work, Joe. So that's where we'll go in."

"But how?" Adie asked.

Jeff smiled. "Oozie."

"Okay. So Oozie blows up the walls and we get in. Then what? We just run in circles?" Adie began to feel nervous as the realization sunk in that they really were doing this.

"I don't know," Jeff said. "But Jora didn't know either until she started sniffing around. So maybe that's what we do. We figure it out once we're in."

Bain's voice rang loud from the monitor. "Jeff's right. That's how Demry worked. With loose interpretations that we would tighten instinctively, relying on intuition and our environment. If he has anything to do with those maps, then they were designed the same way."

"Hold on a dad gum second." Joe squinted his wrinkled eyes. "This isn't some stickler of a labyrinth. This here's a trail system."

Jeff stepped closer to Joe.

Joe started at the gondola room where they planned to bust through. "In the woods, you have a trail system so you don't get lost, right? And lots of times, those trails connect in more ways than one, so that if you happen to make a wrong turn, you could end up taking yourself in circles. We take for granted what's in between these trails, just a bunch of trees, and rocks, and flowers, and grasses, and maybe some little critters scooting around, but most of us ignore all that and focus on the trail itself. But the animals, they cut through all that, diverting from the manmade trail system and creating their own. They let their intuition guide them rather than the trail."

Jeff grinned. "What the heck are you saying, Joe?"

"Bain said Demry reacts on impulse, feeds from his intuition. Like those wild animals. Well, I think these tunnels are set up the same way. I'm willing to bet that once you're in, the tunnels themselves are just the trail system. Our job is to figure out how to maneuver what's in between the trail. The part we would normally ignore."

"But wouldn't that just be a bunch of rock and clay and earth?" Adie asked.

Joe did a quick jerk of his head to the right. "Guess you young'uns are gonna have to go in there and find out."

Jeff turned to the monitor. "Bain, stick tight to that screen. Chaz will take us to Ops to get wired up. Joe will prep Oozie and then get back to you for follow up."

They headed to the exit. Adie turned back. "And Bain, don't let that girl out of your sight."

"Not even for a second."

*

Adie felt like a superhero by the time they got all wired and suited up and met Oozie at the gondola room. There were no suits to fit her smaller frame. She tried to convince them to bag the suit, but the suit had sensors and GPS chips so that they could be located anywhere. Adie told them it would be pretty obvious where she was. Jeff insisted.

Chaz chuckled at the black leather baggy pants and shirt-coat combo she had tucked in down to her knees, though it still billowed over her belt.

She wasn't the only one who looked out of place. Jeff looked like he needed a Harley and the handlebar mustache to match. His frat boy wardrobe had probably never seen the color black. He walked funny in the boots and kept pulling at the crotch of the pants. It was clear that everyone had a place where they belonged, and for Jeff and Adie, it certainly was not Operations at IPA.

Oozie had brought in ten different bombs to try. Red, black, and yellow wires were hooked into rows of metal cylinders. Oozie held up two black boxes to Adie. "You're the psychic. Pick one."

Adie shrugged. "I don't know. What's the difference?"

Oozie smiled and she realized she had never seen his teeth before. Three on top and one on the bottom were missing. His beard was all twisted together and his matted ponytail had the beginnings of dreadlocks. "Well, both of these babies will knock out that wall." He held up his right hand, the black box about the size of a DVD holder and equally as thin. It had a tiny on/off switch. But otherwise, simple. The one in his left hand had the shape of a miniature wine bottle, with several trigger buttons and loads of extra wires.

"You're gonna take one with yous, in case you need it later. All yous gotta do is chuck it at the wall and duck. It's programmed to combust forward and upward, so yous back off and duck, yous is clear." He examined them both closely, puckering up his lips to plant a small kiss on each. "Theys both such masters of beauty, I cants decide which one should go first."

As soon as he mentioned that she'd be carrying one, it was obvious. She grabbed the thin, square one, stuffing it inside a pocket in her coat.

Oozie widened his toothless grin, enough so Adie saw a few more spaces in the back. "Yous a smart one, ain't cha?"

Adie rolled her eyes and started to back away so that

Oozie could blow out the wall.

Adie couldn't believe something so subtle could do so much damage. In seconds, the wall was blasted open, debris flowing into the newly exposed area. The sound wasn't louder than a firecracker. She spoke into her earpiece to ensure Bain was still in contact. She followed the charge Chaz and Jeff had already begun.

"Adios, partnas," Oozie said. "I'd go along, but someone's gotta clean up dis here mess." He added a chuckle.

Once in the tunnel, they had to choose right or left. After the maps had all been taped together, Jeff had minimized them to the size of a legal pad and stolen a Zoomranger from Tech. It was a circular magnifying glass Ops used in the field that with the touch of a button would log in the location of the user, take an inch-by-inch section of a map where the user stood, and zoom it up 500 times onto a 3-D model that hovered in the air above it. He pulled it out and set it over the map. There seemed to be much more of the tunnel system to the right, so they took off in that direction.

At the next cross-section, Adie noticed that there were several bright orange bricks near the top of the tunnel wall and an equal number on the floor. "Hey guys, what do you suppose that means?"

Jeff answered, "Not a clue."

Chaz walked over and stepped on them. "Just plain old brick. Odd color though. Like they've gone rusty."

Adie walked over and tapped on a brick with her toe. It shifted, turned sideways. Adie jumped back. "What was that?" Bain said into the earpieces. Adie placed her hand to her earpiece, and glanced at Jeff as they all listened.

"The bricks. They moved." Adie answered.

They turned back to the bricks as Bain spoke to them through their earpieces. "I think these bricks might correspond with the numbers on the map."

Jeff nodded to Adie as he confirmed with Bain. "Got it, Bain. We'll give it a shot." The first set of numbers closest to their location on the map. "5-4-8-3-2-7."

Adie walked over to the bricks. "It's a pattern, just like the bricks." She counted from left to right and noticed that she had stepped on the fifth brick. That was why it had moved. Five was the first number.

"It's a code," Chaz said.

Jeff punched his arm. "Aren't you a genius?"

Adie put up her hand, wishing the other two would stop acting like schoolboys. "Next number, Jeff?"

"Four."

Adie started at the left and stepped on the fourth brick. It shifted sideways in the opposite direction the previous brick had. She continued to step on the bricks in the order of the numbers. Each one shifted the opposite direction to the one in front of it. She counted to seven for the last brick.

Jeff put a hand up. "Wait. We have no idea what this means, what will happen."

Adie looked at Jeff then Chaz. Chaz shook his head. He had no guesses. She dropped her head. "Bain? Any 'intuition' about what's coming when I step on this last brick?"

There was silence on the other end of the earpiece. Then she could hear a voice in the background. Dannika. She had recovered from her stupor and joined Bain.

Bain seemed to pause before he answered. "Well, I don't know for sure. But my first thought is that it is likely to shift something. When Demry led us on interference missions, his strength was in the metaphor.

Something that the potential murderer wouldn't be ready for or aware of. For what that's worth."

Jeff shook his head. "Doesn't help much. But what do we have to lose? Let's just go for it."

Adie slowly stepped down onto the brick that held the seventh spot. It shifted and the wall went with it. Adie's jaw dropped as an unmapped tunnel system appeared where only rock and dust had been. "Joe was right. It's the in-between."

"Let's go." Chaz charged through the broken entry, following the system to the next fork in the tunnel system.

Adie and Jeff fell in behind him. Beads of sweat formed at her hairline and goose bumps rose from her arms. One hundred yards down, another set of orange bricks lined the crusty walls and dirt floor. Jeff pulled out the map, allowed the Zoomranger to hone in on their spot. The three could scarcely catch their breath as they worked through the map, tried to determine which tunnel system they had moved toward. Jeff read the numbers closest to where the Zoomranger located them as Adie stepped on each brick respectively and unlocked another wall. The ground beneath them shook as the wall shifted to expose the hidden open earth.

Six more codes were listed. The final wall opened up to a large control room. The clay and granite had been carved back to create a room half the size of a city block and the air so dank it made Adie shudder.

A large box that resembled a basic computer server—only one hundred thousand times the size—sat in the middle of the room. Lights at the top blinked on their own with no consistent rhythm.

Adie, Jeff, and Chaz shuffled quietly around the enormous server. Their eyes traveled up and down the monstrosity in an attempt to detect any clues as to what it might hold. As they neared one end of the server, still searching intensely, they heard the wall shift. Adie sprinted back to the corner of the server and poked her head around to see if it had indeed closed them in. It had.

She dashed back to Jeff's side and whispered so both Bain and Jeff could hear. "I think we're trapped."

A set of footsteps crackled on the gritty earth behind them.

"Well, well, well."

Adie froze, moved her eyes to Jeff, whose eyes hardened, but she didn't turn around. She knew that voice.

Jeff pulled Adie to his side, put himself between her and Demry. "What's going on here, Demry?"

Demry reached inside his lab coat pocket to reveal a long syringe. Adie cringed and leaned against Jeff's back. She could feel his muscles tighten. "Just the most innovative combination of technology and intelligence that has ever been created." He tapped the needle with his finger.

"Where's Mayer?" Jeff asked.

"Mayer is quite useful with the patients and the experiments, but I don't really need him anymore," Demry took a step toward them. "The Ram project has verified that we are up and running. All of the Random Access Memory he uploaded into that brilliant new head of his while on his missions has wirelessly downloaded into this server. You may have caught the Ram, but his memory automatically deletes after download. It's a shame, though, he's worth nothing holed up in that jail cell. Everything that downloads from our Human Intelligence Tools will be processed and placed into neat little sellable packages. And guess who has the power then?

He who has the knowledge." Demry chuckled.

"What are you talking about, Human Intelligence Tools? And how does what *you're* doing with those poor people bring about peace of any kind?" Adie asked.

Demry smirked. "You really are all a bunch of silly idiots, aren't you? I can't even believe that the Ram project lasted as long as it did. The Ram was my first HIT. He interrogated and gathered information, stored billions of gigabytes in his own little brain until it downloaded onto this baby. Get it—Random Access Memory—Ram. How brilliant am I?"

"So what, you're making more like the Ram?" Jeff said.

"Of course. Can you think of anything more valuable than a human that can retain as much information as any computer ever could dream of? Every political leader and law enforcement entity in the world will break down my door to get that information. Not to mention the black market potential. Can you just imagine how valuable my HITs will be at election time?" Demry tapped the syringe again.

Jeff spoke under his breath. "But we've got the Ram now."

Demry shrugged. "I've got a whole load of HITs ready to fire."

Adie could hear a faint whisper coming into her earpiece. She glanced at Jeff and Chaz, making sure they could hear it, too.

Dannika had reviewed Bain's copy of the maps and located where they were. She recognized the shape of the room on the other side of the wall behind them. It was the long tunnel just outside the nurse's station at Research. Adie reached up onto her tiptoes and whispered in Jeff's ear. "Stall him."

targeted Demry's masterpiece, broke down his plan, stroked his ego, all while his cockiness grew and Jeff pretended to be blown away by such wit.

Adie listened as Dannika explained to her what they would find on the other side. That the file board might still be stuck in that crack. How it could open the tunnel and take them to where she last saw Ivan. Adie slipped her hand into her coat pocket and set a finger on the trigger of Oozie's bomb.

"You won't get away with this," Jeff said to Demry.

Adie flipped the switch on the bomb and threw it up against the wall behind them. She peeled Chaz and Jeff away from the thin, black ticking plastic and folded her head up into Jeff's armpit.

Demry yelled out, "No!"

But it was too late, and the bomb blew out the wall. Tiny granules of earth spewed back at them. The unexpected force sent Demry onto his back and his hands released the syringe as he covered his face.

Chaz grabbed the syringe and planted it into Demry's neck. His body convulsed, then went limp. Chaz squeezed Demry's wrist. "He's got a pulse. Not sure how much time we have." He tucked the syringe into his jacket.

The wall had collapsed into the tunnel, and Adie could see a large crack on the far wall that ran from floor to ceiling. Inside, the file board was in place, blinking.

Adie wiped the dust from her eyes. "Welcome to Research."

CHAPTER TWENTY TWO

Adie listened to her earpiece, followed Dannika's instructions, movement by movement. She pointed to the file board still crammed in the slot in the wall of the tunnel. "Dannika says we have to get that file board out and insert it above the door on the north wall."

Chaz yanked hard, but the file board wouldn't budge.

Jeff took a stab at it, but his strength was still not a hundred percent. Adie wedged her fingers between the stone and the board and tried to pry the board loose.

"Dannika, it won't budge." She listened for a moment. Disappointment fell over them as Dannika's voice ran through their ears. "I don't know what else to do. The file board worked for me."

"I know what to do." A voice behind them carried through the hole in the wall.

Adie jumped and turned around. "Jocelyn! You're okay!"

"Yep. I'm good. Now let's get to work." She turned to Adie. "We're gonna need to use your ring."

"Why?"

"This is Dannika's file board. She didn't know that's how she got into this tunnel and got us out of the portal, but only the person, or a personal item from that person given to another, can utilize their own file board. Dannika didn't choose this file board randomly. If you're near the electronic cabinet, your file board will blink wildly. The nurse's station holds all the file boards for the IPA employees that Research is keeping an eye on."

Adie inserted the ring into a tiny slot at the edge of the file board and pulled the file board free.

"Now insert it into that slot above the north door over there." Jocelyn pointed to direct Adie as she followed instructions. The door slid sideways and opened up to the nurse's station. Adie pried the ring from her finger, feeling her heart drop as it finally slid off of her fingertip.

"Follow me." Jocelyn hurried through the doorway.

Following Jocelyn at a full sprint through a maze of hallways of pure white, Adie began to feel tired. Then Joceyln turned a sharp left. "This is it. This is where Mayer kept Ivan."

"So what do we do?" Adie asked.

"We go in."

"Shouldn't we have a plan first?" Jeff asked.

Chaz felt around the door. Adie figured he must be looking for weak spots. Then he turned the them. " I say our plan is to get Ivan out of here at any cost, even if it means…"

"Look guys," Jocleyn interrupted, "we don't have much time. We'll have to improvise some, but if Ivan's in here and we are able to get him free, just follow me."

"She knows what she's doing, guys," Adie added.

"Fine." Chaz said. "Step back."

He busted the door open to find an empty room.

"They're gone." Jocelyn paced for a moment. "Okay, we're gonna have to search the entire place."

"That won't be necessary." Demry stood behind them, Mary beside him, each with a gun pointed at the foursome.

Chaz put his hands up and glared at the woman standing beside their new enemy.

Demry nudged Mary. "Aren't assistants wonderful? She injected me with a reversal serum, and Chaz, you sorry excuse for a soldier, if I knew you were so horribly incompetent at your knots, I would have told Ivan to pull you off Ops years ago." Demry snickered.

Chaz balled up his fists. Adie grabbed at his arm gently, hoping Chaz could keep it together.

Demry pressed a button on his collar and a metal contraption six feet tall and twelve feet wide ejected from the wall. It had four spaces, each with straps wired into steel buckles. He pressed another button on his collar and the straps opened up.

"Each of you will step back into one of the open cylinders. Forget about escaping. I assure you, it's impossible."

Adie sucked in deep breaths. She glanced at Jeff. He stared at her with a look she failed to interpret. Should they make a run for it? Jeff turned his head toward Jocelyn and Adie got her answer. They would follow her lead.

"Now!" Demry yelled.

Jocelyn backed up to the first cylinder. "Just do what he says."

Jeff and Adie backed up, eyes glued to Demry. Chaz slowly moved toward the last cylinder. Jocelyn placed her back against the cylinder and the straps wrapped around her. Jeff and Adie were about to step into the cylinders when Chaz made a swift step forward while reaching for the gun at his belt.

Before he pulled the gun from its sheath, Demry shot him through the heart.

"No!" Adie tensed her body, wiggling back and forth as if the straps just might give way.

Chaz's body collapsed to the white tile floor as his

shirt soaked up with blood.

"Anyone else?" Demry asked.

Adie and Jeff stepped back into their cylinders, their eyes glued to one other. Adie cringed at the force of the straps against her chest, arms, legs, ankles, and her neck.

The cylinders were close enough together that Jeff could just touch her hand. He gripped three of her fingers tightly. "It's gonna be okay."

*

"Bain, we gotta get in there." Dannika's head lay against his shoulder as they listened to the chaos in Research.

She could feel his chest rise and fall in nervous breaths. She pulled away and gathered her things. Then she returned to Bain, gripped his shoulders, and looked him in the eye. "These people are my family, now, Bain. You and them, that's all I have. We can't just sit here and let this happen."

Bain's jaw tightened. No other muscle in his body seemed to move. He grabbed Dannika's cheeks and pulled her to him. He kissed her intensely, then pulled back. "Only you. Only you could get me to do this."

*

They reached the tunnel and sprinted through the nurse's station, lost in the pale maze.

"I have no idea which way to go," Dannika said. Then she remembered how she discovered Ivan before. "Wait."

She placed her hand on her gut, closed her eyes, and opened her senses to the energy. That rare pull of a magnet she would feel when deep in meditation.

"What are you doing?" Bain whispered.

"Just shut up. Trust me. It worked before."

Dannika let her body move and guided herself along the walls with her hand. A few turns and Dannika felt compelled to stop.

"This is it. Someone's in there."

"It's a wall. How are we supposed to get through?"

Dannika placed her hands on the wall. "Feel right here. Feel that heat?"

Bain put a palm below hers. "Yes."

"That's where they are."

Dannika began to feel up and down the smooth surface, at the corners, along the trim. Sure enough, just like everything else in this place, there was a strange hidden opening. One piece of trim at the base of the wall had a long crack in it. Dannika kicked at the crack and it widened.

Her heart quickened and she felt that familiar twinge of anger begin to emerge. She kicked it again and again, and kicked it until the opening formed a perfect square. Bain dropped to his knees and dug with his mammoth hands into the open space.

"There's a knob back here."

"Pull it!"

Bain pulled the knob and the wall flipped around. On the other side, Ivan and Mayer were tied to metal bars that dug into the wall, their mouths gagged in cloth.

"Ivan!" Dannika ran to him.

Bain pulled a multi-use tool from his belt and used wire clippers, knives, and mini-screwdrivers to get Ivan loose. Ivan sprang free and pulled Bain and Dannika into his arms. "You two are amazing."

Dannika took advantage of the moment. "Yes, we are. *Together*, we are amazing."

Ivan smiled. "Comment noted."

Dannika filled Ivan in on the others, likely still at the mercy of Demry and Mary.

"I think I know where they are," Ivan said. "Follow me."

Bain had been gracious enough to remove the cloth from Mayer's mouth, but left him tightly in the grip of the hard steel.

He spit the cloth out of his mouth. "What about me?"

Ivan glanced back as they moved down the hall. "We'll deal with you later."

Ivan, Dannika, and Bain sprinted through the maze. Their footsteps echoed from the emptiness around each corner. He stopped at a large closet and grabbed a pistol for each of them.

They reached the door where Demry was still interrogating the others. Ivan put his finger to his lips as they tiptoed to the door. "We'll have to shoot. You know that, right?"

Dannika felt her stomach turn. "We have to kill?"

Bain caressed her cheek. "*You* don't have to do anything, unless we miss. Okay?" He turned to Ivan. "Demry in the shoulder. Mary in the foot."

Ivan nodded. Bain motioned to the door with a jerk of his head to Dannika. She smiled as her body filled with the kind of confidence only he could provide. She jumped into the air, jammed her foot into the middle of the door, and knocked it flat.

Demry and Mary whipped their heads toward them as Bain landed a shot to Demry's shoulder and hit Mary in the foot. Both immediately dropped to the floor in pain. Bain's shots had carried the accuracy and speed of a Navy Seal. Bain cuffed them both and shoved them against the wall. He wrapped the cloth that had bound Ivan's mouth tightly around Mary's foot. Mary began to shake. The cloth around her foot turned a deep maroon.

Ivan ripped the removable collar from Demry and released the others.

Adie wrapped her arms around Dannika and squeezed her as tears rolled down her cheeks. Dannika just held Adie and listened to everything happening around them.

Bain started moving in toward Demry.

"No, Bain. Let him be," Ivan said. "We will deal with him properly." Bain paused, then stepped back.

Ivan turned to Demry. "Quite impressive, really, Demry. But why? What did you hope to gain?"

Demry winced as he shrugged his injured shoulder. "Well, your job, for one." A deep chuckle escaped his gut. "You realize that my Human Intelligence Tools would bring in a hundred times the revenue IPA does now?"

"How so?" Ivan kept the gun pointed right at the bridge of Demry's nose.

"You really are an idiot, aren't you? If it weren't for that tasty little thing of a wife you have, you would never have what it takes to run this agency."

"You haven't answered my question."

"Since your pea of a brain can't figure it out, let me give you the brief version. Data. Information. All-in-one convenient location. The ultimate in Intelligence. Who needs your silly little psychics when we can put someone right in the middle of the action — someone dispensable — and everything they see, hear, and read downloads instantly to one central location. You want to try to tell me that every government agency in the world isn't going to want that information? Wouldn't pay any price for it?" He delivered another deep, scratchy cackle.

"Why Noder as your cover up?"

"Cause sweet tuts over there knew so much about him." He nodded to Jocelyn. "When she was at Head-quarters, she'd spout off all the time about what a nut job he was, couldn't believe a woman smart enough to spawn her could ever be with a man like that. I knew he would be the perfect accomplice. Of course, he had no idea what he was really getting into. I figured a little bust on him would get me in real tight with those Feds."

"How did you think you'd ever get away with this?" Ivan asked.

Demry squirmed. "If it weren't for GI Jane here, and her Charlie's Angel counterpart, we'd not only be nailing guys like Noder on numerous counts of smuggling and laundering, all while the HITs are collecting intelligence that will give government agencies all they could ever hope for. People only get hurt, when they get in the way, you know."

"That's the Fed's job, not ours. You went too far. We do our job. The government does the rest."

"Wait until they get a load of my project. They'll toss you aside like a bottle of dirty rum."

Ivan stepped closer. "The Ram was a murderer, Demry." He jerked his head toward Chaz's body. "And now so are you."

Ivan paced in front of Demry. "And Rens? What do you suppose has become of him?"

Demry hissed. "He's just puffed up on steroids. He can translate every spoken language, like Mayer's freaky lions, but he's no leader. He'll just wander around, clueless."

"Hmmmmm." Ivan thought a moment. "You don't think Rens is a threat, now that the Ram is gone?"

Bain pressed a pistol to Demry's temple as encouragement to tell the truth. Demry jerked his head away from the gun, leaned back against the wall. "You'll have to ask that loser of a scientist you have as a partner. Rens was his idea, to protect the Ram."

*

"Idiots." Dannika kicked Demry in the side.

Ivan pushed her back. "Don't let him get to you." He kneeled beside Demry.

An odd voice rung low from the doorway "Yes, why don't you ask me?"

Mayer stood in the doorway, a large explosive-looking gadget in his right hand. Bain glared at Mary, at her loyalty to these cowards.

"What is with you people?" Dannika said with a tense jaw.

Demry banged his head against the wall lightly. "Mayer, just put the bomb down. We're done here. If you follow through with whatever you plan you've got going through that twisted brain of yours, you will have to go at it alone. Just let it go."

"Twisted? You call me twisted?" Mayer fondled the bomb between his hands, like it was a couple of apples freshly picked from the tree. Dannika watched Demry's eyes follow the bomb carefully as it traded Mayer's hands, back and forth. Demry must know something about Mayer, about how he operates. What he values. What he is capable of. "You're the one that took my animal experiments and broadened the scope. With no real clear goals, just throwing caution to the wind. The Ram was the real bomb. Rens kept our secret safe. Your subject is the one that got us into this mess. Besides, who's the smart one here, eh? You let them get you. You're weak. But me. I'm in control now." He held the bomb with both hands in front of him.

Demry shook his head. "You worthless snake. What are you going to do? Blow us all up, including yourself?"

Mayer tilted his head back into laughter. "No. This bomb has a timer. And as you know, these walls have a secure lining of solid steel interior. All of you will be on one side, along with my lovely creation here, and I will be on the other."

Mayer crept slowly toward Demry, knelt beside them. "All those years of you demanding things from me. Telling me my ideas were absurd. Stinking up our pristine work environment with that nasty quiet ego. That if I just did as you instructed, we would be equally rewarded. Well, *my* subject escaped, and *yours* got caught."

"Yours wouldn't know how to put one foot in front of the other without the Ram. Nothing but a brut without a brain, that's what he is. He'll never find his way back here." Just as Demry finished that final phrase, Mayer slapped the back of his fist across Demry's face.

Dannika could see Adie moving toward Chaz, just a blur in her peripheral vision, Mayer and Demry too heated by one another's stare to notice. Nearly dying of curiosity what Adie was up to, she strained her eyes to see Adie better, but didn't move a muscle. She glanced back and saw Mary with an intense glare focused on her, then Mary's eyes moved to Adie.

Ivan spoke calmly. "Mayer, how much time do we have?"

Mayer smiled. "Two minutes. Or maybe a little less." He glanced at his watch and his eyes lit up. "Oh my, how the time does fly. Looks like I am mistaken. We have less than one minute."

Bain rose his gun, but Mayer counteracted by placing a finger on the trigger of his bomb. "Don't forget that I am a surgeon. These fingers are precise."

*

Adie dug deep into Chaz's super-suit pocket, felt the smooth syringe at her fingertips. She gripped the syringe into her palm, and slowly pulled it out, holding it firmly behind her back. She thought hard about the distance Mayer stood from her, the fact the syringe was empty, so it wasn't likely to do more than act as a minor distraction. But it would have to be enough. Enough to get the bomb away from Mayer and get Mary to disengage it. Surely, Mary was the only one who might know how. It was their only chance.

There was not time to devise a plan. To share with anyone else what she was about to do. They had less than one minute.

Jeff stood just in front of her, and peered over his shoulder. He narrowed his eyes and locked in on her chest. Adie knew he felt something, something in her intensity. He knew she was about to make a move.

Her eyes focused in on Mayer's neck as he and Demry continued to feud over who's project was king. Jeff motioned to her with his head for them to exchange places. She stepped one foot around, maneuvering her own body in front of him, now only ten feet from Mayer.

Mary began to cry. Adie hoped she could hold it together for just a few more seconds. Mayer noticed Adie's movement and secured his finger on the trigger. Adie landed a push kick with the inside of her foot to the bomb, sending it right into Mary's shaking hands. With her opposite foot, she delivered a high kick to Mayer's left ear, his whole body folding over on the hard ground. She leaned down and pressed the syringe deep into his spine, causing his back to arch in pain. Bain moved right in with a gun to his temple. Dannika gripped Jocelyn's hand tight.

"Disengage it, Mary, now." Bain yelled.

Mary shook her head, sobbing. "I don't know how."

Mayer tipped his head outward, yelling. "Yes you do. Pull the integration wire, just like we do to disengage the animals."

Mary's hands fumbled around the circular object, the expression on her face filled with fright. "I can't find it." A high-pitched beeping sound echoed from the walls.

"Twenty seconds." Mayer said firmly. "We will all be dead if you don't let me show you."

"We'll die before let you move." Bain's jaw was tense.

Adie knelt next to Mary, each beep pulsing in her chest. "Mary, think. Where does Mayer put this integration wire?"

Mary's head moved back and forth. "It could be anything."

Mayer yelled. "On the inside, in between the two steel masses that resemble a frontal lobe and temporal lobe, you dumb woman."

Mary fumbled more with the circle of metal and wires.

Adie had counted twelve beeps. Eight left.

She placed a hand on Mary's forearm. "This is what we do, Mary. We are here at IPA to saves lives. So, please, save ours. Save your own."

Mary took a deep breath as Adie realized four more

beeps had passed. Mary dug in with her forefinger and middle finger, bit her lip, and pulled back hard. Her elbow flew backwards with the momentum of the wire releasing. The beeping stopped.

Adie blew a large breath through her cheeks and patted Mary on the shoulder. Mary threw the explosive to her side like a hot potato. Adie gently grabbed it and placed it in the corner of the room, far from Demry, Mary, or Mayer.

Bain kept a gun to Mayer's head, and with the other hand tossed an extra set of cuffs to Adie. "Go ahead. You deserve to know what it feels like."

Adie moved in and bound Mayer's hands behind him, and smiled. It felt amazing. Better than a nine mile runner's high. Better than scoring the game-winning goal at the state championships.

Dannika ran to Adie, hugged her tight. "You are something else, girl."

Ivan wiped at his forehead. "I don't get it, Demry. I trusted you. You were my friend. You are—were—the best in technology. Ever. Your project has potential, but you've gone about it all wrong. It's immoral and illegal. If you had been the person I thought you were, we may have developed something really great here. But you're finished."

Adie watched Bain kneel beside Chaz's body. Bain's head fell to his hands and he began to sob. Jocelyn put a hand on his shoulder, and he reached up to hold it.

"Jocelyn, notify Headquarters so we can get all these guys patched up. We'll need to make arrangements for Chaz," Ivan said.

Adie pulled away from Dannika and grabbed her hands. "Go to Bain. He needs you."

Dannika kneeled next to Bain and wrapped her arms

around him. He fell onto her, tears wetting her shoulder. Jeff pulled Adie in close.

Ivan rested against the wall, his head heavy against it. Adie watched him as he gazed at the scene before him. He watched them all carefully, then he locked eyes with her. She saw Dannika watching Ivan too, as she ran a hand through Jeff's hair. Maybe Ivan would see that the couples were better together. That no one could be their best alone.

Ivan seemed to understand, as he delivered an affirming nod before he closed his eyes and leaned his head back, only the wall behind him to hold the guilt and shame of everything that had happened under his leadership.

Dannika pulled Bain in tighter and he rested his mouth against her ear. They sat this way for a moment, until he whispered 'I love you' to Dannika, loud enough for Adie—and Ivan—to hear.

CHAPTER TWENTY THREE

Adie sat in the oversized chair and stared at Dannika's clothes hanging in the closet. All black or burgundy or navy blue. She would be so glad when things returned to how they had been when she first signed on, working nights with Dannika, spending days with her at the retreat.

A lot of changes would be made, for sure. Mostly about procedure and specifically on their progress at Research, but Adie mostly wondered about Jeff. Could it be different now?

A soft knock at her door led her eyes in that direction. The door opened and Maimey peeked her head around the corner.

"Come here, you." Adie patted the big comfy chair next to her.

Maimey skipped over and plopped next to Adie. She had pulled the headphones down around her neck, and the wires draped over her shoulders.

"Think I'll see Dannika before I go?"

"Don't know." Adie wrapped an arm around Maimey's shoulder. "She'll miss you, though. So will I."

Maimey squirmed for a moment. "I heard about your dream, with me, and um, thanks for saving me."

Adie chuckled. "Apparently you didn't get the whole version of my dream. You were like the extra super-duper spy that saved yourself. You were your own hero."

Maimey smiled, her eyes on her lap. "What do you

mean?"

"You got the bad guy. The world is a better place because of you." Adie smiled at her.

Maimey shrugged. "You and Dannika are my superheroes. I know everyone thinks she's so weird and all, but I think she's cool."

"I think she's pretty cool, too."

"Maimey?" A voice bounced from the hallway walls.

"In here," Adie called out.

Steph came through the door with an armful of their things. "We have to go, Maimey. Go get your sister. She's with grandpa."

Maimey squeezed Adie and ran through the doorway. Steph moved closer to Adie, her eyes glued to the ground.

"You okay, Steph?"

Steph glanced toward the door, then back to Adie. "Yeah, I'm just nervous, you know. To take the memory scan. And for the girls to have to go through that."

"You're doing the right thing. Your girls are better in the city for now. They deserve to see the whole world for that matter. The memory scan will be no big deal. You're all set up with a job at the DEA. The girls will spend their first week in a mountain condo with Ivan and Bethie. They'll adjust. They need to have friends, and go to school, and I don't know, play basketball, and go to summer camps, beat up some boys or something. Maimey was miserable down here, and Macey probably wasn't far behind."

Adie hugged Steph tightly, then backed away. "I understand why you brought them down here, after they lost their dad, but it's time for you to get your feet beneath you again."

"You're right. Even though I won't remember any of

this, at least I'll still be working for the good guys." She tried to smile, but Adie could see the uncertainty in her eyes. "I know Mom and Dad will fill me in on the details over time."

"When you're ready, I'm sure they will. By the way, heard that head DEA guy, Knox, is pretty hot." Adie winked. She was happy to see that Steph could still laugh.

Steph shrugged her shoulders, her cheeks reddened. "We'll see. Thanks, Adie. And good luck. I hope I get to meet you someday." She smiled and left.

Jeff brushed shoulders with Steph as he entered. He yelled over his shoulder, "Look forward to meeting you in a couple of weeks, Steph."

He walked steadily up to Adie. He ran a hand over the top of her head, his hand sliding down her spine until he pulled her in close. He leaned in and kissed her. A jolt of electricity shot through every vein.

"So what? We're just going to break the rules now?"

"Why not? Apparently everyone else around here does." Jeff kissed her again. Then he reached into his pocket and pulled out her garnet ring.

Adie grabbed it and placed it on her right middle finger. "How'd you get this?"

Jeff linked his hands behind the small of her back. "Just a little birdie in Research."

She laid her head on his warm, pulsing chest. "Thanks, Jeff."

He squeezed her and kissed the top of her head. "C'mon. Bethie and Ivan are waiting to have dinner with us."

*

Bethie set a plate full of quinoa and sautéed vegetables in front of Ivan. Adie giggled with Jeff as Ivan grumbled about how he may as well be eating concrete.

Adie glanced at the dining hall "window", the one with the city view, and held tightly to the burning in her chest. It was time for her to go. Two-a-days would begin in a week, and she had a promising athletic career ahead of her. But what about this career? Would she be a coward to do anything else? Was there a decision to make? Would she really leave? Did college even matter now? She hadn't spent a single day on the soccer field at the Wilderness Retreat. She hadn't even thought to go there. So what did it all mean?

She felt Jeff put a hand on her knee below the table and give it a squeeze.

"So, when does Dannika come back?" Adie asked with her mouth full.

Bethie's and Ivan's faces went blank. Ivan set his fork down. "Jago didn't tell you?"

Adie swallowed hard and too fast, which caused a painful lump in her chest. "Tell me what?"

Ivan glanced at Bethie, and she gave him a nod. "Adie, dear, apparently, when Dannika made her way to Research, Demry ordered Mayer to put her under. He inserted the info chip into her brain. He also injected her with the chemicals that cause the transformation to a HIT to begin. We've sent her away for a while, so we can monitor her changes."

"An HIT? You mean..." Adie's jaw dropped and her pulse picked up.

"Yes, Adie," Bethie continued. "She was to be their next 'Ram.' But she will be okay. Jocelyn is in charge of Research now. She'll stay on top of it."

"So, can they remove it? Reverse it? Whatever?"

Adie asked. Jeff squeezed her hand.

Bethie shook her head. "No. But it may be a blessing in disguise. It's quite possible that these Human Intelligence Tools will be useful to IPA, if used appropriately. Since only humans with the brain activity found in those with moderate mental illness respond to the injection, it might be the perfect fit for Dannika. We'd like to think she'll be a new kind of hero."

Adie grimmaced. "So, all those brains in the bank?"

Ivan nodded. "All set up with neuro-microchips, hidden and ready, just waiting for their next host. Well, except those that were removed to develop the memory scan — the ones with Alzheimer's. We'll probably have to dispose of those. But with Demry's influence out of there, we will focus on more humane methods of Research."

"Ugh." Adie set her fork on her plate. "Well, after all that, I think I'm done." She paused. "So, when can I see her?" Adie shrugged her shoulders.

Bethie moved over to Adie and took her hand. "She will be crazier than ever for about three weeks, until her brain accepts the new asset. Then she'll return to Research and Jocelyn will run experiments on her wireless info downloads. Who knows, she may be the next President's undercover angel."

"Maybe undercover dark angel." Adie smiled. "She'd love that."

Bethie moved back to Ivan. "By the way, we have something for you two."

Adie glanced over at Jeff. He just shrugged his shoulders.

Adie grinned. "What is it?"

Ivan placed a piece of paper on the table in front of them. "An addendum to Jeff's contract. It now states he is only permitted to be involved in relationships that prove to be beneficial to *both* him and IPA. We have decided that one area we should not interfere with is love."

Adie squeezed Jeff's hand. "And?"

Bethie clapped her hands together quickly. "And you qualify, of course."

Adie looked over at Jeff. Her cheeks flushed and her heart threatened to burst through her chest. He leaned in and kissed her softly. Then he turned to Ivan and Bethie. "Thanks, guys."

The entrance doors crashed opened, and Adie peered over her shoulder. Lonie was leading the way. A slightly shorter figure followed behind. When they reached the table, the figure stepped out to the side.

Adie froze.

"Hey, guys, I'd like to introduce you to our new Analyst intern, Witt Jennings. He's amazing in his field and will be so awesome for our new Research approach. Witt, this is Ivan and Bethie, Jeff, and Adie." Adie's jaw dropped as she locked eyes with Witt, his eyes wide as a truck as the sight of her.

"Witt?"

"Adie?"

"You guys know each other?" Lonie asked.

"Yeah," they said in unison.

Adie caught Jeff's expression of confusion from her peripheral vision. Her brain quickly calculated how the pieces fit. The recognizable number on Witt's phone must have been Lonie's. How easily Witt could commit to IPA so young, with no connection to his family.

Adie worked hard to maintain a normal smile, rather than the intense flow of energy and heat she felt inside. "Welcome. Wow, um, this is great!" She turned to Ivan and Bethie, careful not to look in Jeff's direction. She wondered if Jeff was picking up their energy, feeling any of Witt's familiarity in either of them. She spoke loudly, as if noise might break through any vibes Jeff might be analyzing. "Witt's worked with my Dad."

Bethie nodded. "Yes, we know. Witt was a perfect choice for our next Analyst position, and we figured with you leaving us for your studies until next summer, it will be a lovely way to stay connected, since Witt will still be working on some experimental data with your father. Your father will think it's University work, of course."

Adie sat back in her seat. "Of course." Adie worked harder to keep calm, hide her shock, not let Jeff catch onto the odd feelings inside of her.

An uncomfortable silence lasted way too long until Witt reached out to Ivan. "Such a pleasure to meet you." Adie recognized a tremor in his voice. The same nervous sound as when he had asked her out.

Adie could feel her palms sweat. "Um, I'm going to go check on Bain. I'll be back." She turned to Witt but no longer made eye contact. "It's great to see you, Witt."

As she exited, she felt all eyes on her, right through her shoulder blades, until the heavy curtain-painted steel doors folded together behind her.

*

Adie crept into the dark cave, a gloved hand on Zeneva's back. Zeneva planted herself next to Tred and they assumed their positions on guard.

Bain sat against the rock wall, his back curved to the lines of the cool surface. A crackling fire lit his face to reveal an expression mixed with relief and defeat.

His knees bent in front of him and his feet planted

firmly into the dirt of the cave floor, he stared at his hands, which held the unopened letter.

"Hey." His voice was soft. Barely there.

Adie moved next to him, rested a hand on his shoulder. "You should open it."

"I know. I'm just afraid."

Adie seated herself and felt Bain's warmth beside her. "She's going to be okay." Her garnet ring glowed in the light of the flames.

He nodded and reached inside a coat pocket to retrieve an antique letter opener. Adie recognized it from the Noder's house.

She pointed to it. "Where'd you get that?"

"From The Ram. Kind of reminder of that day. Finally getting him, you know."

He stuck the sharp end beneath the wax, and it broke free from the paper.

Adie backed away to offer him a bit of privacy.

He held the letter to the dim light of the fire, let the paper fall open. To Adie's surprise, he read it aloud.

"Every life may have value, but where it is in my own seems camouflaged by all things unnatural, and by beings with no understanding. Most days bring brief moments of clarity followed by a mental tornado. My moments with you are the ones in between, the ones where I feel free. If I have to live, I want to live one way and one way alone. I want only one dream to matter above the rest. The one where my life is forever entwined with yours. Where we are woven so tightly that nothing may interfere. In any other life, or any other dream, I am nothing."

Bain dropped the letter, let his head fall into rough hands. He turned toward Adie. Tears rolled down his cheeks.

"Have we lost her?"

Adie crossed her arms, the ring warm against her

palm. "No. The life Dannika was meant to live has only just begun."

Adie pulled the folded addendum from her jeans pocket, the one Ivan and Bethie prepared for Bain, as they had for Jeff. She placed it in his hands.

Squinting against the rising flames, Bain read his new contract. Adie watched as a slow grin peeled back from his profile. He nodded to her, leaned his head against the jagged wall behind him, and closed his eyes.

Adie crept back quietly, left him to process what his new life would be like. She would slowly wander home through the thick, marvelous forest, stepping off the trail now and then, into the in-between, to ponder what might become of her own.

FADE TO SILVER
BOOK TWO OF *THE IN BETWEEN* SERIES
COMING WINTER 2013

CHAPTER ONE

For Adie Brighton, working for a secret intelligence agency was like walking the tightrope. But attending college was the whole circus. At the agency, Adie had felt like she belonged, like she finally had people she could relate to, who could understand how the dreams affected her life. Only a couple of months in at the University of Colorado, and Adie felt like an alien. Classes were tougher than in high school, and her lack of focus was stronger than ever. She was always looking over her shoulder on campus, as if a criminal from her past was tracing her footsteps. And the dorms certainly weren't her thing. They were hot and stuffy, and her roommate, Jazzy, would return between classes solely to spray an extra dose of Juicy Couture perfume around her neck and armpits.

But a roommate was one thing Adie was grateful for, because Jazzy was a night owl, which often broke Adie's sleep patterns and woke her before she fell into the deep sleep when the nightmares usually began.

If Adie did have one of her nightmares — the kind so different from the average young woman — she'd use her voice-activated wireless handheld to 'write up' the report and send it off to Impire Peace Agency. But then she was out of the loop. She wouldn't be there to watch IPA Operations carry out interference on the events of her dream. She couldn't revel in the feeling of accomplishment as IPA used her dream to save a life. It wasn't the same to send off the report of her dream and then immediately delete it from her handheld to prevent someone from finding it. She didn't get to see the end result, an innocent life spared, the only benefit of enduring the dreams. Instead, she had started to feel like she used to before she knew about IPA — she just lived with the nightmares that wrecked her ability to concentrate on anything else, and made her feel like nothing more than a scared coward.

*

Adie pulled her wavy chestnut hair back into a ponytail, gathered up her extra cleats and headed to the soccer fields. She'd been pulled out of red-shirt status when the starting forward got hurt, and the backup was on probation for a DUI. Before last summer, Adie would never had been able to imagine how anyone could do something so out of control and downright stupid as to drive drunk, which jeopardized their athletic career on top of that. But her summer job had shown her a different side of the human existence. The motivations and the ideals that drove some people. And she knew firsthand that not everyone could control their own behavior so easily. For some, free will was a dangerous sidekick.

"Ready, champ?" Adie's dad was, of course, the first person to arrive at the game fields. Even before Adie.

"Yeah, Dad." She wrapped her father in a big hug. "Mom coming?"

"Your brothers have baseball, so we're splitting up today."

Adie nodded. Every time they 'split up,' her father was the one to come watch her. It hurt, but Adie never asked about it.

"Well, I better get suited up." Adie turned on her heels to head to the locker room.

"Good luck," Adie's father yelled to her back.

Halfway through the game, a loud crack filled the sky and the oohs and ahs from the crowd shifted upward. Tiny drops fell as the sky lit up with a bright flicker. The rain began to pelt down as the referees blew whistles and sent both teams to the locker rooms. The crowd dispersed like ants on a disturbed sand mound. Only a few brave ones sought the shelter of an outbuilding to wait out the storm. After thirty minutes, both teams took to the field, but ankles were turning and cleats slipping, and both coaches agreed they couldn't afford any injured players. Adie's father, soaked and shivering, ran onto the field.

"Well, tough luck on that one, Pooks. Can you make it home tonight for dinner?" He held a newspaper over his head.

"Yeah, okay. I've got more laundry than a family of twelve." Adie laughed as her dad ran off to the parking lot. *Pooks.* So much had changed since Adie had graduated from high school. Her summer had taught her about the darker ways of the world, and how she had to face them head on. Any other girl her age would probably die to hear her father refer to her by her childhood nickname, the one she had forbid him to use once she hit puberty. But now Adie welcomed it. It was one simple thing in life that couldn't turn to gray.

*

In the locker room, Adie stood beneath the steamy water, grateful for a hot shower. She wondered where Dannika, her work partner from her summer job, was at the moment. Dannika had been the kind of friend Adie would never have imagined she could be close to, and just as they got tight, things drastically changed. But her boss Ivan had convinced her that Dannika would be okay, and while they might not work together directly anymore, their paths would surely cross—should Adie take up with IPA again next summer.

But Adie couldn't wait that long to see Dannika. To know she was all right. And to see what amazing transformation she hoped had taken place in her once sadly confused and distressed friend.

Adie threw the duffle bag strap over her shoulder

and hunched forward to head out of the locker room. As she stepped through a set of double doors, a hand landed on her shoulder.

She jumped, then smiled. "Hey!" She hadn't seen Jeff Reid in weeks, and the long lapse felt like a hundred years.

"Hey," he said gently and leaned in to kiss her. Adie glanced over her shoulder, making sure they were alone. "Sorry I missed the game. Ivan sent me on a wild goose chase to recruit a woman who was already too far gone." Jeff removed the duffle bag from her shoulder and tossed it over his own, slightly mussing his light brown hair. Adie noticed his eyes had gone a dark hazel to match his button up shirt.

"That's okay. Rained out, anyway. So, um, why was the woman too far gone?" Adie was always curious when a fellow psychic seemed to take a mental dive.

"Well, she was older, you know. In her fifties. I think it just got to her before we could." Jeff fumbled for his keys and held a rain jacket over Adie's head as they stepped into the cold drizzle.

"Great. That's going to be me. I mean, it seems like eventually, the dreams do us all in at some point. You suppose there's any way to avoid it, you know, ending up like that?" Adie sighed.

"By continuing to work with us, Adie. The only ones that stay sane are the ones that put the gift to work."

"Like Dannika?" Adie regretted that her voice was filled with sarcasm.

"C'mon, Adie. Dannika is different. She has a mental illness. Although, it turns out that's going to work in her favor."

"So she's doing okay?"

"Yes. She's doing very well. You'll get to see her

soon, if you want."

"Does she ask about me?"

Jeff lowered his head. "No, she doesn't have recall in that part of her memory yet. But she will. Don't worry."

They reached Adie's car and Jeff threw the duffle bag inside. He pulled her close and kissed her. Adie's body relaxed as she allowed herself to melt into the buzz that ran through her body when his lips met hers.

"You want to grab some dinner?" Jeff asked.

"Promised my dad I'd join the family tonight. I haven't been home since school started so I feel like I should go. Besides, see all that laundry? Mothers are always good for that." She smiled and lowered herself into her car. "Plus, she couldn't make it today. I miss her."

Just as she planted herself behind the wheel, Jeff jerked his head forward and his expression froze.

"What is it?" Adie's heart jumped.

"No way," Jeff whispered.

Adie's voice was thick in her throat. "What is it? Jeff? You're scaring me."

Jeff leaned his head into the car and pointed. Adie peered through the windshield. Forty yards ahead stood the man who'd haunted Adie's dreams all summer long. They'd thought he was no longer a threat. They'd thought she was free of him. That they all were.

Rens, still tall and blond and thick all over, was leaning against a car, one hand resting on a black sedan and the other hidden beneath his jacket, holding still at his waistline.

"I'm going after him," Jeff's voice shook.

"No! Just get in and we'll tell Ivan immediately. Jeff, don't go."

"I'm not letting him back into your head, Adie. No

way."

Adie grabbed his arm and squeezed tightly. "No. Let the agency handle this, Jeff. You can't go after him alone."

Everyone had thought Rens was gone for good. His presence meant only one thing. Everyone that was part of Impire Peace Agency was in serious danger.

Jeff's hand crept around to his back and he grabbed his gun.

Rens must have noted Jeff's movement. He ducked behind the sedan, then bobbed between two Ford trucks.

"That's it." Jeff threw his arm backward to free himself from Adie's grip and began creeping toward the two trucks. Rens exploded into a sprint toward the back exit of the parking lot.

Jeff ran towards him, gun in hand, using the few remaining vehicles in the parking lot to protect him.

Adie jumped out of the car. "Jeff, no!"

At the edge of the lot, a souped-up, white pickup truck pulled to a screeching halt, and the passenger side door flew open. Rens jumped in and the white truck peeled off with a roar.

Jeff turned back to Adie, wiped at his forehead, and stared at her. He panted in quick spurts and his eyes revealed terror. Their fairy tale dream of having a quiet and calm year—until Adie joined the agency again next summer—came to a screeching halt.

ABOUT THE AUTHOR

Catherine Converse is a freelance writer and independent author living with her husband and four amazing children in beautiful Montana. She studied Business at Carroll College and Marketing Communications at West Virginia University. Her love of writing took off in her years working as a marketing consultant using creative writing to sell. Now she uses it to take readers on an adventure. *The In Between* series is her first journey into the world of publishing.

Follow the journey of the *The In Between* series and future books by Catherine Converse at http://catherineconversebooks.com.

Become a fan of *The In Between* series at http://facebook.com/theinbetweenseries

ACKNOWLEDGEMENTS

Thank you, God, for your unbelievable grace, seemingly impossible mercy, and keen guidance (now that I am finally listening). In the words of Britt Nicole: You've been working with me all this time.

Thank you:

Mom, for having an uncanny amount of faith in your children. You are, and always have been, my biggest cheerleader. And Dad, who showed me the way of the rhino, and taught me to 'always look for my shot.' I love you both bigger than oceans and skies.

Stan, my best friend, insanely supportive husband, and biggest fan. You are a saint for putting up with me during those times my mind lingers in space pondering the lives of fictional characters rather than real ones. I'll never forget the day God merged my life with yours. I love you.

Clare, Chloe, Caitlin, and Andrew. You are my everything.

Mother-in-law Nancy Crowley, and her longtime friend Dreamer Clemons, for raising the man who would turn out to be my soul mate.

My editor, Monica T. Rodriquez. Your knowledge and attention to detail is mind-blowing. Working with you was such a pleasant adventure. I hope we have many more of them.

Graphic Artist Eli Clark, for kick-butt book covers. And your amazing ability to get my vision. And Jen Clark, for taking an evening out of your summer to take author photos.

Videographer Brian Easterling, for a book trailer that I have adoringly watched eighteen million times. And will adorlingly watch eighteen million more.

Brian Schwatz, Kindle Expert, for taking over my file conversions, and therefore taking away the technology headache I was sure to have experienced.

Beta readers Carole Mason, Janice Lake, Kelli Gardner, Betsy Carroll, Charlena Toro, and Jen Clark. Your feedback has been invaluable. You all rock.

Best friends Amy Cassel and Kelli Gardner, for the last 20 years. I look forward to a hundred more just like them. As Katy Perry so eloquently put it: Thank you for believing in my weirdness.

Erika Johnson, Deb Johnson, and Jennifer Troupe, for the ever-necessary girl time over coffee and wine. You are essential items in my mommy survival kit.

Chuck and Laurie Mason(and Amelia and Bodie), for being big fans, and for telling everyone else they should be, too.

Discovery Developmental Center, for being our second family. You are my lifeline.

Tyke Town at the Summit, for taking great care of my little peeps. Maybe one day I'll actually workout instead of work when I drop them off.

Teresa and Sari Suhr, for making my house look amazing twice a month, even if it does only last a couple of hours.

City Brew Coffee, for great caffeine. Period.

Jimmy Buffett, for turning me into a perpetual daydreamer.

Andrew Belle and The Xx, for music that inspired this story.

And to T. Greenwood, Tana French, Suzanne Collins, Veronica Roth, Kathy Dunnehoff, S. R. Johannes, Phillip Dick, Sibella Giorello, Dean Koontz, Julia Glass, and Virginia Woolf (to name a few), for writing the kind of books that moved me so much I just had to write my own.

CREDITS

Editing:
Monica T. Rodriguez: A Writer's Source
http://monicatrodriguez.com

Book Cover:
Eli Clark
http://elibclarkdesign.com

Book Trailer:
Brian Easterling: TransArtisian, LLC
http://www.trans-artisan.com/

File Formattting:
Everything Indie
http://everything-indie.com